SPIKIES

CHRISTOPHER LEUNIG

First published 2021
Polite Sharking Publications

Cover Design: Julian Akbar

Catalogue records for this book are available from the National Library of Australia

ISBN: 978-0-646-83249-4

Printed and bound in Australia

This book was written on Wurundjeri Country.

The author respectfully acknowledges the Traditional Custodians of the land, the Bunurong Boon Wurrung and Wurundjeri Woi Wurrung peoples of the Eastern Kulin Nation.

Naarm is sacred and will forever belong to Bunjil and elders past, present and emerging.

Always was. Always will be. Aboriginal land.

Terra nullius was a lie. Sovereignty was never ceded.

Know thy art dealer.
Know thy drug dealer.
Know what you want.
But never pay with your life.

- John the Baptist

Angular moonbeams find openings in the weathered roof, past the brittle skeleton of the structure, and bathe the stained concrete in a blue glow. It is an unusually clear night, and the stars appear like diamonds across a black-velvet sky. If you stare long enough, they twinkle and disappear only to re-emerge in the perspective of another.

The warehouse under the evening's searchlight was probably once a hive of productivity, but it now lies dormant, a mere shell in an abandoned industrial sector on the edge of a busy city. There is little to be illuminated except a stack of rotten pallets, a rusted barrel which possibly once discarded evidence, burnt remains, and a crumpled sheet that hangs from a rafter, resembling a blank canvas that will hungrily consume and refract an artist's folly.

But it is not the only presence awaiting imprinting.

Several feet back, a man reclines in a chair, blood seeping from his mouth, bruises evident around his ankles and wrists where he is bound like a reluctant dental patient in the hands of a doctor frivolous with the administration of novocaine.

A ball gag has been placed in the man's mouth. He appears unconscious; however, his eyes have been forced open with metal prongs. He could be awake. He could be dead. A Schrödinger's cat.

In the darkness, murmurings can be heard. The tip of a cigarette burns as if it desires to become something bigger, with dreams of charring and turning all to dust. Feet shuffle busily as if time is of the essence. It is not an act of anxious pacing or irritation. The steps are directed and meaningful. The clicking heels would walk alone if they could. A second beam of light leaps forth, this one horizontal, only metres above the floor, from the iris of a projector. In the

7

particles, images come to life before they splash across the backdrop like dancers erupting from a backstage dressing room and proceed to tear up the boards. The Moulin Rouge in two dimensions.

The seated man jars upright and his eyes grow wider, which, in many ways, seems impossible. He holds his gaze for a moment to decipher the symbols, the moving shapes, before trying to avert his attention to his surrounds. A pair of hands reach around and grasp his jawline. The paws hold him in position while an assistant tightens a buckle around his temple, his cranium held tightly to prevent breakage or, more importantly, diversion.

The ushers then find exits via torchlight, the doors are sealed, and the popcorn machine is retired for the night. The astral light slowly dissipates, and the warehouse becomes a cinema, a cinema for one. Full immersion is encouraged and mostly unavoidable.

PART I:

MAGNETIC DEVIATION ABOARD THE *PEQUOD*

BURNING CARDS AND
OTHER ACTS OF BOREDOM

Accent walls in otherwise stale, featureless buildings tend to rouse suspicions regarding what may or may not be concealed and why. And the double-sided mirror wasn't fooling anyone.

It wasn't there to satiate a bout of vanity. Not for us to routinely check our reflection, nor ensure our hair was correctly parted. I was being watched, scrutinised, recorded—something I had become accustomed to. I was a bona fide video star with a nice haircut.

But why the attention? Why hours of content when a five-minute loop would say as much? A jury could be saved the boredom.

Seemed like an open-and-shut case. Hardly worth opening at all.

And the unfolding pantomime was redundant and unnecessary. The audience had tuned out and retired to the candy bar hours ago, yet the performers still dreamed of accolades.

I didn't like cops, never had—I was brought up in the glow of the Rodney King newsreel—and I wasn't about to provide a motive or sign a confession for a packet of cigarettes or a chocolate bar. I didn't even fucking smoke, and I'm a diabetic—type 2 but still the real deal.

Not that my resistance would do any good.

The fuzz were already privy to a filing cabinet's worth of eyewitness accounts, surveillance footage from multiple vantage points, and I was arrested at the scene—the weapon prised from my sweaty, taloned grip.

All fairly incriminating pieces of evidence, I would say.

Or, so *they* said.

Perhaps they were trying to rule out temporary or even permanent insanity. Pre-empt any surprises in court in the presence of a cunning lawyer. Perhaps they had protocol to follow and they wouldn't dream of deviating—true-crime docuseries were finally holding law enforcement accountable. Or maybe, just maybe, they loved this shit and it was all simply a game, a game they knew they couldn't lose.

The whole scene played straight from those prime-time detective programs, and because I'd been reared on a steady diet of Caruso and Colombo, I played my part with aplomb. I shrugged, smirked, and grimaced at all the right times. Found the light and paused appropriately for dramatic effect.

Even my head came to rest in my hands. Tears dampened my palms.

I hit the mark every time, and although I knew the lens, along with the above-the-line talent, was present, I never acknowledged it, like a born performer. The ramifications for my actions were far beyond my perception, and unlike my crime, which crashed to Earth like an unsighted meteorite, it all seemed premeditated, stage-managed.

And that's when I fluffed my lines.

When the rap sheet was read, I tuned out, became numb. I didn't have to feign disinterest, it had me by the balls. I didn't mount a defence or plead for a phone call. I simply fell mute. Apathy had become a close ally, and I routinely kept it by my side.

Naturally, this attitude infuriated my apprehenders even further.

Bad Cop—a fellow named Munro—beat his chest and tore at his hair, a show of primal strength, while Good Cop—known simply as Yates—clenched his jaw and offered calming words to halt the hysteria. He secretly seethed beneath a white collar, which had suddenly shrunk two sizes, but he wouldn't show it. It was strange that men in their line of employment would be enraged by an accused killer. It was part of the job, part of the screenplay from week to week, and nobody forced them to sign the academy entrance papers.

You'd think that if you hated dirty, rotten scoundrels, you may stick to scooping ice creams or picking berries and leave the policing to those who liked to wade through the blood and the filth. Those that had the mind to understand a killer but not the gumption to ever become one. But then again, that line was often blurred.

For the record, I am, in fact, not a ruthless murderer. I have remorse. My eyes are not the gateway to a tarnished soul. I had an adequate upbringing. I never beheaded dolls or prised the wings from insects. I never even reduced miniature soldiers to mounds of melted plastic.

The act I committed did render a number of people lifeless—so I've been told—but it was spontaneous, disconnected, a product of boredom. I wanted to throw a grenade over my shoulder and walk away.

You know the guys that ignite bushfires on sweltering hot days?

Apparently, I'm one of those.

I just never intended to turn around and face the destruction. I had no excuse.

In the wider scheme of things, not many people are actually capable of murder, but a majority of us have been in a position where we could have been responsible for the death of another. Be it through negligence or mishap, defence or aggression, it's not overly difficult to acquire blood on one's hands. Indelible stains that last a lifetime. Take, for instance, that time you encouraged others to drunkenly stumble through traffic. Or when you left your child buckled into the car seat at the supermarket before realising your load was a little light.

I'm not trying to proclaim my innocence, but my actions aren't too far removed from the average person, and I don't directly align with those that are programmed to take another's final breath with reckless abandon. I don't read John Grisham novels and root for the psychopath. I'm not riding the shoulders of lions chasing antelope on the National Geographic channel.

It all began when I grew tired with my day job as a croupier—a card shuffler, felt table jockey. The casino was a less-than-reputable establishment that paid out intentionally to get the fish biting, then pulled the red carpet from beneath patrons in seemingly insurmountable positions. They let weak hands build confidence, then shattered dreams.

They occasionally turned a blind eye to cheating, just as long as the chips were slid back to their rightful place—the dealer's slots. If they were cashed, alarm bells sounded, and beatings were handed out by two hard-headed Bulgarian bastards that looked like cookie dough moulded in the palms of children.

Foreign billionaires generally had some loose change to spare, and they could buy their way out of trouble, which was an attractive business model for everybody involved.

No surprises, right? After all, it was a casino and the house always won.

I, for one, wanted to have my own fun, so, instead of mindlessly shovelling out the deck, I began to count cards. It's really not a hard skill to master, and after a few online tutorials, I quickly got the hang of it. It's all just a matter of adding and subtracting and dividing to find a ratio. When you know the potential combinations, it's easy to encourage or discourage other players at the table. A nod here, a wink there, a look of concern at other times. It's blackjack, and nobody could or should be trusted.

Twenty-one can be evenly distributed across the seven deadly sins.

Of course, security got wind of it, their eagle eyes glued to my abacus pupils darting back and forth. But, again, they looked the other way. I was raking in dollars and lining their filthy pockets. I was employee of the fucking month.

That's until the patrons dried up. Grubby little gamblers threw me a stink eye, muttered something to their counterparts, and turned their backs on me. Losers tend to lack ambition and instead of taking me on—perhaps learning a trick or two themselves—they simply looked for easier ways to win, and my unstimulated colleagues held that ticket.

Casino management didn't take too kindly to my newfound inertia—empty seats meant I was a fading attraction at the circus, I was a bull with a sterile cock—and I was taken aside for a few words of encouragement in a thick Eastern European accent.

"If the clown's mouth receive no balls, the clown no use to the fairground."

I nodded, smiled politely and agreed to their terms, conditions, and whatever else they had to say. I wasn't about to get into a pissing contest with two sticks of salami regarding maths, customer service, cutting decks, global affairs, or anything else, for that matter. They had never been wrong, and I wasn't about to break their streak. And, in any case, I was being subjected to tandem exhalations which smelled like a combination of asparagus, onions, and expired meat, and I was just happy to get out of there before my facial pores absorbed Chernobyl levels of toxicity. Beat me down, choke me out, but never try to foul my complexion.

After our conference, I returned to my station, loosened my bow tie (I can't begin to tell you how much I hated that fucking thing), and began flicking matches, setting alight each card from the stack.

Literally.

Although I hated the royals and harboured a desire to blow up Buckingham, I started with numerical diamonds as some kind of protest against greed and the imbalance of wealth. Perhaps I should have leaned towards spades to dig my own grave, because the next thing I knew, Varna and Plovdiv were dragging me to the car park—one arm under each of mine, the remaining hands clutching my underwear elastic and my testicles. I had invited the manhandling, but it still came as something of a surprise. Groping in broad daylight almost always catches one off guard.

The car park scene played out as you would imagine. Punches and kicks now replaced the infliction of soiled breath, and I took nearly all of the blows cowering on all fours before I was stuffed into my car with less courtesy than that offered by an officer of the law. I was told in no uncertain terms to never show my face around there again.

That's where things got a little hazy.

In my mind, I made a wiseass comment that was deserving of its own hashtag, but not before the door was slammed and my tailgate stomped for good measure.

It was all quite childish, and I may have muttered something to that effect through a mouthful of broken teeth and syrupy red saliva.

The car adhered to my quivering hand and purred to life as if summonsed to carry a wounded soldier from the battlefield. Several bunny hops later, I was through the boom gates and onto the street, which is no place for the cheated, humiliated, or vengeful.

Blood streamed from a neat cut above my eye, which made vision blurry but not my thoughts. I can blame neither concussion nor shock nor punch-drunkenness for what happened next, but I was swept along in a swirl of colours and colliding thoughts—a flickering kaleidoscope of horror. I was an astronaut on the grimmest of missions, and no amount of training could prepare me. All I had to do was hold on for dear life.

THE BULLIED BECOME THE BULLIES

"So, why'd you do it?" Bad Cop asked as he prowled around the table. This guy was a fucking caged tiger, and he wouldn't stop pacing until he got a pound of my flesh. I could imagine him raiding the stationery cupboard and tutoring me with a hole punch in one hand and a stapler in the other.

"I already told you," I hummed softly, trying to balance the volume in the room. "I have no idea how I ended up there."

"Were you bored?"

I shrugged. It seemed like an acceptable answer, but the truth was that I had been bored for years and never resorted to such actions. Boredom was the malady of my generation.

"You were bored after taking an ass kicking? Would you have preferred to go a few more rounds? Set your sights on a points decision?"

The ability to talk shit was clearly a prerequisite for gaining a badge, and it became contagious as he shovelled word after word into my mouth.

"The bullied become the bullies, I guess."

I assumed he knew, there was no other way to explain it. Bad Cop had surely been the bearer of one or two fat lips in his younger years. The first few times he would have sobbed out of sight from those that would point and laugh. Then he would have raced home after the final bell to avoid further torment, thrown himself under a blanket, and awaited sleep to provide refuge. It was no mistake that beds were often fortified by children lost in their imagination.

Eventually, he would have crossed over to the junior area to take out his frustration by shaking down kids for lunch money and harassing anybody smaller than him.

It was a cycle.

Abusive parents raised abusive children who recruited even more thugs by repeating modelled behaviour.

So on, etcetera.

Persecution was generational. It was a creative outlet for those that knew nothing of art, of culture. But it wasn't my job to lecture about villainy or centuries of inequality. I had no option but to take my medicine.

"So, you drove into a crowd of innocent people because somebody gave you a hard time?" Good Cop asked scornfully.

Okay. So, my reaction was extreme.

CONVERGENCE

The street was crowded with people: revellers enjoying a time of celebration, sporting ear-to-ear grins and handfuls of bagged shopping contributing to lopsided postures. For some reason, souvenir flags and sparklers were being waved in commemoration, as if inviting the raging bull. Except for the streamers that lay torn and tattered, I neither saw red nor blue, nor any other colour associated with rage or deep sadness. I just planted my foot and pulled sharply on the wheel like a ship's captain attempting to avoid an iceberg. But I wasn't attempting to avoid anything. On the contrary, I used my wheels like a missile seeking out as many targets as possible. I was a rodeo cowboy whose adrenaline far exceeded the initial eight seconds of the ride; unfortunately, however, I couldn't relinquish control to barrel men and walk away.

At first, it was like taking out bugs, hardly registering on the radar. Then a few speed bumps, wayward pedestrians dinting the panels, and a crowd dispersing in the headlights. The vehicle left nothing but carnage in its wake. A body burst across the windshield like a bag of rotten meat, and then another shattered the glass, leaving behind an intricate mosaic reminiscent of a spiderweb or a Jackson Pollock.

The vehicle finally came to rest when it slam danced into a bollard.

Responsibly, I pulled the handbrake and allowed the airbag to recede from the jab it had landed. The global positioning system, evidently damaged, delivered directions in French, and I swatted it aside. It was romantic, and I appreciated the encouragement, but it was no longer needed—it was just another channel in an ascending wave of noise.

I was pulled from the wreck in the presence of an angry mob, not by Good Cop or Bad Cop but by a couple of constables walking the beat accustomed to issuing on-the-spot fines for loitering and littering. The poor bastards didn't know whether to pull out their black books or their weapons, read me my rights or join the chorus of insults.

In the end, they cradled my head into the wagon and threw me into the custody of my interrogators, who had clearly been reading Hardy Boys hardcovers and rehearsing all day.

"So, let's recap," Good Cop intervened. The day had been long for all involved, but he was dedicated to stretching it out a little longer. His personal diary surely bulged at the seams.

"No need." The serve was played back into his court. "We've been through it."

"I just wanted to hear your version of events," he pushed in a sheepish tone.

"You know we have four hundred witnesses outside ready to rough up that pretty little face of yours. Belt the shit out of you if we let 'em." Bad Cop made his obligatory contribution to the script. The remains of his lunch were still visible in the corners of his mouth. "We could vacate the building, leave the keys. Makes our job a hell-ova lot easier."

'Vacate'? Bad Cop's vocabulary was more extensive than first credited. But 'hell-ova'? This guy went from real estate agent to tobacco-spitting sheriff in less than two sentences.

"The paperwork that would result from an assault on an un-manned precinct would definitely *not* be doing you a favour," I responded just above my breath for personal satisfaction and to address the scent of bullshit. I did, however, appreciate being referred to as 'pretty.'

The detectives stole a glance at each other. Insanity was off the table. Motive now had to be established, and boredom wasn't gon-na cut it. Why? Because without motive, manslaughter becomes a very real part of the playbook.

Either that or they were testing me. For what, I couldn't say.

"You seem to have all the answers, smart guy, but there's one question you haven't answered. Why did you let the Bulgarians get close to you? You had it all worked out: fuck over the casino by fucking over the punters. But you weren't prepared for the pum-melling." Good Cop chewed on his words for a moment. I let them rise overhead, hoping the rotating blades would cut them to pieces, scattering meaningless letters randomly across the floor.

"You know what I think?" he quizzed. It was rhetorical, and I allowed him to continue without offering a quip. It wasn't the time. "I think you wanted to be provoked. I think you wanted to be pushed, slapped into action. You had this heinous act in mind, and you just needed someone or something to push you over the edge." Yates paused to see if I would take the bait. "A mass murderer only ever commits the deed when they are scorned by a lover, or when God or the bank turns their back.

There is always an instigating factor. It's all sparked by hate, but hate is never enough. 'Shifting the hurt' is what we call it, and it's all quite desperate…juvenile, really."

Bad Cop leaned back against the wall, enjoying the chill down his spine and the thrill of the chase. Good Cop rested forward on a foldable chair, ready to tie another lure.

They had heard this thesis in a lecture many roll calls ago, and they loved reciting its machinations. It made them feel smart. Superior.

Cops think they know psychology, but they didn't know shit. They were insurance brokers with a badge and a uniform, and a comparatively lower salary in accordance with their level of education.

"Not to mention the property damage," Munro croaked.

Case in point.

"Some would argue nihilism, but there's a calculated target here," Yates mused, one hand on a stethoscope, the other on the safe's dial.

Talk about making a mountainous case out of a brain snap. I smashed the façade of a Starbucks, and I'm a nihilist? I ruined an elderly man's afternoon, and I'm an assassin?

"The Bulgarians may have made it physical, but there was an emotional catalyst. Someone or something set the wheels in motion." Good Cop added: "Something close, someone you cared about." He swiped at the air and squeezed his fist.

The fly hadn't seen it coming and nor had I.

NATHALIE

The linen blew in the breeze beyond the flaking window frame, its previous pearl complexion now blushing a rose hue in the sunlight. From the sofa, I stared at the white wall hoping the contrast between fabric and painted plaster wasn't too great. It was undeniably notable.

"It's supposed to be Egyptian. Four thousand thread count," Nathalie screamed from the kitchen. She was now taking it upon herself to assume domestic responsibility.

"Who the fuck counts threads?" I asked, truly mystified. "What does it even mean?"

"I ask you to do one thing, and you fuck it up," she continued unabated. "It looks like *menskonst* on our fucking bedsheets."

She had a foul mouth when she wanted to.

Nat entered the room with heavy steps. Her head was like a swarm of bees aggrieved by the loss of a queen.

"I don't know why I bother." Her posture was enviable, with her chin held high, and again, she looked down on me. "You can't do a thing right."

"What are you talking about?" was my only response. But I knew what she was talking about. These were not the ravings of a lunatic but rather somebody that had been nudged too close to the edge of a cliff and the precipice was beginning to fracture.

Nathalie was Swedish, but she only ever spoke to me in her native tongue when we were making love or when she was furious. She was also too good for me, and she knew it. She wasn't the stereotypical blonde and bouncy ski bunny most associate with Scandinavia. Instead, she was the product of migrant parents—her father Croatian, her mother Czech—and was, thus, only partly a product of liberalism. This gave her a short fuse but also the disarming features one associated with the exotic: dark hair with a Cleopatra fringe, opaque blue eyes like mined opal that never gave you the satisfaction of contact, and a smile that could persuade world leaders to sign peace treaties.

And she hated me.

"This is it. I can't do it anymore," she continued in a controlled manner which indicated prior rehearsal. "It is the stick that breaks the camel's back."

"Straw," I corrected.

"What?"

"It's the straw that broke the camel's back."

"Whatever. You never listen anyway. I meet halfway, but where are you? Nowhere. Never anywhere I need you."

"I am sitting right here."

"I have wasted too much time already." She was exasperated and had been fighting the tide without a life vest for far too long. It was an argument that had played out in her mind time and time again, and it always ended the same way.

Nathalie placed her hands on the counter, where a small unit of ants fossicked for sweet remains and peered out towards the clothesline which stood beside the lemon tree that hadn't produced fruit for years. She longed for more, but the surrounding soil had turned foul and threatened to infect all in its proximity. Her crescent moon earrings, a gift from a time when I was undeniably smitten, glinted in the afternoon sun as if showcasing an inner spark.

I bit my nails and stared at my reflection in the blank television screen. It was true. Nat was right. I was a lost cause, and I had never provided the stable home she had desired. Perhaps I was afraid of settling down. Perhaps it was because I had seen how badly things could go beyond the point of no return. Perhaps I was a self-destructive pessimist and all relationships were bound to reach the same inevitable conclusion.

"Do you remember the first time we met?" Nathalie asked.

"It was the kebab stand, wasn't it?" I turned to face her for both confirmation and to prove I wasn't completely reticent.

Nathalie didn't answer, she just continued to stare into the backyard. The permanently discoloured sheet wasn't the issue, but it was symptomatic of carelessness and dissatisfaction. If she could will change, she surely would, but she also wouldn't sit in the shit.

"Yeah. It was the kebab stand," she finally said, reflecting on a moment that had offered hope but was now filed under 'regret.' It was fate, but sometimes fate had a way of leading you astray. Nat wiped her hand across the benchtop and swept away a stream of ants, causing confusion and calamity in their ranks, and without another word, she exited the room.

A question of hygiene was always raised when buying dinner from a street vendor. Especially those that only came out at night and parked in back lots where the general public, apart from the drunk and starving emboldened with local knowledge, feared to tread. But those questions were set aside in the presence of beaming smiles that greeted all customers, and all but forgotten upon the first bite. The only real question that mattered was what ingredients to select.

Lightbulbs of various colours hung from the caravan offering an oasis on an otherwise gloomy night. It was as if a travelling sideshow had taken a wrong turn and decided to stay a while. As I approached, I was happy to discover that rush hour had yet to commence—the bars and clubs would hold the hungry masses a little longer yet—and I wouldn't have to engage in conversation with those experiencing the effects of uppers or downers, or both.

I placed my order and watched spellbound as they shaved meat from a rotating skewer, shovelled an array of colours into pita bread, and rolled the delicious cacophony in tinfoil as if it were a scroll of precious papyrus to be received by somebody of a higher order. It was a thing of sheer beauty, and the mere sight lubricated jowls.

Approvingly, I took the parcel, as heavy as a brick, to the awaiting plastic table and chairs, which sat beneath a crooked umbrella branded with the logo of a tamarind-flavoured soft drink. It was alfresco dining at its most relaxed, and the loyal clientele wouldn't have had it any other way. I slid into the seat, it threatened to break, and I let the scent consume my airways as I imagined I was somewhere else, far from the concrete that loomed large.

"Do you mind if I sit?" a voice asked as I drifted further and further away.

Slightly startled, my eyes slammed open and I sat upright.

A woman, similar in age, in an oversized turtleneck sweater and torn black jeans hovered at my side. Her smile was restrained, along with her use of makeup, but her eyes…her sapphire eyes sparkled as if to mock the melancholy surrounds.

"Sure." I liked the concept of solitude, but her presence was welcome.

She took a seat, leaned back, and stared up at the glowing pinpricks in the sky. It was as if she wanted to navigate her way through the wispy clouds and escape. I could sympathise.

I crossed my legs and tried to assume an air of cool, which meant I didn't dare fumble with the sandwich in my hands—they had a way of transforming dainty eaters into pigs at a trough, and first impressions would last long after my screaming appetite.

"No party tonight?" I asked and immediately winced. It was probably worse than asking if she came here often.

"No." She broke her gaze and turned towards me. "A date."

I looked around to see if her companion remained. He or she did not. "Not a keeper?"

She shook her head with a forced pout and a scrunched nose. 'Keepers' it seemed had been elusive.

"Tinder?"

She nodded and her eyes darkened like her mood was pooling to the surface.

"The right person will show up," I offered, but I knew nothing about affairs of the heart. Maybe the right person would never show up. Maybe they resided only blocks away, but they would never cross paths. Maybe she would only ever encounter the wrong people, and she would settle for less or wallow in loneliness. Destiny, for some, could be a vindictive and unaccommodating fiend.

"And you?" the woman asked. She had an accent, but geography wasn't my strong suit and I wasn't able to place it.

"Me?"

"No party?" She seemed genuinely interested.

"I stayed in." It sounded lame coming out of my mouth. Twenty-something and nowhere to go on a Saturday night. "It was my axolotl's birthday, so at least there was cake." I had plummeted to new depths.

"Axo—what?" She coughed.

"You know Mexican walking fish?"

She nodded. "I do."

"Same thing." I'd had Doug for five years, and, although I didn't know his exact birth date, it was as good a day as any. He hadn't changed much over the years, but I'd been promised he would live to the ripe old age of fifteen, so we still had a few good years ahead of us and a decade of Saturday-night celebrations.

She turned her head skyward again and laughed without restraint. She didn't care about her good side, about opening her mouth wide and chortling in defiance of her crumby evening. At least I was cause for some entertainment. I wondered if her date had seen her in such high spirits, in such raptures.

"Where are you from?" I said, bringing her back down to Earth.

"I'm from here," she said as she straightened her posture, her face turning deadpan. "How else would I know about this place?"

"I mean your accent. Where were you born?"

"Sweden." She said it like one may say, *I'm late*, which may be worthy of an apology, but she wasn't willing to give it.

"Stockholm?" The range of my knowledge was exhausted.

"Göteborg. West. But I think my name is more important, no?"

I nodded. She could have been extraterrestrial for all I cared.

"Nathalie." The corners of her mouth turned upward, and the word sat high in her mouth before rolling off her tongue.

"And what are you doing at Mustafa's Kebab Stand, Nathalie?" I asked.

"Well, isn't that obvious. I'm here to meet you, silly."

For the first time in a long time, I blushed. I was disarmed. Doug's celebration was the furthest thing from my mind, and the kebab in my hand could most definitely wait.

In no time, Nat returned with a packed bag. Along with the confrontation, it seemed premeditated. Random acts had never been part of her modus operandi.

"This is it," she said, clutching the suitcase in front of her waist like a cynical passenger waiting to see the bus driver's credentials. "Now is the time to say something." She scratched at a birthmark no bigger than a freckle above her lip—many called it a beauty spot, but she knew it was a mole and she had grown self-conscious of it.

I held the gaze of my image on the screen, Nat just over my shoulder looking for an excuse to stay or to go. I thought it was a bluff. She had nowhere to go. Although there was that older guy… she had mentioned him in passing a few times. He sounded sophisticated, well to do, albeit a little crafty. Perhaps it was for the best.

Silence prevailed until the door was slammed. Then, and only then, did I find my voice: "I can change," escaped my lips no louder than a whisper, but, of course, the darkened reflection had heard it all before.

I reached for a deck of cards and began shuffling. The odds were always in favour of the dealer, and I was late for my shift.

"You know we have Nathalie in the other room," Bad Cop cooed like a poker player with a full house. "She seems to think you are a fucking loser. 'In crisis' were her exact words."

"I'd say this is a prime case of a privileged thirty-year-old male trying to make headlines the only way he knows how," Good Cop chimed in.

They wanted me to bite, but I didn't like that they were chumming the water with Nathalie.

"We also tried to contact your parents..." A silence fell across the room. "It sounded like a tragic accident. It must have had a profound effect."

"I honestly don't remember," I uttered slightly louder than the whir of the ceiling fan.

"Trauma has a way of getting under your skin...and then peeking out when you least expect it," a cop said, specifically which one eluded me. Yates and Munro were starting to blur into a single two-headed beast.

"Will that help me beat the rap? Trauma?"

"No. But it may provide people with some answers. Give them peace of mind."

"You owe them that much."

"Some questions have no answers," I offered, channelling adolescence.

"Well, when the judge asks how you plead, you best have a clear answer."

"I think we all know the answer," I conceded. There was no use in mending a broken dam with a spool of tape.

"Then sign the fucking confession." That was unmistakably Good Cop. He had finally switched sides.

MONOCEROTIS

Somebody, somewhere, was arriving home after several nights away from the comfort and nurturing powers of a couch or a bed. Their reality skewed by riding synthetic highs in clubs that appeared like bomb shelters illuminated by mind-altering strobe lights and throbbing sounds that could throw a pod of whales off course miles out to sea.

Employment duties could wait, and guilt-free sickies would be taken—local GPs only too happy to sign 'release forms' if patients presented with symptoms of anxiety or simply sleepless nights, most due to hangovers, comedowns, or benders that saw no end in the short term. Weekends melted into weekdays, and clocks did little more than act as a proof of life.

Others avoided work altogether, preferring to crack open nest eggs laid by parents that toiled tirelessly for the youth they had spawned, and state money, which ultimately greased the palms of club owners and drug dealers that lurked in the shadows promising alternate realities, one free of rules, regulations, and responsibility. It was millennial economics, and the leading proponents had everything, and nothing.

Falling onto a couch after hours of dancing, after hours of chewing the inside of your cheek and engaging in overly loud conversation, was like pulling on a fresh pair of new socks. Invigorating. Life-affirming. It breathed a sense of hope into your soul. It reminded you that all would be okay. But when the couch was occupied and the socks sullied, the pits of despair became more prominent and its swollen circumference more difficult to avoid.

Hungry mouths widened, sharp teeth protruded, and gullets that knew the taste of hopelessness all too well eagerly awaited company. Resistance was mostly futile and the chemical remains, the unnatural harbingers of doom or euphoria, decided when the grips would be loosened.

YOUR FACE WILL CRACK ONE DAY, THAT'S JUST A FACT

A second fly buzzed around the room, searching for its deceased soulmate. The absence of a window or active door meant it was imprisoned until its dying breath—a death sentence for committing no crime at all. As I stared at its mounting distress, I noted a small fracture running from ceiling to floor, across the wall. It was symbolic of the situation, but I didn't know how. The crack was destined to get bigger over time, and that fact made me feel uneasy, on the verge of an anxiety attack, and I suddenly understood why innocent people signed confessions or agreed to plea deals.

When the possibility of buildings turning to rubble became a reality, it was best to take cover, even if that meant accepting a helping hand from those that had caused the destruction. It was a short-term solution without considering the long-term pain.

I slid the chair back, stood, and made my way across to the one-way mirror—the dimensions of which dominated much of the wall—installed to catch a glimpse of predators in their natural habitat. I pressed my face to the glass and tried in vain to turn the lens on those observing my sweat ducts, my twitching eyelids, the number of times I bit my nails and wiped my brow. But all I could see was my own reflection squeezed into a fishbowl.

I moved across to the door, flicked the switch on the lights, and returned to my position—cupped hands forming a viewfinder around my eyes as I squinted as if to blur the pixilation. Finally, a number of outlines appeared. I was unable to compute their features, but their burly silhouettes stood in a line like a train of humans cut from the same cloth.

I planted my hand once, then twice, onto the glass to get a response, but not one of the figures flinched. They were like shadows that had lost contact with their bodies long ago. I stepped back and shook the image from my mind. I had made my point. By breaking the fourth wall, I had made it clear that none of my actions had been candid and their data points were tainted. Yes, I had done something terrible, but I wasn't ready to be used as a case study for fresh interns. Cro-Magnon man forever reduced to a frame within a textbook.

The chair shrieked noisily as I dragged it back into position, and I resumed my place at the table. They could continue to stare, but I had to be sure they couldn't penetrate. I placed my head in my hands, as if in need of consolation, and began to count (electric) sheep.

The door then swung open, I instinctively sat upright, and the fly produced a rapid figure eight, unsure whether to dart towards the draft or stay and wait for a rescue party.

Bad Cop's face had changed.

If possible, he appeared even angrier, a sterner version of his former self.

THE PROPOSITION

Here's the deal…

Both cops re-entered, stood at the table, placed hands on hips like a game of Simon Says, and pointed their crotches in my direction. Sweat stained the stretched fabric beneath their arms, and collars had been loosened.

"What if we said there was a way out of this?" Good Cop scanned his hand.

I had stopped counting cards long ago. "I'm listening."

"An opportunity has arisen."

"An opportunity we don't think you deserve, but it's one we don't think you can refuse." Bad Cop was an unnecessary annotation in an otherwise pleasant dialogue.

"When you say opportunity, you mean a deal that fucks me harder than I'm being fucked right now?"

"You have fucked yourself, Elijah."

It was the first time they had uttered my Christian name, and I felt like I was being dressed down by my father after being sent home from school for emptying Angelo Pagnani's pencil case into a urinal.

"We need somebody to join a task force—a task force only a handful of people know about," Yates pitched.

It was unexpected, but I guess it's what I was being primed for. All roads led here. All creases had been ironed, and it was time to hand over the servant's new clothes.

"And the alternative?" I asked.

"You know the alternative."

Again, I felt like a child at the mercy of adults making decisions on my behalf.

"Drugs in this town are a problem," Good Cop continued without being asked. "A big problem. And no matter how many labs we bust or shipments we intercept, we don't seem to make inroads. The major players are still lining their pockets and peddling poison to kids that will ultimately become a burden on the system."

"A burden?" I knew kids that did drugs, and they had only ever become a burden on themselves, and those that loved them. They were mostly pariahs, victims of disassociation.

"Have you ever seen somebody chew on their arm because they were being eaten from the inside?" Munro painted the macabre image like Henry Fuseli dining with Dimitri on a businessman's trip.

I hadn't seen such a thing, and I wasn't about to pretend I had.

"That's what ice does. After the cravings, the violence, the willingness to bury your own mother for a hit, then come the bugs, the parasites that crawl beneath the surface. No amount of scrubbing can relieve you of that shit."

Welcome to Kafka's basement.

"Okay, I get it. So, where do I come in?"

"We want you to target the demand," Yates continued. "If potential customers get a whiff that a bad batch is doing the rounds, then they're more likely to avoid another transaction."

"And how do you propose you do this?" I queried.

"*We* get on the inside and give the users a sniff of our product."

I chewed on this information like a stubborn piece of gristle. *Did they intend on harming innocent people? Some kind of reckless social cleansing?*

"A product that will make headlines and hopefully send shock waves through the scene." It was a two-man weave of Harlem Globetrotter proportions, and I was the point guard for the hapless, and hopeless, Washington Generals.

"Wars are won by showing no mercy," Munro supplemented. "By clearing villages, terrorising civilians. A sniper pulls the trigger after consulting his head, not his heart."

"And you want me to be the one that administers your dirty dose?"

"*Bingo!*" Bad Cop enthused.

"You are our sniper," Good Cop affirmed.

"Why me?" Puzzle pieces were being scattered and nothing was slotting together.

"You fit the demographic. Not too far removed from the battlefield. Young, white, access to a few notes to throw across the bar. You'll go undetected."

"And what do you have to lose?" There was no chance of hiding the obvious.

"Surely, the trail will lead back to me. Dead people don't just go away."

"I guess we're in a fortunate position to monitor that."

My eyebrows jumped, sensing that my rap sheet could get considerably longer.

"Forgive me if I say this doesn't seem plausible." I shook my head as if I'd been offered short odds on a three-legged horse.

"Oh, it's been happening for a while now," Bad Cop said proudly.

"Haven't you noticed the rising death toll? We have considerable momentum," his partner added.

They were masquerading under a guise of nobility, but it seemed like anything but. And, it was true, I had noticed the rise in drug-related deaths. I had read the obituaries dressed up as feature stories, but just put it down to sensationalism.

"So how does it all go down?" I was curious.

"You attend the traditional haunts, keep an eye on whoever is using, and when their back is turned, you give them a taste of our product."

"*Our* product?"

"Carefully formulated to take effect several hours after being administered. A single measure will prove lethal, so there's no need to follow anyone home to ensure the job is done. It's clean."

It sounded predatory, and the two alpha males in the room were practically beating their chests. They were entering wild terrain, and they needed to prove that they were at the top of the food chain.

"Clean? I'm gonna guess it gets pretty messy in the end. Vomit? Faeces? And who knows what else."

"We hear it's quite peaceful actually."

"Is that what your lab rats told you?" I quizzed cynically. I was starting to feel like a rat in a maze myself.

"And those people you turned into roadkill?" Bad Cop reminded. "You don't seem to be in a position to hand out moral lectures."

My high horse had ridden off into the sunset long ago, and I wasn't about to beckon its return. A big mouth only ever led to big trouble.

"And correct me if I'm wrong, but you don't seem to be in a position to question the technicalities of the operation."

"I'm not yet shackled," I said as I clasped my hands and raised them above my head.

"We can arrange something."

I lowered my hands. "I have my rights."

"Wrong again."

The two-way mirror caught my attention, and I turned to face it. I wondered how many fuckers were now watching this exchange. Waiting. Swallowing too much air like old men tended to do. Handshakes at the ready. Lusting over scattering roofies like confetti.

"How do I know I can trust you?" I said, still facing the glass.

"You can't."

"Look, we're not in the business of doing deals with lowlifes, especially those with a complete disregard for life. But if you do this, if you make people think twice about what they're ingesting, then you will be a free man."

I chewed on the prospect for a moment. "And if it doesn't work?"

"Fearmongering has been responsible for having heads delivered on platters, for deciding elections, for launching missiles and invading countries. It will work."

"Scaring people into submission doesn't seem like police work." I had heard of wild sting operations, but this had to take the cake. This wasn't a simple honeypot, it was a goddamn quagmire.

"We're here to help people make better decisions."

"And if I don't agree?"

"See that?" Munro turned his head and pointed at the wall. "That's the best view you'll have for the rest of your natural life.

That's paradise."

Panoramas of holiday destinations glided by in the forefront of my mind. Postcards sent from better times.

"All you have to do is sign?" A folder slid across the table.

I carefully opened it as if it may bite. I flipped the page. Singular.

"Not as much small print as I expected." Not even double-sided.

"It's all pretty straightforward."

"And if I run?"

"You won't get far. You'll be fitted with a tracer."

"Like a collar?"

"A microchip. It's not 1984, asshole." Bad Cop was growing impatient.

"Listen, if you leg it, it's a breach of contract. Any breach of contract results in reminiscing about the beauty of this room." It was blunt, and sometimes blunt was best.

"Is there anything else I should know?"

"If you talk to anybody about the assignment—you're dead. If you fail to report—you're dead. If you tamper with the product or question our practises—you're dead."

Blunt had become downright forceful.

"And if it proves ineffectual?"

"Well"—Yates hesitated—"I guess you can see a trend forming here."

"So, I do this for how long?" A deal was on the table, but I really needed to pour some sugar on it. The length of my imprisonment needed to be definitive.

"Until we see results…or when the funding runs dry."

It wasn't exactly a bowl of Cocoa Krispies, and I would have to negotiate a sweetener at a later date.

"And who exactly is funding it?" I asked.

"There are things you don't need to know," Bad Cop stated. "Just concentrate on what's before you, and that means getting the job done."

"And then I'm free?" I had no idea how I had arrived at this juncture.

"Seems like a good career move."

"Aren't people going to recognise me? I don't need facial-reconstruction surgery, do I?"

"Facial reconstruction surgery?" Munro looked dumbfounded—a sock puppet with its mouth agape."No, Elijah." Yates fielded that one. "Thankfully, the first detectives on the scene placed a hood over your head before the cameras arrived."

"So, there's nothing in the papers?"

"Oh, there's plenty in the papers, just no headshots."

"And in any case, people quickly forget a face. An angry mob could have taken to you with bats and fists and spat insults, and the next minute they wouldn't have been able to identify you in a lineup. It's like going to a party with a houseful of strangers."

"Eyewitness accounts mean nothing?"

"Most of your eyewitnesses ended up strewn across your windshield."

"I remember all of their faces." It sounded like a lie. The words of somebody pushing remorse. But it was the truth. I'd been given their names, shown their personal photos. I wouldn't forget.

"Well, that's something you're gonna have to live with, kid."

"Look, are you in or are you out?"

"In." I sighed from somewhere deep within, as if somebody again had taken the controls. A rat pushed into a corner under the piercing glare of those beyond perception.

Have you ever felt lost or completely out of control? Like when you're following a map and the battery on your phone dies and your petrol gauge drops to a new low. Or perhaps you've spent days on end without speaking to a family member or a friend and you feel incapable of piloting your own destiny? Well, that's how I was beginning to feel.

I searched the room for the frantic fly—its own plight made me feel a little better about the world caving in on me. It was nowhere to be found.

Fear. As a means to manipulate. It worked.

A ballpoint pen was produced and handed my way. It felt light in my grasp, and it raced across the page, rising and falling like a heart monitor. I fastened the lid and dropped it like a weapon in the hands of somebody surprised by their actions, somebody that had no idea how they landed smack bang in the middle of a crime scene. My signature, with its sharp twists and turns, stared back at me like a toothy grin. The devil was sure to rubber stamp and file this one under 'continual fuckups.'

WITHOUT YOU (WE'D BE NOTHING)

A tall guy—hair parted with a refined silver streak, curated facial stubble, knitted sweater—swivelled on his chair as we entered. He looked up and offered a tight-lipped grin. He was handsome, the type that didn't have to say much to disarm those in his company, and exuded threatening levels of class.

"This is Kelvin, he will be your case manager," Munro stated, excitedly waving an arm as if I'd won a prize pool.

I nodded firmly, acknowledging that it wasn't the time for pleasantries.

"I would not say 'case manager,'" Kelvin said each syllable intently. "Let's just say, I'll be overseeing your time with us."

The room was neatly furnished and looked like it had housed a number of successful mediation sessions over the years. But this clearly wasn't a time for negotiation or compromise. There was an established hierarchy, a procedure set by precedence, and they had clearly executed the dance on more than one occasion. The demands would be explicit, undeviating, and consent would be expected.

"You will report to him daily, providing detail of your whereabouts and your activities. Imagine a loop: Kelvin is at twelve and you are at six o'clock."

It was a lot to take in, and it suddenly felt like I was doomsday prepping.

"Everything before six is a directive from Kelvin, everything post six is relayed back to Kelvin. In other words, Kelvin is your moon and your sun, and if you neglect his importance, tomorrow may never arrive."

"So, you're telling me if things get hairy out there, I have to call on a guy that looks like he should be on a yacht in the Mediterranean?" I raised a hand in a peaceful gesture like a guy that had kicked a rabid dog and offered a truce to warn off retaliation. "No offence."

"None taken." Kelvin had heard it all before, right back to schoolyard bullies the likes of his colleague. His tone was soothing, his words measured. I suddenly realised he wielded more power than I had credited him.

"Like we give a shit who you call. If things go awry, you have K. Or in extreme cases: Batal." Bad Cop inserted himself into the frame.

"Batal?"

"Last resort," Munro warned.

"Consider him nine o'clock," Yates added.

Kelvin raised his hand, held it for a moment, demanding silence, and then slowly lowered it like a musician straining a sustained note from a theremin. It was captivating and commanded attention. He cleared his throat to ensure his words weren't diminished.

"You are going to see a lot over the coming weeks," he said. "I encourage you to stop and draw it all in." He inhaled deeply to demonstrate his notion, and I couldn't help but replicate his actions. Kelvin spoke like a hypnotist and his words had a similar effect. "Joseph Goebbels once said, 'You can't change the masses. They will always be the same: dumb, gluttonous and forgetful,' so we must prey on those same qualities to advance our cause. We are standing on the precipice of greatness, and one day you will thank us for this opportunity."

"So, when do we meet this Mister Nine O'clock?" I asked, falsely eager, deliberately choosing not to address the propaganda, or any form of mind control.

"First you get chipped. I have a feeling that you have a tendency to wander," Yates, still the good cop, scolded like a headmaster with a soft spot for the bad boy.

The 'gun,' for want of a better word, much like the type that pierced ears, inserted the microchip like a tick burrowing beneath the skin. My neck pulsated for a moment while the foreign object made its place at home. I scratched at the pinprick and realised if I were to escape monitoring, I would have to get pretty handy with a scalpel and probably shed a pint or two of the old red ale.

The thought of bones colliding with the windshield and already bruised panels re-entered my mind, and I shook my head in an attempt to dispel the demons.

"Problem?" Kelvin asked. It wasn't a sign of compassion; he was merely kicking the tyres on his new acquisition.

"I'm just not used to having things inserted into my body." It wasn't a lie.

"This tells us where you are at all times," Kelvin said like a doctor detailing a procedure. "When you sleep, shit, boil an egg… we'll know."

"We'll also know if you haven't followed co-ordinates. You know that 'find my phone' feature?" Yates queried.

I nodded. Like most millennials, I knew my phone intimately.

"It's like that, but from the future."

"So, if I stray too far, it explodes?"

"If you stray too far, I greet you at the end of the path and my revolver blows your head off." Munro's response was as expected: hostile.

"Please, Detective." Kelvin intercepted the barrage. "Must we resort to that type of vulgarity? Mister Caulfield knows the implications of his actions. He knows that if he plays nice, then we play nice."

"I've stitched a few merit patches in my time," I joked. Nobody laughed.

"We know more about you than you think, Eli," Kelvin continued. "And we know that you were never a Boy Scout. That's part of the reason why you are here."

I scratched my neck again, this time pondering how I had got there. Two days ago, I was a schmuck stuck in a dead-end job casting disparaging stares at what I considered to be the bottom-feeders of society.

I was drowning in a loveless relationship and harbouring no friendships to speak of.

Things were okay.

But now I had a streetscape of blood on my hands, a SIM card of sorts resided too close to my central nervous system, and I had to abide by a curfew dictated by the Lord of the Manor a soft-spoken jerk-off who lauded his clout over me.

I had become a pigeon with a hood over my head and my wings clipped. For now, I was the subject, but I would soon be administering toxic doses. I would be the poster boy for a fucked-up scheme that had been cooked up by psychopaths in a think tank.

ACAB, right?

My thoughts swirled and collided like stars being devoured by hungry black holes—I needed a jelly bean or a can of fizz—and, in that moment, my arms grew heavy, my head slumped forward, and my chin nestled into my chest. I lost consciousness, and it was finally a moment of respite, a moment to enjoy the drugs, before I took my work home with me.

THE EXCHANGE

Hands met one another like those holding a matador's cape drawn towards the horns of a bull. The body turned, the gaze fell onto something in the distance, and the grip tightened when contact was made. The dance partners then parted, only to reunite when the desire to stimulate the synapses re-emerged.

MDMA was a synthetic drug otherwise known as methylenedi-oxymethamphetamine, or traditionally, ecstasy, and more recently: pingers. German scientists originally synthesised the drug in the early nineteen hundreds, but it wasn't until the eighties that it really came to prominence amid the European rave scene, resulting in increased visits to the dentist—due to the fierce grinding that resulted—and the essential, yet criminal, nightclub fashion accessory: sunglasses, which were required to conceal eyes that resembled the peepers of excited goats.

The dosage commonly affects the users' dopamine, norepi-nephrine, and serotonin levels and, thus, results in increased energy levels, feelings of empathy and affection, and a general willingness to dance like Travolta.

In other words, it's a good fucking time, and unequivocally the most popular product in a dealer's toolbox for good reason. Not that Kelvin would admit as much.

The cap is dropped like a diver entering a pool. A stream of effer-vescence and energy in its wake. Its journey is one of anticipation and growing excitement. As it bounces from one precipice to the next, it slowly dissolves, capturing the attention of those that reside on the walls of the fleshy tunnels and nooks that only surgeons, perhaps forensic pathologists, will gaze upon. When it becomes nothing—just an additive to a steady bloodstream—that's when the real fun begins. A vagabond finally realising a purpose, finding a meaning.

Toes, ears, and brows bristle with euphoria. Eyes widen. Teeth clench. A hug from within wraps itself around the body, forming an outer glow that forces sweat ducts to act accordingly—a physical response to the crashing waves in the brain.

And when the swell dies down and the calm returns, the divers take to the canals again—the streaks of solvency illuminating the dark passages along with the night.

The next morning, many report that the previous night raced by, a steam train refusing to take passengers. Memories condensed into fast-paced vignettes.

During the comedown, they become aware of their heartbeat, questioning if the knocking on the rib cage will become a cardiac arrest, or if the colliding thoughts that prevent sleep will manifest into a stroke. They also regret intimately embracing those that they wouldn't give a second glance in the cold, hard light of day. A hole in a chewed cheek doesn't necessarily sit well either.

When a sense of normality returns, thoughts turn to the next score or even just a quick dab of what remains. Of course, after persistent use, normality (and a sense of equilibrium) may remain more elusive for longer. In that instance, a hit is the only way to drag oneself from the depths of despondence. Thankfully, it's relatively inexpensive and has found its way unabated into poorer communities, aiding the necessity of escapism but also contributing to multiple tiers of depression that already exist.

Of course, not all users know their dealers, and the tablets, or caps, can sometimes house substances like ketamine, plant fertiliser, or bath salts.

This is when a good time becomes a very, very bad time.

This was Kelvin's favourite part.

Victims, during these occurrences, could slip into permanent hallucinations, behaving as if possessed, or even losing the function of vital bodily organs. These filthy yokes changed lives and occasionally damaged brains and reputations beyond repair.

MDMA doesn't account for many hospital admissions—especially when compared to alcohol, tobacco, and crystal—another fact that didn't quite fit the Operation: Spikies narrative and, hence, was discarded. But when junk finds its way into the equation—paramedics fear the worst. And a whole heap of junk was about to wash up on the shores.

Kelvin prowled the room. His back rigid, head held high. Proud like a faun. His hands were folded together as if he were kneading a ball of clay.

The room was lined with desks much like a classroom, and equally stiff students sat with unwavering devotion. Their facial features weren't recognisable, mere thumbprints protruding from collared shirts, and hair was cut militantly short. Fraternising was outlawed.

I scribbled something on my page. It seemed important to take notes. Habit perhaps. Possibly just a good distraction.

The blinds were drawn, and the time of day was anyone's guess. Were we already prisoners? Or was this the price for freedom? Would there be a test?

Talk of illicit substances turned to over-the-counter products, those acquired with a prescription. These were no less harmful, no less a strain on productivity, and society needed to be rid of such shackles if it were to prosper. Antidepressants. Painkillers. Cough medicines. If it could be abused, it fell under the Spikies umbrella and had to be treated accordingly.

Kelvin spoke in short bursts. Every new piece of information was to be registered and indexed in the hippocampus. Confusion led to mistakes. Uncertainty led to idle hands.

He scrawled a passage across a blackboard, and each strike of the chalk sent shudders down my spine. I had always been a good student, so I squinted to bring the ribboned text into focus. It read: *The great protagonists are those who fight for their ideas and ideals despite the fact that they receive no recognition at the hands of their contemporaries.* I copied it onto my notepad.

Attendees in close proximity raised their hands and asked questions, others answered to a pointed finger or a nod of acknowledgment. It was like I was part of a colony, all working towards a shared goal, a greater good expounded by a man in a turtleneck sweater and pleated trousers. He was the voice of authority, and we were entrusted with building the bridge towards his version of Utopia. But first, the foundations had to be laid.

A man from the back row was called to the front. It may have been premeditated, it may have been random, but, in either case, he had been chosen, and he willingly rose to his feet and strode to the head of the class. Whatever the collective noun for fauns was, it would have been apt. I felt a twinge of jealousy.

The two men, who could have passed for father and son, stood side by side. Kelvin ran a finger around the student's torso as if he were outlining the best cuts, and further notes were taken, the sound of frenzied nibs scratching paper filled the room.

Kelvin grasped the man by his broad shoulders and turned him to ensure they were facing one another. Again, it felt militant, and they stood tall before Kelvin held out both of his closed fists. It was an offering. Hesitation was a sign of weakness, and after only a brief moment, the nominated pupil pointed to the concealed item in Kelvin's right hand. The teacher raised an eyebrow, turned his palm upright, and a small pill was revealed. A nod endorsed the need to swallow the gift, and the student did so without protest. He unfurled his tongue for inspection, which was met approvingly, before making his way back to his seat in the shadows.

Kelvin clapped his hands together and continued the lesson which included projections of math formulas, tactical diagrams, and heat maps. It meant nothing to me, and I felt like an imposter on campus. A student that had paid his way without completing the homework.

After several minutes, the sound of the volunteer's head hitting the desk roused me. Whatever he had taken wasn't a placebo. Nobody blinked an eye. Nobody turned to check on his well-being. The paper soldiers knew their place and they feared the flame. And, as if on cue, Kelvin drew back the blinds and the arresting daylight beamed into the room. It was a rude awakening, but, unlike some, at least I could say as much. At least I was alive.

JUNK STAINS

No posters lined the walls. No flowers or cards had arrived, imploring me to *Get Well* or *Come Home Soon*. And thankfully no cuffs had been applied. But I was now horizontal, and the stretcher beneath me wore pristine sheets—they weren't freshly washed, they were brand new as if to replace those that had been soiled and incinerated.

The artificial implant must have messed with my biological circuitry, and a voice roused me from my slumber.

"While we are here, we would also like to do a few other tests." It was Kelvin, and he loomed large in my field of vision like an undertaker as I receded into my coffin.

"What kind of tests?" I queried in protest, becoming alert once again.

"Nathalie mentioned that you didn't mind occasionally experimenting. We just want to ensure that you are of sound body and mind."

"In other words, we want to make sure we're not handing over our lucrative stash to a fucking junkie." Good Cop and Bad Cop had again merged, and it was hard to tell who was actually speaking as I turned my head and stared up at their strong jaws and flared nostrils.

"Nathalie? Where is she? Can I see her?" I blurted, hoping to find a link to the real world, my world.

My requests for information were naturally ignored, and a doctor, or whatever you call the people that unapologetically plunge needles into your veins in police headquarters, stepped forward and exchanged places with Kelvin. He was the overseer, and it was apparent that he didn't like the sight of blood on his hands.

The physician was pencil thin, and her warm expression almost felt ironic given the circumstances. Despite her slender frame, her grip was firm, expertly forcing a tube of blood to the surface almost immediately. She slapped my forearm in a gesture that resembled friendship and produced a syringe no bigger than a ballpoint pen from her breast pocket. I knew the smile that she wore had no doubt proven instrumental in willing submission, and even in my state, I couldn't help but register her beauty.

"What is your name?" I pressed, hoping to find civility amid the intensity.

"We can save the 'getting to know you' routine until later," she said with a neat smile. It was enough to put me back in my place.

I then realised that blood wasn't being extracted but rather a transparent liquid was being injected. Any attempts at flirting could wait.

"Is that…" I slurred before drool flooded my words.

"Just a little something to help with the nightmares," was the only explanation given.

Before I could mount an argument, the room spun. All four faces of my newfound associates along with wall charts and pill bottles tumbled to the floor, and in the swirling mass of colours the overhead fluorescents became my anchor point until the blackout returned.

"This is no longer your story," a voice said as I faded into the spiralling darkness.

PART II:

MAKING FRIENDS WHILE
CIRCLING THE DRAINPIPE

MYSTERIUM COSMOGRAPHICUM

The cigarette between Nathalie's long, delicate fingers had dwindled in size, and she suddenly understood why so many referred to it as a 'roach.' It was now mostly soggy tobacco, but there was still some weed to be savoured, a luxury she hadn't been afforded under some of the strictest laws in Europe—the national cabinet, along with a majority of the populous, believed cannabis made you lazy and stupid. They obviously hadn't heard of Carl Sagan, Bill Gates, or Willie Nelson.

She winced as she took another hit, held it a moment in her lungs, and exhumed it into the air. It was a brisk evening, and the smoke added to the low-lying fog resembling a billowing chimney. Despite the cold, she was warm beneath a crocheted quilt in her reclining acacia beach chair with Elijah by her side. For some, it may sound naff, to her it was paradise.

The café had closed hours ago, but the owners never forbade employees climbing onto the rooftop for a little rest and relaxation, or to blow off a little steam after a lengthy shift. As long as they watched their step, shut off the lights, and locked up when they left. The sky was clear and magnificent and seemed to mock the limits of human perception, of how small and futile everything else was in comparison. Thankfully, on the outskirts of the city, light pollution hadn't tempered the appearance of constellations and drifting satellites, and Nat and Eli could pretend they were part of something bigger, something more intricate, even if that something cared little about their existence.

Elijah accepted the wilting joint and drew back on it deeply, expertly, in order to extract all its gifts, much like an asthma sufferer sucking on an inhaler in a time of need. He wasn't what you'd call a pothead, but he did enjoy the occasional indulgence. His head swirled under the effects of the dope as he gazed up at the shimmering stars, drawing lines and mapping their correlation. He knew Nathalie's and his zodiac signs were compatible, but he had no idea where to find the armed centaur nor the twins. It was nothing more than a random scattering of glistening coins thrown into a wishing well.

"If only five people at a dinner party, would I be one?" Nathalie asked. Her head was light and felt like it was full of Styrofoam peanuts, the type used for packing fragile items. She was also starting to feel peckish.

"It depends," Elijah responded after a moment of contemplation—an act he wasn't overly acquainted with.

"It depends?" Nathalie hated the indecisiveness of the word. She had heard it often.

"Yoko may want to accompany the Beatles." Elijah had a way of teasing Nathalie, and it never failed to get a reaction. On this occasion, though, she faced north and let her eyes rest on the brightest object. It wouldn't offer a signal, but she was tuned in anyway. She liked the idea that she wasn't looking up at the sky but rather across the solar system.

Nathalie pondered for a moment if Elijah would invite his mother if given the opportunity, but that was a seed better left unwatered.

"If stuck on a deserted island," she continued unperturbed, recalling a scenario from her youth, "would you want me there?"

"I wouldn't do that to you." Elijah's face was blank. His commitment to not committing was resolute.

"You take nothing serious." Nathalie turned her attention to Elijah. The marijuana had spread warmth through her body, warding off shivers but not uncertainties, and her boyfriend was unable to allay her anxieties, her apprehensions for the future. She was an 'all-in or bust' type of person, and she was constantly being stonewalled.

"Okay, give me one more," Elijah pleaded. He was the king of second chances.

"No. You are high. And you say stupid things."

Elijah feigned a sulk, but it wasn't in his nature, and it came off as half-assed, much like everything else he did.

"Did you ever have a microscope?" Nathalie asked. She thought of a brass clockwork mechanism she had been shown recently that depicted heliocentrism—planets orbiting the sun. The new friend had called it an orrery, and it reminded her that they weren't the centre of the universe—a concept Elijah constantly forgot. Nathalie checked her watch and realised he would be calling soon, this new acquaintance, and she would have to excuse herself. The model in motion was intended to impress, and it had worked.

"Telescope?" Elijah pointed upward to clarify.

"Same thing."

"That's not much of a hypothetical. But no. My family could never afford one."

She knew the answer before asking the question. Rich, poor, whatever. The point was he had never looked closely at anything.

"Okay." Nathalie drew back on the last of the spliff and flicked the glowing remnants over the edge of the rooftop to the street below. The roach could join its own kind. "If you were arrested and had one phone call, would you ring me?"

"No."

"No?"

"No," Elijah replied. "Because you would be my partner in crime."

Nathalie's face softened and she remembered why she loved him. She wanted to lean close, kiss her cellmate, and unscrew his skull so she could tinker with his wiring. But above all, she wanted to ask him what he would do if she left. In many ways, however, she knew the answer and it would never be enough. One day she would leave, but today wasn't that day.

A star shot across the sky as if another nickel had been skimmed across the galaxy, and both Nathalie and Elijah made two very distinct wishes before he drew the blinds and gave into tired eyes. Nathalie was again alone, and she could take the call knowing that Elijah was drifting away to the sound of his own irregular heartbeat.

L'APPEL DU VIDE

Paranoia gives way to unadulterated fear when the senses of those in your company shut down and become unresponsive. Those responsible for continued companionship and selfless supervision can only nurse and offer words that encourage regaining consciousness, words that are desperately wishful rather than being drawn from any true place of wisdom or understanding. Bursting forth from such a state of enforced inertia could leave one sheepish, but, as they said, the only way to avoid a knockout blow was to get up and fight another round, even if fragments of your mind were scattered across the canvas.

"Welcome back, Mister Caulfield, you've been out for quite some time," said the jab-happy nurse, whose pixie haircut neatly framed her face and complemented her demure features. Her complexion was porcelain, and she radiated an air of intelligence, emotional and academic. She was anomalous in many ways but still exuded a pleasant familiarity.

Elijah blinked rapidly and drew a deep breath into his lungs. The room was exorbitantly white. So blinding, in fact, that it was difficult to make out edges, find corners. Had it all just been a dream?

"I don't believe we officially met," the woman continued—more syringes now evident in the pocket of her lab coat. "I am Yumi Chiba, but you can call me the Pharmacist."

"The Pharmacist?" Elijah quizzed through the haze that remained.

"And this here to my left is Batal Kautista." The Pharmacist gestured to the foot of the bed. "But you can call him B."

Elijah directed his gaze to a space just above his toes. There stood a hulking man. Six four, 260 pounds. A bespoke suit threatening to come apart at the stitches. His head sat on his shoulders like a bowling ball on a pedestal. His pupils shaded by a heavy brow. His nose crooked from repeated repairs. The man could take a punch. Probably a sledgehammer.

"Nine o'clock," Elijah said softly, trying to place the name, slowly gaining clarity.

Batal said nothing.

"As you wish," Chiba continued. Brains and brawn had been plated, and the contrast between both had never been more acutely sketched. "You have been briefed on the task force, its objectives, its parameters. You know us, our roles, but we know so little about you. Tell me: Did you enjoy killing those people?"

Elijah blinked heavily as if the lids weighed a tonne, roller doors with well-oiled rails. Although Chiba appeared congenial, she was all business. Data for KPIs stacked up like long division on her finely tuned frontal lobe.

"I just remember the car taking on a life of its own. The brakes failed. The steering locked." Elijah continued breathlessly: "The vents spoke to me."

Chiba looked towards Batal, who returned her gaze as if she were glass and there was a telling vista beyond.

"What did they say?"

"Don't stop," Elijah cooed. "It was very soothing."

"And that's why you accelerated for almost a mile?'"

"The pedal was pinned. But my foot…" Elijah scanned archived visions. "But my foot, it wasn't planted on the gas."

Chiba stroked her chin which had never known a blemish.

"So, this is all a setup?"

"I didn't think of it earlier," Elijah murmured, lost in thought.

"How many times did you beat your girlfriend, Mister Caulfield?" Chiba changed the subject. She had boxes to tick, and she couldn't linger on, or encourage, trivial details. Cultivation of a model employee had to proceed unimpeded.

"I never beat her." Elijah was still chasing memories, but he was sure of that.

Again, Chiba and Batal exchanged glances. Lies? Perhaps the intel was inaccurate.

"One more question." Chiba referred to a clipboard. "If you could kill everyone in this building to escape the noose, would you do it?"

Elijah raised his head and locked eyes with the Pharmacist cum interviewer.

"Absolutely."

A chill tiptoed into the room, but not one of the three in attendance shivered at its arrival. Desensitisation, it seemed, was contagious.

THE VIRTUE OF YOUTH

Katie Vincenzo didn't take too kindly to being told what to do. Especially when it was her father doing the telling. Two nights a week, she snuck out through open windows or anything left ajar; other nights, she just avoided her father altogether—you can't lecture what you don't encounter.

Katie was six months shy of her nineteenth birthday, but she could easily pass for somebody five years her senior. She didn't look old, she just looked ready for the world. Confident. Assured. Fierce. Not that it mattered. All the club owners knew her father and wouldn't dare refuse her entry, wouldn't dare deny her every demand. Not the child of such a prominent figure. And no matter how poorly she behaved, heads nodded, grins held firm, and concessions were made. Of course, word got back to Pops, but it just mitigated the cycle, and all consequences were met with chagrin, all words of warning met with defiance—it was enough for a parent's frustration to manifest into violence.

Her father was a disciplinarian at heart, and he lacked the ability to be flexible, even empathetic. It was a trait that made raising a teenage girl an arduous task, one filled with dirty looks, raised voices, and the threat of irreparable damage.

"When he was my age," Katie said, holding a sequined top that would later expose a midriff, "he would have been out 'til all hours. Now he's forgotten what it's like to be young, to be reckless."

Nadia sat on the corner of her friend's unmade bed and nodded, feigning interest. She had heard it all before, and she knew Katie just needed to clear her airwaves and blow off a little steam. That children's song about body language and the rising temperature of a teapot, it was also about Katie.

"He's lost his zest, his lust for a scrap and a good time."

"Didn't you say he had a guy tied up in the bathroom the other day? You heard him screaming through the vents," Nadia recalled while leering at the dazzling crop top, hoping it would fall to the floor and make its way into her handbag.

"Yeah, but that was business. And it was definitely not off the cuff." Katie examined her reflection in the mirror affixed to the wardrobe door, fabric held for appraisal to her naked skin. "It's not like Dave Parsons came over, asked for a cup of sugar, and ended up getting his teeth extracted. That bastard owed money and he was holding out."

"Extracted?" Nadia quizzed her friend's developing expression.

"It's what Dad does when he's chasing debts. He asks nicely at first, but some people just don't respond to *nice*."

"Katie, it's pretty cool that your dad gets shit done by ripping dudes' teeth out," Nadia gushed. "My dad spends the whole day pushing pencils. He even grovelled to the teachers when they were calling me out on my behaviour."

"Well, he can't intimidate me, I'm not one of his piss-weak associates. We're going out tonight with or without his blessing."

"Didn't he say he would cut access to the trust fund if you disobeyed him again?" Nadia warned selfishly. There was always the chance of excess runoff when bank accounts overflowed, and catchment needed to be strategic.

"Do I look like I give a shit about his trust fund?" Katie spat, like a seasoned brat. Veruca Salt raised with a knowledge of blade artistry.

Nadia took the fifth and simply eyed Katie's open wardrobe which was lined with the season's finest and looked like a Saks' pop-up store.

"And, anyway, tonight we're drinking Copagne."

"Copagne?" Nadia hated not being privy to all the new trends. It really had become hard to keep up sometimes. Hashtags worthy of one's attention changed daily.

"Bubbles dusted with cocaine. You really should follow Hannie Carson's blog—she knows all the ways to get high."

"Did you know Stevie Nicks used to have coke blown into her arse through a straw to avoid a deviated septum?" Nadia tried to assert a certain level of social nous.

"Stevie Nicks?" Katie cocked an eyebrow. "Who the fuck is Stevie Nicks?"

"Maybe it was Miley Cyrus?" Nadia scrambled.

"Miley Cyrus?" Katie jammed her brows together—the upper third of her face really was hyper-expressive. "Miley Cyrus is soooo yesterday, Nadia, the bitch needs an upgrade. I think she's officially black and white."

BIG SHARKS EAT LITTLE SHARKS

The grainy image between Elijah's fingers looked like little more than blurred blobs, as if mould had taken hold and spread across the page. It was void of colour and discernible figures. Perhaps the courier had exposed it to direct sunlight or dropped a milkshake on it.

"What exactly am I looking at here?" Elijah quizzed into the phone, turning the frame one way and then the next.

"This is a guy we're working to shut down. A prime mover on the club scene," Chiba said, proud of her intel. The Pharmacist had many strings to her bow.

Elijah had been allowed to return home, the implant keeping him grounded. The package and the conference call had arrived almost immediately.

"There's a guy in this mess? I thought you were testing me with some Rorschach bullshit." Elijah squinted to form an outline.

"You're a kid, you know how hard it is to get a well-lit shot in these multiplexes."

"It's been a long time since I was a kid."

"Sure still act like one," B muttered his first words. Elijah glanced at the phone but knew better than to poke that bear. It was a three-way conference call, and three-ways never worked as well as one may imagine.

"So, what do you want me to do with this? Make a citizen's arrest? Post it around town to drum up some support for his business?"

"You monitor his interactions and act accordingly. Take out the mouths that he feeds. We need to sculpt consumer perception."

"Why can't you just go after the scum? You're police, right? Do police shit. Take off the head and watch the supply dry up."

"Because it won't." B was becoming talkative. "One will replace another. It doesn't take the product off the streets and the feeding frenzy continues."

"Plus, these guys are protected," Chiba added. Their reach is far and wide, and we have a tough time getting a conviction. They deal in junk but are treated like diamonds."

"Everyone is dirty, and you want me to punish vulnerable people that spend their hard-earned on a dab here and there? A recreational hit on the weekend is hardly an offence."

"It's the only way users will curb their ways." Chiba had studied the psychology at length, and she had an answer for everything. Her intentions were pure even if her actions weren't. "And it sends a clear message to the top dogs. Abolish demand, bankrupt supply."

"These dealers aren't gonna just pack up shop and become gardeners and yoga instructors, they'll find a way."

"And we will too. We will adapt our methods if and when it's necessary."

"And this is necessary?"

"For now."

"We're talking about people's lives."

"We're talking dozens to save thousands."

It suddenly became clear to Elijah that even if Yumi Chiba wasn't the brainchild of this reform, she sure as hell was head of the class. He could imagine the PhD graduate presenting to a boardroom of cops that had been on the beat too long, salivating at the prospect of taking out a few long-haired delinquents. It was the green light they had eagerly awaited. An opportunity to jack-off on the job and crack a few skulls along the way.

"Kid. You've been chosen for a reason. Just hours ago, you flattened a crowd of people. Your scruples are questionable." B planted his feet so his moving jaw wouldn't result in him toppling over.

"I was angry," Elijah offered like a grade student in the headmaster's office.

"Marwan al-Shehhi was angry. Mohamed Atta was angry."

"Who are they?"

"They are the men responsible for steering two planes into the World Trade Center. They were terrorists."

"Makes your motive sound pretty feeble, doesn't it?" B and Chiba were playing a convincing game of tag.

Elijah looked defeated. His actions had deafened all ears in his proximity, and he had forgone all rights, including the one to voice an opinion.

"Your card is stamped, champ. It's time to go to work."

Elijah held the phone to his ear as the dial tone reinforced that a brick wall had been erected at the other end.

The handpiece fell to the floor with a soft thud, and Elijah caught sight of his grazed feet and bruised lower leg from being dragged into custody. He had once had fight, the tenacity to stand up to the vocal tormenter on the train, but at that moment, he felt like nothing more than a wounded cub stranded in the woods.

MANNERS ARE FOR THE MEEK

But fuck being a cub.

No level of scratching and tampering would uncover the crown of the implant, and Elijah wasn't willing to dig deep in the vicinity of vital wiring to seek freedom. Jugular veins were best left to do their thing, and meddling was ill advised.

He had three choices: stay put, wait for the armed squadron to arrive and get thrown in a cell to rot for the rest of his days; eat the prescribed medicine and ride the wave to an arguably untimely death; or slide a razor across his face, splash on some aftershave, step into his finest yet tired threads, and make his way downtown where he would proceed to poison hordes of poor bastards all in the name of 'raising social awareness.'

In no time, Elijah was tightly buttoned into a freshly pressed shirt and making his way out the door with an empty wallet and a vial of liquid—a liquid that was hell-bent on ruining evenings and ending lives. At least the recipient wouldn't have to endure the crippling effects of a hangover. It was a substance Death would happily trade his scythe to get his hands on.

He took the stairs three at a time and passed the customary faces that he customarily ignored. When he pushed through the building's main entrance, the cold night air embraced him like an old friend and he immediately felt at ease. Elijah had always been comfortable in nocturnal surrounds, and he took a deep breath, accepting the various possibilities that accompanied the hours between dusk and dawn.

The electronic tracking device felt warm in his neck, and although it reminded him of the deal that had been made, it also felt strangely supportive—a crutch during time of injury, an accomplice during times of deception.

That feeling had all but evaporated by the time Elijah arrived at the club. In fact, he had never felt more alone. His hands were clammy, throat dry, and his armpits burned as he stood in line with the mostly beautiful young things, some already feeling the effects of a pregame bump. It was an arduous wait, and it reminded Elijah of why he no longer wasted his time on such establishments. Social distancing had been a godsend, and he felt uneasy, even betrayed, when it was forgotten or neglected, which had become most of the time.

When he did finally reach the head of the queue, a cynical eye scanned his presence from head to toe before a demand for identification was made from a stone-faced asshole sporting a mouth that seemed incapable of a smile or anything other than a snarl.

In a past life, he would have been called out for the wrong footwear or a stained collar, but he now knew the score and there were very few access points for discrimination. He even bit his tongue knowing that it had been a crippling appendage and not an asset during his youth.

#PARTYTIME

"ID? I don't need a fucking ID. Do you know who I am?" Katie queried in a way that indicated that she was more than willing to make a scene.

"Everyone that enters needs to be scanned in, Katie," the guard responded, arms crossed, attempting to maintain a strong resolve.

"See, you know my name. Why do I need a card to prove it?"

A figure appeared over the guard's shoulder and spoke into his ear—although he wore an earpiece and communication could have been done remotely, a point was being made, a peace gesture, and apparently protocol could be relaxed. The guard's stance relaxed, and he stepped aside while unlatching a red rope which separated the sidewalk from the exclusivity of the brick barracks, which looked as if it had once housed government secrets.

A cursive neon light buzzed overhead as Katie bypassed the counter for entry fees and rubber stamping and made her way towards the heaving trance music that emanated from the bowels of the building. Protests again fell on ears accustomed to deafening buds, and Katie, with Nadia in tow, made her way to the balcony where they could powder their noses, scream over the music in conversation, and make themselves comfortable amid a growing forest of empty bottles. They had only the bare necessities, and cloaking was for the ill prepared.

Eyelids drooping, hair a little ruffled, mascara smudged, Katie stared out over the crowd that rippled in the shimmering light of reflective mirrors. Every night was opening night, and the club was bursting at its seams.

"I've double-dropped and can't feel shit," she exclaimed irritably. "Did Henry say we had to shelve these caps?"

"You can do whatever you want, Katie, but I'm not sticking anything up my arse," Nadia responded, loudly enough to capture the attention and imagination of those standing at the bar. The music always knew when to drop at the most inappropriate time.

Katie gave her a wry look to suggest that she knew her friend was more anal receptive than she would ever care to admit.

"We need to find Tony to get something that will actually work. The stuff we get from Hank and Flex and Nuisance are vitamins at best." Katie took a seat beside her friend and lamented the elusive nature of their high.

"It could be for the best, Katie, I don't want to feel like a used mop tomorrow. I'm getting tired of crashing so hard."

"Fuck that! If we pay to get wasted, I expect to get wasted," Katie concluded, venom dripping from her fangs. "I don't have time to swallow blanks."

Katie intently chewed her bubble gum and rapidly flicked her eyelashes. The scent of ignited hormones and alcohol filled the air.

"Ladies." Tony sidled up to the girls' makeshift lounge room. "Are you in need of my services or are we already amped?"

"Speak of the devil," Nadia said at a barely audible level, not bothering to compete with the pulsating atmosphere.

"Jesus. Are we glad to see you," Katie cried in a more euphoric timbre.

Tony slid onto the leather sofa and placed an arm around both women. "I am neither Jesus nor the devil, but I can certainly help you meet both."

"One trip to heaven, please." Katie raised a finger and pointed skyward. Nadia couldn't help but giggle, unable to evade the contagious nature of her friend's rapture.

Tony smiled and reached into the lining of his jacket. He was a typical drug dealer: self-assured, instinctively alert, charming, and seemingly at ease. Some might say that he could be volatile and contemptuous when necessary, but that was like calling a reptile too scaly or a wolf too carnivorous. Tony handed over a small plastic pocket containing the powder the girls so longingly desired. Katie snatched it without a moment's hesitation, rose to her heels, and began to enthusiastically skip her way to the bathroom, relinquishing her usual catwalk strut and composed demeanour.

"Do you want me to put that on your father's tab?" the resident dealer enquired through the thick fog of angular synthesisers and rumbling bass tones. But by that stage, nobody was listening. Drugs had a habit of doing that.

The toilet seat looked like a piece of abstract art comprised of haphazardly applied white lines against the midnight black of the closed lid. It was Joy Division's *Unknown Pleasures* reimagined by somebody with OCD. Katie hoovered what she could as soon as she could, each time pulling her head back like a ravenous botanist savouring the scent of a recently pollinated flower.

Sounding distant, yet in close proximity within the same cubicle, Nadia spoke incessantly about music and boys and clothes; after all, what else really mattered? Katie responded with another swift and deep inhalation of the chopped synthetic particles.

Nadia paused briefly, noting her friend's rapidly expanding pupils, before adding: "Maybe you should take it easy, Katie. I'm not sure you're supposed to have the whole bag in one shot."

The walls drew closer and Katie found a sense of clarity.

"I know when I've fucking had enough," she snapped before holding her hair back and dropping to her knees for another hit. "And anyway," she said between healthy doses of snow trails, "I think I'm becoming immune to this shit. It's like stuffing my nose with flour. Maybe we need to channel that Stevie Nicks bitch."

"I'm not going anywhere near your asshole, honey, so you can forget that right now." Nadia's hands pushed forth an artificial barrier.

"You should be so lucky." Katie pinched her nose to remove any stray particles and crashed through the door of the stall, leaving Nadia standing against the wall to bear witness to her best friend's growing erratic behaviour. The surrounding tiles seemed fragile in the whirlwind that had been summonsed.

"Feel free to clean up that mess," Katie's voice echoed through the bathroom as she twirled her finger in the air. "Hopefully it has more effect on you." And with that, she disappeared back into the enveloping darkness of the club with a spring in her step that landed with an occasional stumble like a wounded ballet dancer that wouldn't dare disappoint.

Tony was now entrenched in business at the bar, so Katie made a beeline for the dance floor; she was a valued customer and payment could wait. Her credit would hold for now. The pounding beats and bright lights had a magnetic pull, and Katie had no time for banal chat or strained hookups. She needed to ride the wave she had worked so hard to catch, a wave that would carry her towards temporary enlightenment, even a sense of accomplishment. Katie had read in a glossy magazine that amphetamines had been pre-scribed to sufferers of depression in the nineteen seventies, and she could understand why. She was an icon, an entertainer, the life of the party, a stunning vista at the end of a gruelling hike, all in that moment.

A deep house record familiar to the attending crowd spun beneath the stylus, and a loud roar erupted. Although the name of the track eluded her, Katie Vincenzo threw up her arms, and she felt the warm embrace of the flailing bodies that now moved as one. Pulses dictated by subwoofers and chemistry.

COLOSSEUM IN RUINS

Legs crossed and ass firmly glued to the chair, Elijah admired the fake ID in his hand. His image and birth date remained the same, but he was now Patrick Svoboda, a name that he would have to become accustomed to. Of all the names that could have been selected, he felt very little connection to Patrick; now, Jack or Antoine, he could have gotten behind, even Michel—he'd been told he had French traits—but Patrick? Patrick reminded him of a prep student acquainted with polo and rowing, pastel collars and loafers. And the Czech surname was even more mystifying—he would never be able to explain its origins—pronunciation in itself was a chore. No doubt it all amounted to a proto-offspring for that prick Kelvin, he thought. An accumulation of all that he wanted in the son he'd never had.

Elijah's wardrobe would need to be adjusted, hair product purchased. A Svoboda also sounded like it should sport impressive jewellery, of which he had none. He cringed as he noticed the mass of people on the lower level of the precinct—cardboard cut-outs pulled by strings in the hands of a pogoing DJ, high on the effects of an inflated sense of self-worth. It had been a long time since Elijah had attended such a venue, and he felt like a prickly cactus in a sea of dim-witted sunflowers solely focussed on reaching for the sky and each other.

Surely, he thought, this was a fate worse than prison and his decision had been ill advised, made in haste. He knew, however, that his cheque had been cashed and he needed to present the head of one of these young shmucks, otherwise it would be his own.

The vial sat snugly in his breast pocket, firmly pressed against his rib cage. He thought momentarily about the stories he'd heard of sweaty festivalgoers absorbing sheets of acid through clothing and falling into deep psychosis, a realm where giant yellow canaries tormented and held their prey captive. Elijah shook his head and hoped the vessel was airtight. He had never encountered a bad trip, nor the hallucinogenic effects of psilocybin, and he didn't plan on joining the ranks of Syd Barrett and others that had fallen from the stage.

"Tony Maslow!" a young woman at the next table called out. Elijah's attention was instantly piqued, and he couldn't help but notice her natural, although manicured, beauty, along with her skimpy skirt, glittered blouse parted at the sternum, and impossibly high wedges secured to her ankles by gold buckles. The air was snatched from Elijah's lungs, and although he didn't want to stare, he couldn't take his eyes off the radiant presence that spoke too loudly and spilled her drink as she began to lose the battle with gravity and the content entering her bloodstream. Elijah had only recently been dumped, and he felt the first impressions of a rebound as he admired her slightly turned upward nose, pixie-pointed ears, and pouted lips which provided a gateway to perfectly straight white teeth reserved for the genetically gifted or financially secure. Her tousled hair shone as if she had just stepped from a steam room. Boy, did he miss Nat, and it had only been a day or two.

The girl must have been at least ten years his junior, and he felt like a creepy voyeur, but he quickly did the maths anyway: half one's age plus seven years equalled a potential sexual partner. The numbers didn't lie, she was too young for Elijah.

Naturally, Elijah noted that she was joined by an attractive young chap—one who walked and talked and sat back as if he owned the place. 'Big dick energy,' they called it, but he was probably just the head honcho's son or somebody who liked to bask in the glory of being considered a VIP. No matter his story, he seemed to have the scantily clad lady, and her friend, wrapped around his little finger, much like the diamond-encrusted bands he paraded.

According to the girl, this was Tony Maslow, and unbeknownst to them, he was going to be the cause of somebody's death tonight.

Elijah kept one eye on the shimmering swell of figures under the music's spell and one on his object of desire. He feared that she may combust and disappear, perhaps be consumed by the monster made of people. Surely, if she stepped into that mob, she would be circled by sharks and ultimately ripped apart, predators savouring limbs, clumps of hair, even ripped sections of garments would suffice.

In his periphery, Elijah noted the exchange: a hug around the neck for a bag of nose candy. He turned his head to watch the mirage skip her way to the private confines of the bathroom and in doing so caught eyes with the distributor—the guy that got all the girls because his stash was a baited lure, a precious gemstone in the eyes of those that craved a sniff. The two men didn't share a smile, a nod, or any form of friendly acknowledgment—they were strangers in the night, and no level of mutual appreciation would bring them together. Elijah knew there was one guilty party involved in the transaction, and he wasn't about to give undue credit.

Elijah recognised the man. The photo didn't do him justice. He was apparently the king of the scene, and Elijah could throw him from the balcony and end it all now. Cover-ups were all the rage at the moment, and he felt confident that his superiors could clean up the mess, even if it did spread across the dance floor.

But he had his directives. The contract stipulated that he should now spike the drink of the angelic presence, albeit of the foul-mouthed variety, which, according to the brain's trust, would create hysteria in the clubbing-scene/social-drug-using community and thus put slick out of business. It was a conclusion scribbled on a blackboard, but a wrong turn had been taken along the way. Nevertheless, it was a novel way to tackle what they called the 'drug crisis,' and Elijah couldn't help but smirk at the prospect. There had to be a simpler way, one that didn't involve a roundabout killing spree that put dealers on the poverty line and users in body bags. But he also knew they had eyes on him. Every move would be transcribed, and he would be portrayed back at HQ as one of the team or a rat in their midst. Kill or be killed. It was the law of the jungle, and The Weeknd offered the perfect soundtrack from the two-tonne speakers.

A stranger would be best. Somebody Elijah hadn't overheard in conversation—definitely not somebody he instantly felt an attraction towards. But how would he know? Drug users didn't just sugar-coat the décor and vacuum their way through blow in front of adoring fans like some kind of stage spectacular. And behaviour commonly associated with alcohol or a high Red Bull intake could easily be confused with being drug addled. The path to euphoria had many possible stimulants. Elijah hadn't been trained in this shit. A nasal sniff could just be a common cold, a scratched arm just eczema, or swollen pupils just the by-product of exposure to intense light. That was why official drug testers swabbed cells and bottled urine, and didn't just diagnose upon performance or appearance.

"Four caps, a sheet of Hillbilly, and some dexies if you've got 'em," a sweaty-ass punter asked the resident supplier during a lull in the blasting beats. His shirt had become almost transparent like a parcel of greasy fish and chips, and the collar and cuffs had soured to the colour of brown vinegar. He had either perspired, dried, and then perspired some more, or he simply hadn't soaked or bleached in quite some time. Elijah stood casually, smoothed his pants, and made his way to the bar. He need not hear any more of the conversation.

"What will it be?" the bartender queried beyond the sanctity of the bar, which was lit up like a lone truck stop on a desolate road.

"Two Jack and Cokes," the damp guy said over Elijah's shoulder. Elijah turned to face the gentleman that had just scored and was greeted by a beaming smile that featured a set of teeth that lit up the room. Elijah suddenly became aware of his own cut lip and chipped molars.

"Sorry to cut the queue... I hope you like JD," he said just inches from Elijah's bemused expression. Social distancing was certainly a thing of the past.

For a moment, Elijah was dazzled by the row of pearly veneers that consumed his vision before he eventually squeezed out a response. "I'm strictly a bourbon man."

"Take it, dude," the man emphasised. "It's an apology for being rude. I hate people that skip the line." Elijah shrugged. He wouldn't argue, but he still wasn't there to make friends.

"I ain't never heard of anyone refusing a free drink," the overly friendly stranger said as he leaned across the bar to retrieve his drinks.

"Just put it on Cleo's tab," he said with a wink before offering the glass of black fuel to Elijah. He finally accepted it and raised the vessel along with his eyebrows as a sign of courtesy. The gift giver mumbled something, it may have been gratitude, maybe not, and he vacated Elijah's company before taking a seat with the illicit human vending machine.

Elijah looked down at the drink in his hand. He imagined the fizz that would erupt from his solvent, he pictured panicked faces attached to waving arms, drowning in the stormy liquid concoction. Elijah placed the glass on the bar, suddenly losing the appetite to whet his whistle.

Could he really turn a harmless drink designed to lift one's spirits into a cup of poison?

Sure, it wasn't like emptying a tub of Drano down somebody's throat—he didn't have to witness the fatal repercussions—but the result would be similar, and he would still be responsible. Culpability lived on beyond a blind eye.

Interrupting his thoughts, the girl with tousled hair, with a thin coating of white powder on her nose, who could be cast as sex bomb or flirtatious stoner, crossed the room and headed straight for the pit of writhing bodies that was fast establishing its own ecosystem. Elijah reached into his pocket, took the canister, and poured a small portion of the chemistry experiment into the palm of his hand—

Don't scratch your face. Don't eat a meal. Don't even hold your dick. Before washing your hands. Thoroughly.

—and placed it into the lonely glass sitting patiently. He held his hand steady for a moment as if feeding fish and watched closely as each particle fell to the whiskey's surface. He had been given two vials—one liquid, one powder—both would do the job effectively.

"Can I get a straw?" Elijah asked the bartender in a voice that rose above the surrounding noise, a little louder than even he expected in the wake of his stealth act.

"You know those things kill more than a million marine animals each year?" the barkeep said as she handed over a coloured tube prised from a secret stash.

"And how many humans?" Elijah wasn't in the mood for lectures.

"What?"

"Never mind." Humans could fend for themselves.

The bartender turned away and busied herself with another customer. Elijah inserted the harpoon and stirred the contents, keeping one eye on whoever wanted to steal a glance. There were no rising bubbles, no science fair explosions, no demons that appeared from the mist to snap at his fingertips. It was an agent of subterfuge formulated to inflict death without leaving a trail back to its distributor.

Elijah planted his feet, descended from the lofty perch of his stool, and made his way to the two jovial men sharing a joke—one nursing an alcohol-infused soda, the other enjoying the lucidity of his recent acquisition.

"On second thought," Elijah said, leaning over the men and placing his own drink on the small wooden coffee table, which had probably never been used for coffee, "I really am a bourbon man. It's silly, but I guess my allegiances run deep."

The two men looked at each other and then down at the drink, and when they lifted their gaze, Elijah had disappeared into the crashing swell.

NO NEWS DURING MACBETH'S REIGN

The empty vial was the first thing Elijah noticed when he awoke amid crumpled sheets and scattered pillows. It had been a restless night. The grey entered the room through a closed window like an obnoxiously bright television screen that had lost its signal. The world beyond the glass seemed to personify nothingness, offering only a restricted view of wretchedness for those who chose to embrace the cloud-filtered day.

Elijah wiped the remnants of what little sleep he'd had from his eyes. It was as if tears had dried in his lashes and weren't easily brushed aside. Staring at the projection of light shouldering its way into his bedroom, he couldn't help but picture the faces of those he had run down. Looks of pure terror, pure disbelief. But instead of strangers, each face took on the appearance of a past lover, friend, acquaintance. His mother.

Had things really gotten so bad that he had to resort to such measures?

Nothing would really ever explain or justify it.

It was an act so devastating that he had changed the course of his existence in the blink of an eye. From zero to Hades' drinking buddy in less than five minutes; that's all it took to ignite his past and abandon all hope for the future. Bridges in all directions had been demolished. His whole being was soaked in blood, and it wasn't a stain that would easily come out in the wash. The red ran deep.

Elijah's newly acquired phone came to life, dancing to the sound of its own melody. Immediately, the night before came into vivid focus: the girl, the club, the drink. It was a scene he had avoided for much of his adult life, and he found it laughable that he was being instructed to 'blend in.' Elijah stared down at the trembling handset hoping for nothing more than to be greeted by Nathalie's songlike cadence. He missed her hazy morning eyes. The way she smelled like cookies after being wrapped up in blankets. The hint of saliva that sat in the corners of her mouth. Hair fashioned by the dreams she chased.

He would give anything for that moment, but the unfamiliar sequence of numbers on the screen indicated it wasn't to be. Not today anyway.

Elijah snapped open the device and rested it on his exposed ear, the other still submerged in the pillow. A mono signal was more than enough.

"Were our instructions not clear?" the tinny yet forceful voice quizzed down the line. It was Bad Cop.

"What?" Elijah responded dimly, feeling praise was the order of the day, and not the contemptuous tone that greeted him.

"Have you seen the news?"

Elijah sat upright. "News? What news? ODs don't make the news."

"You are very good at making headlines, young man, maybe you should read them sometime." That reminded Elijah, he hadn't seen or heard anything about his joyride. His face hadn't been plastered amid cover stories or breaking bulletins.

"I did what you asked," he said like a delivery boy that had been given clear co-ordinates and even clearer directives. This, he thought, was his life now.

Elijah peered through the blinds. It was still morning. The news could wait.

"It's three in the afternoon, Caulfield, it's time to wake the fuck up."

Elijah shot a glance at the bedside clock, the fragments of illuminated digits confirming the cop's words.

"A car is outside. Get dressed. It's been waiting long enough."

Elijah tossed the sheets from the bed.

He winced as he recalled the microchip that had been planted in his body—a foreign agent sending messages to enemies that masqueraded as accomplices.

Elijah swung his legs across and leapt from the mattress. It felt good not to contend with a hangover that so often accompanied a night at the club, but his head was still far from a fit state. He parted the shades and noted the black Bentley, motor running, windows tinted, parked on the curb. A grim reality flooded into Elijah's consciousness, and the sanctuary of sleep became a distant memory. He was now very much awake and the blood on his hands was still wet. The nightmare was very much real.

VERISIMILITUDE IN THE AFTERNOON

Every inch of the car's leather interior was polished and soft to the touch. Too sharp for a government vehicle, unless the funding was much better than Elijah had anticipated. On the other hand, it could have been plucked directly from Kelvin's private fleet. He seemed like a man with deep pockets and exquisite tastes. He must have built a healthy nest before descending the ladder to become a public servant.

Elijah slid into the back seat and lowered the window. The fresh air would do him good. The car had been modified and a divide separated him from the driver to afford privacy and security. It was much like a chauffeur-driven limousine, and Elijah felt compelled to request a bottle of champagne, except the destination offered no reason to celebrate·

The wind blew in his face and he felt the fatigue wash away. If he closed his eyes, he could almost imagine that he was aboard a magic carpet ride and all that had unfolded was part of a fantasy land, an alternate existence.

"We need to make a stop," a voice rattled from an overhead speaker, grabbing Elijah by the neck and yanking him back into reality. The man was forthright, and Elijah immediately had the feeling that they weren't ducking in for cigarettes.

"What do you mean stop?" he said in an omnidirectional fashion like an elderly commuter that had lost his bearings. "We have an appointment."

The Perspex screen that cut the vehicle in half lowered and the driver came into view. Although he didn't turn his head to acknowledge Elijah, it was clear that he was a younger, fitter, and more fetching version of his passenger, and perhaps more importantly, wielded the ability to drive in straight lines.

"It can wait." He snapped his wrist and held up a small envelope without diverting his attention from the road.

Elijah leaned forward and snatched it from his gloved grasp before nestling back in the seat. He stared down at the envelope to discover that it hadn't been addressed nor sealed. He then removed the contents—a card shrouded in floral designs which simply announced that he was invited to a garden party in Silian Rail typeface.

"A garden party?" Elijah raised his eyes disapprovingly. He wasn't in the mood to sip Pimm's or play croquet. And he most definitely wasn't dressed for it. His whites hadn't been soaked in quite some time.

"More an outdoor rave," the driver clarified. He still didn't turn his head and wasn't concerned about receiving a sucker punch.

"We're going to a rave?" The clarification hadn't changed his attitude.

"*You* are going to a rave. I'll be waiting."

"Nothing was said about a rave." This was Elijah filing a complaint.

"Well, now you know. You have thirty minutes. The motor will be running."

"I'm not sure if you know, but I have to work tonight." He had no idea if the driver was acting autonomously or under Kelvin's command, but in either case, it seemed in breach of workers' rights.

"Consider it a double shift." The man was listening to the words, but he couldn't hear the sentiment. Elijah caught a glimpse of a dull pulse in the driver's neck – a buried beacon – but before he could query its insertion or compare hardware, a button was pushed, and the privacy screen was reactivated. He could have been one of the thousands that had sat across the blackjack table during those long shifts at the casino.

Elijah shook his head. A rave. He didn't know they were still a thing and he had no idea what to expect. Drug overdoses were part of the scene, and he felt his attendance was extraneous. Why strangle a person when they were already bleeding to death?

Fifteen minutes later, they arrived at the parklands where revellers were filtering into a section cordoned off for the party. Elijah looked out the window at all the beautiful young things—women in sundresses, men in short shorts, and all with flowers in their hair and Venetian masks concealing their identity.

"You want me to blend in here? It's a masquerade ball." Elijah again voiced his concerns. What was next? Administering droplets into snorkels at pool parties? Dressing as a leprechaun on St. Patrick's Day? Bursting from a novelty cake at retirement celebrations? A stand had to be taken. Clubs were one thing, but he couldn't be expected to follow the drugs to every social event on the calendar.

"You have thirty minutes," the speaker crackled. It was final. Non-negotiable.

Elijah sighed, swung the door open, which he was surprised to find wasn't child locked, and stepped into the dappled afternoon sunshine.

As he made his way towards the entrance, he glanced back at the car, which was, in fact, still purring, and then down at his wristwatch. He had twenty-nine minutes to endure.

At a divide where the fence line began and ended, Elijah handed over the invitation, which was torn and set aside as if it held little importance, and in return, he was given a bejewelled mask featuring rounded cat's ears. It was playful and extremely feminine.

Elijah chewed his lip for a moment and stared down at the bored-looking attendee who seemed to share his disdain for the unfolding carnival.

"No mask, no entry." The gatekeeper pointed to a sign that supported his statement.

Elijah tightened his lips and shrugged. So be it. He placed the elastic over his head, slid the eyewear into position, and immediately felt like a tragic Greek figure rather than Renaissance royalty.

"Now you have a chance of getting laid," the guard complimented derisively.

Elijah appreciated the encouragement, yet couldn't feign a smile, and made his way into the paddock of grazing merrymakers.

Naturally, at an outdoor event, the vast majority of people stood cradling their drinks, mostly plastic champagne flutes and pre-mixed cans, which made the act of spiking a complex one indeed.

Elijah checked his watch. Twenty-five minutes remained.

Hastily, he made a beeline for a picnic table that sat among a gathering of sycamore trees. If he could sit with momentarily benched cups, he could spike, even in broad daylight.

The seat offered a good vantage point to observe who was there to conform to social obligations, and maintain appearances—*hello, how are you, so nice to see you again, oh, maybe one drink, I really must be getting home before it gets too late*—and those who were there to get fucked up and dance into the wee hours of the morning without any thought of what tomorrow may hold.

The targets would paint their own bull's-eyes.

Before Elijah could scan the expanse of the palatial grounds, he was joined by a man whose morning routine clearly included eating steroids, lifting weights, and applying fake tan. He sat too close and already smelled of perspiration. He was in it for the long haul. Target engaged.

Nineteen minutes.

"Do you do amyl?" the man asked without offering a greeting. His own mask had a low brow and a long nose. It was gold.

"Only on special occasions," Elijah lied. He had never taken amyl.

The man peeled back and sized up his acquaintance. He seemed curious but also agitated. Whatever inhalants he had in his possession had sizzled parts of his limbic system.

"And today is a special occasion, right?"

"Not yet," Elijah replied, "but it could be."

"I am going to call you *She.*" The man changed tact and tapped Elijah on the head. "Because *She* is the cat's mother."

Elijah withdrew from the man's touch, he didn't need to be reminded of the pinnas that adorned his mask, and he most definitely did not need to be touched.

A sustained drone emanated from oversized speakers, and a mass of bodies surged towards the stage like bugs drawn to a flame. Things were heating up.

"He's from Nairobi," the man said as he nudged and nodded towards the sound.

"And what's your name?" It couldn't hurt to become better acquainted with the mark. It was the least he could do.

"Cindy," the man with an impressive beak said.

Elijah nodded his head as if to acknowledge a completed transaction. Now that the formalities were out of the way, he could get down to business.

Thirteen minutes.

"You don't believe my name is Cindy?" Cindy said. His tone was abrasive, shocked.

Elijah shook his head and shrugged simultaneously. He didn't doubt the name given, in fact, he didn't care.

"Morgan," he called to an impossibly thin woman who was standing nearby with a group that had aspirations of becoming influencers. "He doesn't believe my name is Cindy."

She cocked an eye, shrugged, and turned away. She didn't give a shit either.

"Is it short for something?" Elijah tried to massage his pride. "Lucinda? Cynthia?"

"No. It's just Cindy. Cindy Lee." He reached into his pocket, removed a small amber medicine bottle containing a clear liquid, and placed it on the table. It was much like the one Elijah had in his possession, right down to the black twist top.

"Prescribed?" Elijah asked, gesturing to the glass vessel.

"Hardly," Cindy replied as he busied himself with rolling a cigarette. The name, it seemed, was his party trick and it had fallen flat.

The drone intensified, and the crowd clapped and cheered and threw their hands in the air. Beyond the noise, a subaudible throb was beginning to take shape.

A gust of wind rustled the overhead leaves, and Cindy's sheet of paper, which contained a neat trail of tobacco, blew to the ground.

Now was Elijah's chance.

He could swap the bottles, and his dance partner would be none the wiser.

Cindy swore under his breath and reached down to recover the scattered loot, and in one swift movement, Elijah swept his hand across the table and removed the glass bottle and replaced it with his own identical product. It was magic. Calisthenics performed by the hands. It was what a croupier may call a Herrmann pass.

Eight minutes.

Cindy sat upright and returned to the task of constructing his nicotine hit.

Elijah's job was all but done and he didn't need to see how it went down. It was time to say his goodbyes and make tracks. "Well, I guess I should be go—"

"Why did you take my bottle?" Cindy cut in.

"What?" was all Eli could muster.

"My amyl, you swapped it with whatever this is." Cindy Lee held up the lethal dose like it was a replica of his Fabergé egg.

"Oh…"

"It's okay. I don't mind. Just tell me what it is."

Elijah didn't know where to start. *It's a synthetic product cooked up in police headquarters that is later administered to unassuming partygoers in order to create fear in the community. Yep, the same people that receive our hard-earned taxes are out to kill us. In their eyes, with death comes trepidation, and, thus, transformation, or some such bullshit.* "It's a bittersweet symphony," he offered poetically.

"Give me my poppers," Cindy demanded as he held out his open hand.

Elijah dug into his pocket and returned the liquid to its former owner. There was no point denying it. No point in kicking sand in the man's face. His job was to make a scene but not while he was present.

Cindy removed his mask and placed it on the table beside the two jars. It suddenly became apparent that he was in the throes of a major bender, and his eyeballs threatened to burst from their sockets. Elijah hadn't noticed earlier, but his bottom row of teeth protruded abnormally, as if he had lockjaw, as if he sported a second Japanese-inspired Oni mask. His cerebration was doing somersaults and his inhibitions had jumped ship long ago.

"I'll tell you what." He turned his gaze to Elijah. "I'll mix the bottles up, and then you can choose which one you want…and then I'll try the other. I have yours, you have mine. Whatever."

Elijah held the man's gaze and swallowed a gulp that threatened to expose his deceit. It was Russian roulette. Certain death for whoever got the bullet in the chamber. But he knew he wouldn't have to pull the trigger.

"If there's nothing to hide, there's nothing to hide."

Elijah nodded. Although his thoughts raced like a hamster in a wheel, he reminded himself to breathe and keep his eye on the poison. Yes, the stakes were high, but he had been trained in observation, in identifying good hands, bad hands, and everything in between. He could deal with a globule of cleaning product, that part was child's play.

Cindy smiled to confirm the deal and began rearranging the bottles in a way a street urchin may conceal balls beneath upended tin cups in order to prise money from ignorant pedestrians. He sped up, slowed down, reversed the pattern, and even spun the bottles on their side. He was a showman. He was a true capitano, and this was his *Commedia dell'arte.*

It was a sight to behold, and Elijah was happy to play his part. Firstly bamboozled, then convinced, and finally hesitant, like he was choosing a puppy from a litter.

Cindy watched smugly. He was enjoying the game, and, in his mind, he couldn't really lose. No matter the result, he would be getting high.

Elijah naturally knew otherwise, and he was no bunny. He had calculated the risks, and they were marginal at best. By the time the canister came to rest, he had followed the comparatively safe nitrate without diversion through its various manoeuvres, and it beamed at him like a long-lost friend.

"So, which one will it be?" Cindy asked, a hand gesturing to each as if he were offering a selection of fine jewellery.

"Left." Elijah pointed to clarify. "My left."

Cindy took a pipette from behind his ear, which Elijah hadn't noticed in his mane of hair, and, despite his trembling hands, delicately extracted a dose from the ampoule.

Elijah tilted his head back and unfolded his tongue to receive the droplet. It had a distinct banana flavour, and his taste buds savoured the undertones before it converged with saliva and slid down his throat. It wasn't the unpleasant experience he had expected.

"Tell me, what does *She* do?" Cindy asked as he shook the remnants off the dropper.

"I go to parties," Elijah said coldly, "and put drugs in people's drinks."

"And how's that working out for you?" Cindy had stopped processing information, and all communication was now helmed by autopilot.

"I'm not sure yet," Elijah said as he took in his surrounds and considered the ease of contaminating the water supply and cleansing the gene pool. "It beats flipping burgers."

Cindy threw back his head and drank from the bottle. He didn't do things in half measures. "Whoa, that is some seriously rank-tasting amyl," he said, slamming the bottle down like an empty shot glass.

Six minutes…

"Wait, what?" Elijah asked. The hamster had fallen from its wheel.

"Nasty shit." Cindy shook his head in an effort to chase away the aftertaste.

"You said amyl." Alarms were sounding "It's amyl?"

"Yes, sir."

Fuck. Fuck. Fuck. Fuck. Elijah's own internal pilot was in the crash position and bracing for impact. He began to cough, trying to extricate the poison.

"No. I'm joking," Cindy said, slapping Elijah on the back. "That ain't anything I've had before. Kinda tastes like stewed bugs."

Elijah breathed a sigh of relief. Hell, he exhumed his entire lung capacity.

"I'm keeping both of these." Cindy scooped up the glassware. "I'm going to the bar." He placed the mask back over his face and quickly disappeared into the growing throng.

Elijah wiped sweat from his brow and gathered his bearings. A drink sounded like a wonderful idea, but he had two minutes to reach his ride, and he most definitely didn't want to keep Kelvin waiting. That was a patience he dared not test.

As he made his way across the outdoor theatre, the sound of the music dropped momentarily, and a scream carried on the breeze. Bodies ran in various directions, towards and away from an epicentre of catastrophe, and influencers called upon their many talents to do just that. It was an act familiar to the scene, and everybody knew their roles.

Elijah checked his watch. He was cutting it fine, but the car would still be running.

The speakers again roared to life, and the crowd refocused their attention. Nothing, not even a death in the ranks, could ruin the vibe. After only a temporary disruption, the party would go on, and Elijah, now feeling slightly euphoric, smiled and befittingly pulled the cat's head back into position as he exited the stage.

THE HOUSE IS ADORNED WITH NONSENSE

Kelvin sat behind a heavy mahogany table, flanked by Batal and Chiba and a number of thick hardcovers, their spines providing very little detail of their content. Yumi had slipped into a zip-up, bodycon mini, and the men wore fine suits and even finer cologne.

Elijah, neither in a suit nor cologne, and feeling somewhat sun kissed after his detour, took a seat on a comfortable leather Hans Wegner and immediately slid into a slouch. He didn't have much time for authority, and he wanted to make that clear. He also had very little backbone, and that, too, was apparent. The amyl had offered a slight, momentary buzz, but the effects had worn off on the ride over, and now only a dull headache lingered.

The office was befitting somebody of the highest order, and the walls had no doubt heard and seen some shit over the years.

Elijah expected a drink to be offered, a shiraz gin, perhaps a cognac, but that would mean they were equals, and that was far from the case.

"Do we need to remind you that you have a job to do?" asked Kelvin, his demeanour that of an angry neighbour that had tolerated loud music long enough.

"I did exactly what you asked of me," Elijah wined, his voice reaching new heights.

"And what did we ask of you? Or didn't Yates and Munro make it clear."

"Wait. Which one is Munro?" Elijah momentarily sought clarification.

"Heavyset fellow, wide mouth, receding hairline, short fuse," Chiba interjected.

"Right, got'cha. So that would make Yates the family man, an accountant in a past life?" No response was forthcoming. Kelvin paused to wet a fingertip and flicked through a stapled document. His eyes seemed to be trying to crack a code, solve a crossword.

"Daniel Burson," Kelvin read from the page. "Four priors. Rich parents. A fucking dealer himself." He raised his eyes to meet Elijah. "The kid wasn't what you'd call squeaky clean. Probably would have keeled over without a push."

"How was I to know? And who cares?" Elijah protested. "It still sends the same message. You should be thanking me." He couldn't believe he was toeing the company line.

"What you don't understand is that when you take out one of these cronies, the next in line will take their place. Sometimes it's better the devil you know." Kelvin knew the playbook. "And, even worse, now they're going to know something is up. A dealer isn't going to plough through a batch of bad blow. They'll come sniffing. It's like smashing the bulb in a lighthouse, someone is going to fucking notice."

"You hold me hostage, inject me with some mechanical parasite and who knows what else while I'm out cold, and now you're worried about your ass?"

"I don't worry, Mister Caulfield, I act, and your performance last night makes it hard for me to act in a manner that is conducive to getting results." Kelvin enjoyed getting his own way, and when he didn't, the guillotine was wheeled into position. "We have a dead drug dealer—great—but it doesn't advance our cause, and we are on borrowed time. I'm sure you don't need me to tell you that the 'Spikies' cadre hasn't exactly been rubber-stamped by those at the top of the tree. We can't afford to fumble the ball."

That explained the unmarked police car; a patrol vehicle would have alerted suspicion, and neighbourhood watch didn't need an excuse to pry into the business of others.

A melody skipped through Elijah's head: *Criminals catching criminals catching criminals*, as he considered his place in the food chain.

"What about today's sojourn into the park? I did what had to be done. At high risk, I might add. A word of praise wouldn't go astray."

Kelvin shot a glance towards Chiba. She shrugged.

"You do as we ask, when we ask." Kelvin didn't mince his words. "Remember the alternative is a four-by-four jail cell. And I wouldn't be wrong in thinking the prosecution would push for consecutive life sentences."

"Easy, Kelvin," Chiba again arbitrated. "We don't want to upset his state of mind."

"Oh yes, we must preserve his mentality," Kelvin mocked as he leaned onto the desk, his hands folded before him like a chess player deliberating over the pawns at his disposal. "Tell me…do you feel stressed, burdened, victimised?"

"You don't need to answer that, Elijah. You answer to me, not Kelvin, at this juncture." Chiba spoke like a defence lawyer protecting her client.

"Exactly, Yumi. I shouldn't even be here today." Kelvin shuffled the papers before him and began to rise to his feet. "I should be playing with my granddaughter, enjoying the afternoon sunshine knowing that *our task force* is doing its job."

"I saw your man, from the photo," Elijah said as if seeking validation, a pat on the back, an 'attaboy.'

Kelvin craned his head and promptly sat back down. "I thought you couldn't make heads or tails of that image."

"His name is Tony Maslow. He was rubbing shoulders with our dead dealer."

"Did he see you?" Chiba queried.

Elijah cast his mind back to the girl that had held his attention captive. She was an acquaintance of Maslow's, a potential target herself. "No," he lied.

Chiba and Batal's eyes met.

"I thought this clown, Burson, was a customer. He was definitely feeding off Maslow," Elijah continued.

"That may be the case, but Burson is still a known pusher. Granted, he is not a big fish like Maslow, and snorts as much as he sells, but he's not a target—he's not even on the dartboard."

"What's so special about this Maslow guy anyway?"

"He's connected. Goes right to the top," Batal weighed in on the conversation.

"And his stuff is of the highest order. Premium," Chiba added. "He's well liked and he's well trusted."

"So, you're gonna pin this all on him?"

"And his associates." Batal liked to ponder which crayfish to pull from the tank and drop into boiling water.

Kelvin elaborated: "He is a chief supplier. If we slice through his dependents, we drive him and his superiors out of business. Run them out of town so to speak."

"And it becomes somebody else's problem?" Elijah ventured.

"If our operation works here, it can work anywhere. The government will have no option but to provide funding," Chiba said, to which Kelvin responded:

"We just don't need any bad press. If we're going to fill the morgue, we need the corpses to tell a tale, a cautionary tale."

"Would you prefer I strung them up in the streets with a personalised note from the coroner, even the local PD?"

Again, nobody found it amusing.

"You know why they call her the Pharmacist and me the Anaesthetist?" Kelvin hissed, his eyes piercing, lips moist. "It's because I decide who lives and who dies. I decide who gets the antidote and who gets the poison."

Elijah sat up straighter. "Is that a threat?"

"No." Kelvin rose to his feet with spritely conviction. "That is simply a parting word." He extended a hand to both Chiba and Batal, who accepted it obediently. He then rounded the table and placed a bony grip on Elijah's shoulder. "Do not become a fly in the ointment," he whispered before exiting the room like a gentleman well adjusted to washing blood from his hands. Elijah recoiled at his touch and the chill of his breath.

As the door closed, Batal threw a number of photographs onto the table—the type one develops under red lights with chemicals and tongs and a clothesline.

Elijah leaned forward to critique the composition.

"They have you on tape," Batal informed. "These will be doing the rounds."

The images were mostly indecipherable. Underexposed. Infrared. Pixelated. A mere hot spot in a desert landscape.

Elijah looked towards both his nine and six o'clock to gauge whether he should be concerned. The survey was indecisive.

He wanted to ask why his car, which had been used as battering ram, hadn't appeared in the newspapers. Why it hadn't been lauded over like a prize catch on the Amity beach boat ramps. He wanted to ask about the toxicology report. About Burson's final moments. He wanted to ask about the angel he had encountered at the club and the problem with using a fucking straw. But Elijah said nothing. All he could do was try to identify his features in the prints by tracing lines with his finger on the glossy frames. If they had anything at all, it wasn't much.

"B, would you excuse us?" Chiba said as she sidled up beside Elijah.

Batal nodded without protest and quietly vacated the room. He had a way of entering and exiting without raising a stir, and he was even better at adhering to requests.

Chiba scooped up the pile of photographs and threw them into a wastepaper basket before taking a seat across from the young man that looked like a drug mule preparing to board a flight over the Bermuda Triangle.

"They're just trying to scare you," Chiba said as she picked at stray hairs that clung to the fabric of her dress. Her appearance was manicured and pristine, but curious tabbies had a way of finding their way into the clothes basket.

"I know." Elijah had very little to offer.

"Is it working?"

"I think you know my profile. You can probably answer that better than I can."

"And do you know why they're doing it?" Chiba crossed her legs and folded her hands as if she were truly interested in the answer.

"Because they're drunk on power." Elijah turned his head towards the woman, and for the first time in a long time, he felt like somebody was actually listening. "Because they know I will stick to the path, if what lies beyond has bigger fangs with a bigger appetite."

Chiba nodded her head, and an expression of praise, even admiration, crept across her face. The gears behind her eyes were clicking into place, and she restrained from verbalising her many thoughts. She was cunning. A black widow spider that could make love and behead in the same motion.

"Am I right? Do I pass?"

"Partially. Kelvin is trying to evoke a coping strategy. He believes you will solve future problems by staying true to the cause. If it becomes a game, you will find a way. Kinda like counting cards."

"And what do you think?"

"I think this was never part of your five-year plan." It was Chiba's attempt at humour, and it brought a smile to their faces.

"I'm not sure I've ever thought five days ahead." Elijah cast his mind back to a calendar he had hung to cross out the dates. He had lost the red marker before the week was out.

"You will. Someday. When you know who you are and what you need."

"Are you a clairvoyant or is that on my file as well?"

Chiba shrugged her shoulders. The key to unlock her secrets had been hidden long ago. "Just remember: 'We cannot escape ourselves.'"

"Sartre?" Elijah was fond of the existentialists.

"It's Henri Le Chat Noir," Chiba said forming the words in her throat in her best French accent. "He's a YouTube sensation."

Both smiles turned to a nasal snigger. It was a nice release, which was soon followed by a deep sigh.

"You know when I said I'd kill everyone in the room?" Elijah needed to clear his chest. "I wouldn't."

"I know," Chiba assuaged. "Around here, we call it 'gunslinger delusion.' You were just trying to play the role you were cast in. It happens."

"And you...are you really a pharmacist?" Elijah asked.

"I just do what they can't, and I do as I'm told. You should think about doing likewise." Unlike Kelvin's parting words, this wasn't a threat. Chiba was merely offering some friendly advice to somebody that looked like they needed it. She rose to her feet and again ensured she was fur free. "Here, take this," she said as she placed an eyedropper on the table where the photographs had laid strewn. "It helps when administering the liquid doses." And with that, she made her way across the room and disappeared behind the closed door.

Elijah tucked the dainty glass canon into his top pocket and dragged himself upward. The sun would soon be setting, and there was work to be done.

PART III:
THE FIRST DOMINO

DON'T LOOK TOO FAR BEYOND YOUR NOSE

Most of the shop assistants were former school friends—acquaintances, really—who greeted Katie with giddy enthusiasm and who were generally met with a scowl or complete indifference in return. Katie thought of them as prisoners, no-hopers who hadn't aspired to anything beyond becoming a slave to the retail machine—retailers she financed on a weekly basis. It was an attitude spawned from privilege, from the daughter of a father that had always taken what he wanted and avoided benevolence at all costs. Katie didn't have what you'd call a lot of friends, she had patrons that cheered from the sidelines who longed to be drawn into her orbit. These women were simultaneously obsessed with and terrified of her.

Saturdays were often spent at the mall with Nadia in tow. Although Katie had erected barriers between herself and others, Nadia had always stayed close. She liked Katie's 'sass,' she liked the way she gave 'zero fucks,' and she liked her association with a crime family. Gangsters never went out of style, and Nadia romanticised the underworld, envied the way power and prestige could be attained by force as long as you had the tenacity to back it up. In many ways, she wished her own parents had the mental fortitude to oppose the system, to go where others feared to tread.

Nadia had been accepted by Katie for two reasons. Firstly, during their final year of school, Nadia had stolen notes to a forthcoming exam from right under the teacher's nose and had shared them with Katie, who rarely studied, rarely even attended class. Both girls received 'Distinctions,' which was good enough, and Katie was rewarded by her father with a shiny new Jeep—resprayed and replated only days prior. And secondly, Katie needed somebody to tell her how good she looked upon stepping from the change rooms of boutique outlets. Mirrors lied, and Katie didn't care to discuss such matters with manic assistants. Nor did she care that her loyal sidekick feared to offend. It was all just a matter of perspective, after all, and hers was the only one that mattered.

"What the fuck happened last night? That shit was lit," Katie said from beyond the slats of a saloon-style door. She was semi-naked and admiring her figure in the mirror.

The changeroom only had one hook, and a small mountain of clothes gathered around her bare ankles. Although she was nursing the remains of a hangover, she looked good—her complexion concealing the nausea that bubbled beneath the surface.

"That coke was next level. I think I danced myself into shape." She placed her hands to either side of her waist and squeezed the flesh as if she was holding two cheeseburgers. Her fingers nearly reached from spine to midriff.

"It's fucked up what happened to Dan, though." Nadia was leaning against the wall on the other side of the door, sucking on a lollipop. The sugar wouldn't be good for her daily intake, but she thought it looked cute. Cute was important.

The door quickly swung open, and Katie pranced into the foyer, parading a backless minidress that looked like it was made of tissue paper and would fall apart just as easily. She tilted her head and threw up her arms like a homecoming queen acknowledging her adoring fans. "How do I look?"

"Is that gonna hold?" Nadia quizzed, taking the candy from her mouth.

"The possibility that it may not is part of the appeal," Katie said, her mind already made up. She bent down to slide her feet into a pair of heels. "What were you saying about Daniel?"

"He OD'd last night. They found him in his bed this morning. Puddle of sweat. Shredded sheets. They tried to resuscitate him, but he was long gone. Stiff as a fucken scarecrow." She held up the stick and saliva-covered confectionary as a point of comparison.

"No surprises. The cunt was always a lightweight," Katie said as she strapped herself into the Jimmy Choos. "Who knows what he was on. He roamed the clubs like a feral dog."

"Yeah, but it's a bit close to home, don't ya think? I mean, he was probably in the cubicle beside us when he took that shit."

"You know Hendrix, he used to take eight tabs of acid at once." Katie stood straight, trying not to topple in the three-inch heels and a foggy head. "He would cut his forehead and place the drug on the wound—apparently it would absorb quicker that way. That's why he always wore a headband."

"How do you know this?" Nadia was shocked.

"Dad has affiliates in NY, they used to smoke all kinds of shit with those dinosaurs."

"You know Jimi Hendrix, but you don't know Stevie Nicks?"

"I know Hendrix because Benny Benassi remixed the shit out of 'Purple Skies,' or whatever the fuck it's called. Fucking banger, Nadia."

Nadia rolled her eyes in jest, but again also because she thought it would look cute. "You really do just live for the weekend, don't you?"

"Nadia, the clubs are open every night. We decide when it's the weekend."

The girls took a seat at a table in the food court and began slurping green shakes that promised vitality and well-being but packed more sugar than a regular soda. They were surrounded by bored teenage mall rats, consumers steadfast on finding a bargain, and families stuffing their faces with junk because it was far cheaper than cooking an actual meal. A popular song, albeit slightly obscure, wafted across the complex promoting a 'cool-by-association' type vibe. Apparently, consumers would consume if their egos were stroked and the mood was moderated.

The mall on any given day would be home to hookups, breakups, and everything in between, and most were oblivious to the actions of their fellow bag swingers. Some were experimenting with shoplifting, others looking for the perfect gift. It was a place to be seen and a place to hide away from the world. It had its own ecosystem, and no two inhabitants truly seemed alike. The best and the worst of the species were truly on show.

"So, does that mean we're still going out tonight?" Nadia queried between sips of her medicine. She had heard such facial exercises sharpened features and tightened sags. She hadn't been blessed with perfect bone structure, so a straw was a constant ally.

"Hell yes, it does," Katie responded, peering around the floor on which they resided. "Why do you think I just bought this dress?"

"You buy a new outfit every weekend, Katie. I wouldn't call this a special occasion."

"I wouldn't be complaining, Nadia, you know you'll become the beneficiary of this little number. My excesses are your prized takings."

"Your excesses," Nadia countered, "keep sweatshops in business." She grinned, knowing full well that her friend knew nothing about ethical or moderate consumption.

"Oh well, those little fuckers need the pay packet. I'm doing them a favour."

Both girls laughed, the green slime threatening to burst from their noses. Privilege really was a warm hug, and ignorance was the accompanying slap on the back.

CHARIOTS IN THE HANDS OF SKETCH ARTISTS

Upon exiting police headquarters, Elijah had been given the brief. Maslow would be at a place called Jove that evening—a name derived from the persistent swirl of energy that gestated in its core. Elijah wasn't familiar with the venue, but according to the notes, it was owned by Cleo Rodriguez, who also had shares in the shithole he had visited the night prior. In other words, his photo would be on file, and Elijah would have to keep an even lower profile. Not a profile that featured thick-rimmed glasses and a fake moustache, but he wouldn't be high-fiving teamsters or photo-bombing selfies.

Naturally, his protests fell on deaf ears. The punters didn't stop to grieve on weekends, so neither could he. They lived for Saturday. It was rush hour. And the queues for illegal substances would not diminish until word got out that the supply was tarnished. Cooked in unsanitary labs, cut with salts and spices and paint strippers. Due to its reputation, not many tourists in India stepped foot in the Ganges, and the police force would stop at nothing to replicate this 'health first' way of thinking.

Elijah was weary and needed sleep.

The hot spots didn't kick off until after midnight, so he had time to find some shut-eye. Not that it would prove restful. On the contrary, as soon as Elijah put his feet up and entered the dream theatre, his unconscious psyche was submitted to a beating.

A heavy roller door was pulled aside to reveal bovine carcasses hanging from the ceiling—the remains of a recent slaughter. Elijah was strapped to a wheelchair, and as he became aware of the tethers holding his wrists and ankles in place, he was pushed forward into the storage warehouse. It was cold and drained of colour, and as he progressed, his breath turned to mist and the slabs of meat withdrew from his path. A chill ran up his spine—a combination of excitement, intrigue, anxiety, dread.

Elijah squinted, but he could see very little other than a darkened cube that seemed to envelop him. He craned his head to peer over his shoulder, but his navigator, the one pushing him forward, also remained elusive. Light and clarity receding at every opportunity.

Finally, the wheels skidded to a stop. A modest television screen then came into focus, first projecting frenzied static, interference that was foreign in a digital world, and then a crisp image of a spinning roulette table. The sound of the plastic sphere bouncing from one slot to the next rattled around the room as if ricocheting from wall to ceiling, floor to wall, and back again, and the television, a square artifact from a bygone era, slid forward, the wheel on the screen slowing with its movement. A hand reached around and prised Elijah's eyes open. Toothpicks were jammed into the sockets to ensure the lids gave the retinas no place to hide. A pair of isolation headphones were fitted over his ears.

The ball fell into position—the winning colour and number not clear to Elijah, whose pupils had dried and stung as if he'd spent a whole night gaming. And then the picture disappeared into a pinhole, consumed by the black glass. Elijah began to test his restraints, he began to shake his head, he tried to speak. But all of it was futile.

A pair of hands grasped the sides of his face to prevent any further restlessness, and eye drops were messily dripped from above. His tongue did a backflip and he could taste bile in his throat. The television again roared to life, a montage of lifeless faces and distorted bodies hijacking the transmission. Elijah bore witness to the horrors of war. Children missing chunks of flesh. Soldiers relieved of limbs. Wounds that would never heal.

He witnessed land mines and ammunition inflict unspeakable

injuries, and he saw families mourning, sobbing for the departed, sobbing because they could never *unsee* the atrocity. The reel switched, and the footage juxtaposed with shots of a passenger vehicle mounting a footpath and mowing down pedestrians. Horn blaring like Jericho sirens. Tyres screeching like swooping eagles. Debris strewn in its path. The cabin held high from harm's way, riding the crest of a wave.

Nobody was immune. Families walking hand in hand. Lovers on first dates or celebrating anniversaries. The young. The old. The abled now disabled. Nobody was spared.

Bodies tumbled through the air like stuffed mannequins. Torsos became speed bumps. And as the instrument of death careened through alfresco dining areas and shopfronts, some valiantly gave chase while others fled for safety.

Elijah tried to look away. He tried to blink it from his memory. He tried to shake himself free. But he couldn't avoid the trauma. He was responsible for the carnage and he had earned the guilt. This was his legacy and he had to lay claim to what the road left behind.

In that moment, an oversized white sheet descended, and it felt as if he'd fallen beneath churning surf, air eluding his gasps. Elijah tried to swim to the surface, but it was useless. He became more entangled the more he thrashed.

And then, he woke up.

Covered in sweat. Head pounding with pain. The suppressant hadn't worked, it had simply added to the cocktail of chaotic thoughts and intoxicating guilt. The amateur concoctions composed by the cops couldn't be trusted.

Somebody had been bought a science kit for Christmas and had failed to read the instructions. Vaccines could now be formulated in less than eighteen months, but a simple thought suppressant was still hard to come by. It was a curse for the neurotic, the hyper-imaginative, and those wrestling demons in a squared circle.

PROVIDENCE

The taxpayer-funded laboratory was like most others. Refrigerated test tubes. Finely tuned scales anticipating measured doses. Beakers sanitised and neatly shelved. Jars containing pickled specimens on display to highlight failures and curiosities.

Four figures sat in a circular formation, straddling stools and awaiting confessional insight—an AA meeting without the overwhelming feeling of despair or guilt that comes with falling off the wagon. Everyone in attendance wore pristine white lab coats as if there were a stereotype to fulfil. Under the pretence of academia, if you weren't carrying a clipboard or the latest dissertation, you at least needed to be sporting the appropriate uniform. Looking the part was two-thirds the job.

A man of subcontinental appearance, with a head of hair that had benefitted from years of direct sunlight and henna, glanced around the room, surprised by the level of sophistication for a 'police department.' Although, somewhat taken aback, he was seemingly the most relaxed person in the room, and his stonewashed jeans and faded black tee were testaments to such a fact.

"Nice place you have here. It's much better equipped than what we have over at the university," he said as if he were happy to make small talk.

"You must have the best if you wish to achieve the best," Chiba said in her characteristically enchanting yet utilitarian manner.

"Is that why I'm here? You need the best," the man asked. He was the subject, and all eyes were pointed in his direction. Chiba had read his work and had made contact about a 'new and exciting' opportunity. Fearing boredom itself, the man had accepted the invitation. After all, his one true love was mixing chemicals, and if somebody wanted to pay for the raw materials, he was more than happy to cook whatever was on the menu.

Naturally, the interviewee was no fool, and although he wasn't afraid of the spotlight, he also knew it was important to have an exit strategy at the ready. Security had been fastidious upon entry, but as he glanced around his surrounds, he knew there were chinks in the armour, you just needed to know where to apply pressure.

"Perhaps. But that remains to be seen." Chiba chewed on her lip as she searched for a place to start. "What do you know about cherries?"

"Cherries?"

Chiba nodded.

"Full of antioxidants. Cost a pretty penny when they're first harvested. Didn't George Washington take to a cherry tree with a hatchet when he was a boy?"

Chiba shrugged.

"It's safe to say I didn't indulge in too many cherries when I was growing up." The man knew he wasn't there to discuss his knowledge of former US presidents.

"Did you know they contain cyanide?" Chiba asked.

"I may have read it once," the man offered. "But I read a lot."

"Don't you find it incredible that something so delectable, so unassuming, so sought-after, can be a poison chalice."

It was the man's turn to shrug. He liked berries but he didn't need his time wasted.

"One minute, you're inhaling a handful, the next minute…" Chiba clicked her fingers to indicate a sudden and permanent change. She was testing him.

The man didn't bat an eyelid. "When your number is up, there's no point fighting it."

Chiba made a note. She liked him. In ten words, he had passed.

Kelvin craned his neck forward and squinted his eyes to read the man's name tag. "Doctor Ricks, do you know why we've brought you here today?"

"Oh, I'm not a doctor," the man corrected. "In fact, the prefix has never sat well with me. Not since I learnt of the real monster in Frankenstein."

"Not a doctor?" Kelvin turned to Chiba. "Why exactly are we dealing with an amateur?"

Chiba shrunk a little under the patriarchal glare. She had completed the background checks on the man in their midst, and she was accountable for his potential recruitment (and blameworthy for his incompetence).

"You can call me Casey," the man continued, commanding the attention. "And I'm here because I can acquire things off the black market others can't—perhaps also for the sordid company I keep."

Batal shifted his weight. The stool was doing his top-heavy posture no favours.

"And I'm willing to go to certain lengths to get results. Some in your organisation may find that…desirable." Casey Ricks turned his gaze to Chiba and applied a little pressure.

"And you're a chemist?" Kelvin queried. He was slowly catching up to the passing train.

"Correct." Ricks had always felt sympathetic, evenly strangely impressed, by art benefactors. Sympathy because they didn't possess the creativity or talent to make something of themselves, and strangely impressed because they were still willing to set aside their inadequacies and shamelessly ride the coattails of somebody more adept. He was of the opinion that his current company was much of the same ilk.

"But we already have a product. As you can see, we're more than capable of manufacturing and trialling our own recipes right here," Kelvin said as if to justify his credentials.

"From what I've been told, you have a cherry bomb, when, in fact, what you really need is something…"

"Nuclear," Batal finished the sentence as if it were the solution to any and all problems.

"Exactly." Casey Ricks nodded as he clapped his hands together. "I can do nuclear." All he needed was forty-eight hours. In that time, he would create something abhorrent, take his payment, and gladly leave this wolf's lair without looking back. If they wanted something that would stir up trouble, he was more than happy to give it to them, but the bad karma would be on their heads.

Kelvin turned from Batal to Chiba and then back to Ricks with a look of restrained glee. He knew that all victories in war were dependent on industrial might, and before him was somebody that understood the code of conflict. If Casey Ricks could increase their potency, then the morgues would tell a sorry tale indeed. Kelvin was now on the same page, and a new chapter in the Spikies story could be written.

Chiba breathed a sigh of relief; providing the ink never seemed to come easy but appeasement made it all worthwhile.

J♥VE

An imposing woman, athletic, six feet tall in heels, stood in the entrance to the club holding a clipboard close to her chest. It was a list carefully compiled to indicate those that were welcome and those that were not, and, opposed to popular opinion, Saint Peter was every bit female. If Eli's snapshot was anywhere, it would be among those documents.

Elijah handed over his sham ID, allowed his eyes to wander, and tried to settle the spin cycle in his stomach. He was getting used to bad ideas, but this was just downright foolish.

The woman scanned his photo with a handheld device and read his name aloud: "Patrick Svoboda." Her lips formed a funnel, and she elongated each of the vowels like a ring announcer.

"Sorry?" Elijah blurted, his gaze regaining focus.

"You're Patrick Svoboda?"

"Oh yep, that's me." It wasn't overly convincing, and Elijah wished he could repeat the roll call response with more poise.

"Czech?"

"*Ano.*" He had done some Googling.

"I have friends in Prague. Beautiful city. But the absinthe isn't what it used to be."

Elijah humbly nodded his head. His research hadn't extended to the culinary delights, and he would agree with all that she proposed.

"Tell me, what are you doing here, Mister Svoboda?"

The gatekeeper before him had a long, slender figure that indicated she had never missed a training session. She wore leather from top to toe like it was a second skin, and her short hair was cut to a razor-sharp tip. She was more than just a door bitch. She had clout. She had aura. She had authority. She was fucking border security.

"I migrated with my family just prior to the dissolution."

"Your parents didn't care to hang around for the Velvet Divorce?" Security was worldly at Jove.

"They wanted more and had grown impatient." Elijah was out of his depth.

"Don't we all?" the woman mused. "Well, welcome to Jove, Patrick." She unclasped a rope attached to a golden bollard. "Enjoy your night, and steer clear of the hurricane."

Elijah again nodded, this time with gratitude, and advanced down the long hallway towards muffled bass lines that threatened to be unleashed like a caged animal.

Elijah paused and turned: "You know so much about me, but I didn't catch your name?"

"Cleo, Cleo Rodriguez," she said without diverting her eyes from the clipped papers.

Elijah gave an approving grin and turned back to the throbbing heart of the club. He lowered his head and flipped his collar upward. He wouldn't tempt fate again.

The club was a construction of molten flesh. Bodies pressed into bodies like La Tomatina fiesta, minus the projectiles and any signs of sexual misconduct. It was difficult to make out where one person ended and the other started. Faces were lost amid waving limbs and skin, lots of skin. A smell of perspiration hung in the air. A workout was in effect, and beautiful people, much like the woman at the helm, were sculpting desirable physiques.

Elijah didn't particularly feel like a drink—he was still recovering from his dreamscape—but he knew that he should liquor up to blend into the crowd. Everyone here was on something, and a straightedge *x* painted across the back of his hand may have drawn unwelcome attention.

Elijah also knew that Maslow wouldn't be found within the quivering mess of humans. He would have a private booth with an extensive rider—hell, the way B and Chiba spoke of him, the man would demand a throne at Berghain. And the coveted spots were usually elevated above the heathens below. He would have to make his way upstairs and draw back the curtains.

Tony Maslow, as it turned out, wasn't too hard to find. He held court on the third level on an oversized sofa in a tiered dugout. His entourage was small and well groomed, well heeled, and well high. These people made no secrets about their habits, and they had full access and very little moderation.

There was no need to press flesh at those lofty heights, but it was cosy, amicable, a tempered form of social distancing. Elijah could watch from afar with an unrestricted view without being swept away in a tide of people. Although it was jovial and inviting, Elijah knew it was also a snake pit and he had to treat it accordingly.

And then she appeared.

Like an apparition.

Far more breathtaking than an untamed animal in the wild or a portrait in a gallery. Second only to Nathalie, she was one of the greatest views Elijah had ever encountered. This was the hurricane he had been warned about.

HIGH LIFE

According to Katie's warped perception, her hand had grown in size and rippled slightly like the vision of a starfish in a rock pool. She chewed a stick of bubble gum and pondered the sight. She knew the gear was kicking in, but it was still a spectacle to behold.

In recent months, the club scene had grown stale—mere hookup joints for the desperate and bored beneath a barrage of unoriginal house music. Gone were the days of charisma, both in the mixing booth and the dance floor. But this new crop of drugs made it bearable. Better. Exciting again. Earlier in the night, she had taken a Love Potion—a combination of MD and mescaline—and she was riding a wave of euphoria, a wave that could not be replicated via any other means.

Cleo had warned her not to play too hard—the condition of entry was 'to be cool'—Rodriguez didn't want a repeat of the Burson incident on home soil. So that's what Katie would do: she would *be cool*. She would sit quietly and enjoy the moment without hanging from the rafters. Against strong urges, she would remain clothed without tearing the tissue paper from her skin. And she would only re-dose when she felt the effects begin to wane. She would be a model drug user, and, if her fingers became tentacles, she would take it all in her stride. Katie had once had a bad trip. Only once. But it had wiped her out for several days. On that occasion, she had dissolved a sugar cube laced with acid on her tongue and was tormented by what she could only best describe as 'swirls,' pulsating gateways that invited her to the 'other side.' These hyper-coloured portals appeared on the walls, ceiling, and floor, and she refused to move for fear of falling into the abyss. She stayed in that one room for two days, not even leaving to use the toilet. To say it was unpleasant would be an understatement. Katie made a pact with God to get her through it. Swore she'd become a devout believer, that she'd go straight and never take drugs again. She broke her promise five days later. And God still hadn't demanded her soul.

Katie sometimes reflected on that agreement and wondered if the big guy would be there again if she ever had to make a deal.

As she made her way to the bar, her eyes met with a fellow who was clearly checking her out. Nothing strange. Especially in the outfit she was wearing. Especially given who she was. It would be downright odd if he looked the other way.

He was notably older, but Katie was drawn to him. He was cute in a brooding kind of way. Sure, he was a little too skinny and his hair was slightly unruly, but he had piercing blue eyes and cheekbones that most women would die for. She slid into the cushioned stool beside him and said: "Three months ago, this place was gonna be a craft brewery, now it's a fucking meat market."

The man cringed at the reference and took a sip from something brown, something cheap. He forced a smile but remained aloof.

"Nobody drinks anymore. Well, they don't binge anyway," Katie continued.

"What do they do?" The man turned to face her, and her assumptions were realised, he was cute in a skater, possibly stoner kind of way. He could use some dental work, but it added to his dissociative vibe.

"Anything they want really."

The man cracked another grin as if the answer confirmed what he already knew. Lines appeared beside his eyes and he would be an old man soon enough.

"What's your name?"

"Patrick Sv…" The man trailed off. "Just Patrick is fine."

"Well, it's nice to meet you, Just Patrick. I'm Katerina, but my friends call me Katie." A glass of clear liquid and a slice of lime glided across the bar and landed in her grasp. "I'll be seeing ya." And with that, Katie took her drink and proceeded back to the bunker, knowing that Patrick's eyes followed her every step of the way. Without voyeurs, there was no show.

She took a seat between Nadia and Tony on the plush furnishings to see what he was holding. Tony wasn't a pusher, he was a provider, and the apothecary was open for business.

SLAP SHOT

In no time, the crowd found its way to the upper levels, spreading like a fungus. Revellers encroached on one another's personal space yet still had to shout into ears to gain attention.

Elijah was familiar with the venue, although he had never stepped inside before. It was undeniably like all the others—humid, garish, and an excuse to dissimulate feelings of worthlessness. For a moment, he questioned the load capacity of the second, third, and fourth floors, all of which featured circular walkways that allowed a central cavity to exist in the building. Those that wanted to sweat joined the throng below, while those that wanted to watch, sway their hips, wave their arms, and nod their heads lined the balconies above. It was like a hive. A living organism that buzzed with energy.

Elijah was oblivious to the unfolding party, and he kept one eye on Tony Maslow and the other on his new acquaintance, Katie. He silently seethed that she was in the company of not only a kingpin, but a handsome one at that. There was another girl—not without her own charms—but he also paid her little attention.

None of them looked grief-stricken by the loss of their friend. In fact, they looked exuberant, their faces distorted by the cocktail of drugs they'd consumed.

If he wanted to get out of there, he would have to get the job done quickly. Discreetly. Maslow was the target, but the remoras cleaning the shark's gills had to go first. The natural selection would be Katie, but there was no way he was taking her out. Not only was he heavily attracted to her, but it would be like poaching a white rhino, destroying a thing of rare and unparalleled beauty. Her friend perhaps. The other young thing that was cut from the same cloth but lacking the finesse.

Elijah thought about it for a moment.

Kelvin had said not to make contact with the mark. It would arouse suspicion. Fingers would be pointed. The death of Katie's friend was an indirect link, and was, therefore, best avoided. He couldn't afford the wrath, and if Chiba was right, and this was all just a game, he would have to work out the best way to win.

But what other options did he have? He hadn't witnessed any other transactions. He hadn't seen sly hands give or receive. And even if he had, there was a very real risk that the right drink could end up in the wrong hands.

Tonight would not be the night. Regular partygoers knew the feeling: when the stars fell out of alignment and Mercury shifted into retrograde, ruining any chance of a celebration. And nothing, not even booze or music or appeasing one's bosses, even those that demanded perfection, would resurrect the situation.

Elijah threw a crumpled bill onto the bar, swivelled on his seat, and disappeared into the mass of faces melded together by rapturous movement and intimate conversation. He briskly made his way down the tunnel that had earlier digested him into a realm of hysteria and thankfully avoided any further correspondence with the establishment's proprietor.

The cold night air embraced him as he exited the building—an exterior that revealed nothing of the bio-network within its forti-fied walls—and as he walked into the enveloping darkness, he felt, for a fleeting moment, like a free man.

KICKING SANDCASTLES

The sound of the morning traffic was always a pleasant way to wake. The sporadic blare of horns and the hum of engines contributing to the tones of a soothing orchestra. Even the sound of sirens failed to kick a hole in the affable atmosphere. Elijah opened his eyes and yawned, still groggy but satisfied after a good night's sleep. He threw on a pair of sweatpants and a shirt, which were easily located in the exact place he'd left them, the floor, and made his way into the kitchen. For somebody whose life had been in turmoil, he still had a box of cereal and a full carton of milk. Nathalie had been his rock, his lighthouse whenever he was lost at sea, but maybe he could survive without her. Elijah filled a plunger of coffee and thought about where she may have gone. Perhaps a friend's place. Her family was abroad, and she wouldn't be boarding a plane anytime soon. No clothes remained in the wardrobe, and her toiletries were all cleared out, even the hair dryer, which she simply couldn't live without, was gone. She wasn't coming back, but he would still like to know her whereabouts, know that she was safe. Possibly patch things up, even if it was with a blunt needle and a frayed thread.

A framed photograph of the two sat on a mantle. She hadn't bothered to take it, but Elijah knew she had her own albums which were split at the seams. Unlike so many others, she still liked to print her memories.

Nathalie had wanted it all—marriage, kids, a home in the 'burbs—and she had given him every opportunity to go along for the ride. But he was scared. It meant upheaval. Change. Too much change. A definitive departure from his comfort zone. And, although he would never admit it, he was the product of a broken home and he had seen the damage a failed marriage and the impediment of a child could inflict on all parties. It was not the future forecast in his tea leaves, and not the path he had wanted to take, despite Nathalie being the 'one.'

Of course, he never explained any of this to Nathalie. When the subject arose, he became tense, a clam without any pearls of wisdom, and he only opened his mouth to accuse her of being selfish, of only wanting a visa, of not considering his wants, and not valuing what they had together without conforming to societal expectations.

Elijah looked a little closer at the picture and noticed a strained expression on Nathalie's face. Although they were happy, and the photo had been taken at the peak of their relationship while on vacation in the Iberian Peninsula, there was a void, something missing. She needed more, and their life, as it was, hadn't been enough.

Perhaps he could call her. Confide in her. Explain what the fuck was going on. But he didn't want to embroil her in his mess. He had done that enough. And he knew *they* were listening; he couldn't afford to test the validity of their threats.

A loud thud entered the apartment and a window that looked out onto the street trembled in its frame. Elijah flinched, hunched his back, and wrapped his arms around his knees to form a smaller target—they couldn't hurt what they couldn't see.

He waited, and when he realised a second attack wasn't forthcoming, he put down his breakfast and ran to the front door. He stepped into the morning light and peered into the garden, which had been neglected for longer than he cared to remember. Expecting to find a wounded bird or even a message tied to a rock that had failed to penetrate the glass, all Elijah found was a rolled-up newspaper heaved from the hands of a BMX bandit that was long gone, probably already terrorising the next block over. Tomorrow they would have words.

Elijah retrieved the early edition and retreated to the safety of his kitchen.

The front-page headline didn't mince words: "MOB BOSS DAUGH-TER DEAD." The ink was still wet, the pages still warm. The accompanying picture featured a young girl in her school uniform, bright eyed, teeth perfectly cut and polished. She was a senior student and she glowed in a way that only the youthful could. It was an archival photo, a little outdated, but Elijah immediately recognised her as Katerina, the girl that had taken an arrow to his heart. His head spun. His feet felt numb. Surely, he was still dreaming. There were too many parts to the equation that didn't add up. He ran to his room and rifled through his discarded clothes. The vial was still in the pocket of his pants, and more importantly, it was still full.

Elijah skidded back into the kitchen and began reading the article—his index finger following the lines to keep his eyes steady. A combination of words branded onto his brain: 'lethal cocktail,' 'popular nightspot,' 'found by a street sweeper,' 'friend fighting for life.' 'Another victim of bad choices.' The sentences rolled around in Elijah's mouth like rotten meat. He simply couldn't swallow what was being served up. And then the phone rang.

Elijah answered without a word like an East Berliner accepting a call from the Stasi.

"Mister Caulfield, we need you to come in for a debrief." It was Kelvin. "There have been developments and we need to ensure that we progress in a *tactical* manner."

Elijah stared out the window. If the news hadn't arrived, then none of this would have happened. He would have been blissfully ignorant. A kid that didn't have the answers because he didn't understand the question was never wrong.

"There is a job to be finished," Kelvin persisted.

The words marched into Elijah's ear like a horde of unwelcome ants.

"We will be expecting you."

"How did this happen?" Elijah found his tongue. He leaned his weight against a kitchen bench to leverage his failing balance.

"A plan was executed."

"But how?" Elijah glanced down at the vial in his palm.

"The drug was administered to the target. Somehow a second civilian received a smaller dosage—perhaps from the lips of the first—which didn't have the desired effect."

"I didn't administer your poison."

"We know."

"You know?" Elijah was puzzled.

"Do you really think we would let you out of our sight? You are what we call a junkyard dog—you do a specific job, we throw you a bone or two, but we wouldn't dare loosen the leash."

"Then who? How? What the fuck am I missing?"

"You don't really think that you are the only one, do you?"

Silence fell over the conversation. Elijah's stomach dropped steeply before it threatened to leap from his mouth. He had no idea that others were in a similar situation, their sentences pending, futures held to ransom. *Is that how Chiba had learnt her craft?*

"Thankfully our other deployed operatives are only too happy to pick up your slack. They understand the importance of their mission. They also understand the consequences of noncompliance."

"But why her?" Elijah pleaded.

"We knew you were developing feelings. We don't need you to act on feelings."

Elijah felt like a clone, a carbon copy of his former self, minus free will, independence, autonomy. Minus any characteristic that made him believe he was in control.

"And the good news is she was using Maslow's gear. You don't need me to remind you that we're here to hack the limbs until the blood runs dry."

Elijah felt like his own extremities had been severed and were being used to beat him over the head. He had to do something before he was reduced to a crumpled mess, before he became a victim of this death squad masquerading as a task force.

Elijah dropped the phone—the trail of ants racing across the tiles—and ran back to the bedroom that had descended into a disparaging gloom. He grabbed his clothes from the previous night and stretched the fabric over his body, pocketing the ampoule for safekeeping. Batal would be on his way and he had to be quick. Elijah had to run like he'd never run before, and he was willing to push the parameters of the bug in his neck.

AMBERGRIS

The grit between the tiles was hardened and black—old motor oil grout. Elbow grease wouldn't do the job. A jackhammer perhaps. It formed a grid across the off-white partition.

Nicolai Vincenzo stared at it from the edge of a gurney as he fiddled with a jewel-encrusted ring. His eyes were stern, piercing, his thoughts elsewhere.

To his left, his daughter lay beneath a crisp white sheet. She was at rest, but it wasn't the type of rest a young woman needed. Sleep had never been her ally, and the permanency of death never a consideration, but how easy the choice would be now given a moment of reflection.

This wasn't just another Jane Doe. Another neglected victim of the opioid crisis. This was a little girl that had grown into a woman with fierce resolve. A resolve much like the one possessed by her father. *Too much like her father.* For Nicky, she was his purpose, his reason for rolling out of bed each morning. And now she was gone.

The morgue was as you'd imagine: vacuum sealed, smelling of disinfectant and slabs of meat, buried beneath a hospital teeming with the loss of life. Business was booming.

The matron on duty had left him alone to gather his thoughts, to say his goodbyes. The toxicologist would put together a report, but he already knew the findings. In many ways, he had introduced her to the t(h)reats that lead young girls astray. Her dealers were his dealers. She had been exposed to too much, too soon, and he had never given it a prolonged thought. Never considered changing his ways. Never considered discretion. But it was too late and none of that mattered now. All that mattered was finding the source. There was a faulty distributor on the market, and it needed to be located, recalled, stomped on, and thrown onto the scrap heap. It was a liability, a homewrecker, a murderer.

He stared across at the glitter-painted toenail that protruded from the end of the covered mound. She had died with company, but it was a lonely way to die, poisoned from deep within, demons screaming in her head. Everything hard and sharp. No comfort in sight or reach. Nicky knew what it was like to be held in the clutches of an overdose, having escaped a near-fatal encounter with heroin, an experience that steered him towards the false security of white powders and pressed tablets. The idea that amphetamines were harmless was laughable.

His little girl's heart had given out, a power grid sent into meltdown by a bug in the system, a bug that had warmed the palms of Tony Maslow—a friend, a business partner, a man he would have welcomed as a son. But that now all meant naught, less than naught.

In a perfect world, the toe would twitch, and Katie would sit upright. A false alarm. A drowning swimmer expelling water from flooded lungs. A mistake. A close encounter. But nothing more. If only coins could be added for extra credits.

Nicky reached for his phone which was pressed firmly to his thigh. He punched the screen and held it to his face like a frozen bag of peas relieving a swift punch to the jaw.

"Get Maslow in," he spat, finding his voice for the first time since receiving the news. "That cunt knows something, and we need to know what that is." He turned a nostril upward and cleared the passage. "Also grab that bitch, Cleo—she might have something we can use too. We'll sit 'em both down and turn the world upside down if we have to." The silence at the other end suggested that the message was clear. "And, Jakey, make sure the place is clear. I don't want any reporters hanging about while we get our affairs in order." Nicky lowered the phone and turned his gaze again to the foot of the stretcher. Nothing had changed.

For a moment, he considered ringing his wife, his estranged ex-wife, Katie's mother. She had a right to know. Perhaps it would lessen his own grief if they could share the load. But she had her own life now. This is what she had run from. No point grabbing her ankles and pulling her back in like a fat fucking python in need of a cuddle. He had a job to do, and it wasn't the time for a family reunion. She had chosen a sea change in the company of a straight arrow, an accountant or some shit, and that's where she could stay.

Look up from the abyss. Stiffen your lip. Gather your thoughts. And restore order.

He rose to his feet, slipped the gold ring from his finger, and peeled back the linen to reveal Katie's sunken expression—still a beautiful young woman while bereft of life. He took her hand, which was cold to the touch, and placed the heirloom in her palm. His soul would be buried with his only daughter, but hers wouldn't be the only funeral on the calendar.

THE BETRAYAL OF PAWNS

The backpack bulged, but in truth, he had taken very little. A sweater. A drink bottle. A bag of half-eaten dry noodles. A flick knife and a rolling pin. He didn't much like the idea of poking somebody with a sharp object, but he had no problems with swinging around a lump of wood fashioned into a baton.

Leaving was a no-brainer, but finding an adequate escape route required a little more thought. Eli had never been a runner, but it felt like the right time to test his stride and his ability to remain incognito.

He sported a faded baseball cap, which was pulled down around his ears, and a pair of ear-hugging headphones—that remained silent—to discourage any would-be conversationalists. It was strange not to pack a phone and his pockets felt empty, but he knew the consequence of travelling with a SIM card. Towers would ping and satellites would lock on to his location before he had the chance to disappear into the urban sprawl.

Eli had also taken a pair of scissors to his credit card before leaving to avoid the temptation of a traceable transaction. He knew the net would be cast far and wide, but he was willing to take a chance on the location monitor embedded in his neck. It was government issue, undoubtedly superseded technology, and, when called upon, would probably prove faulty.

He didn't yet know where he was going, but anywhere was better than occupying a room in a house of cards. He had heard of people falling foul of the police, but this was truly next level and

Elijah didn't want to bear witness to how far they were willing to go. His coping strategy was now to avoid and retreat and, with any luck, slip off the radar.

Chiba and Kelvin could psychoanalyse his response all they liked. The only way he knew how to win was to not play their game at all, and, for the first time, he understood why those on a losing streak feared strong opposition. There was simply nothing to be gained. Unless, of course, the roles could be reversed.

ECDYSIS

Casey Ricks stared down at the corked centrifuge tubes lying horizontally on a smooth square of brown paper. Well within schedule and under budget, his hypothesis proven correct: it had been easy. No need for paint stripper or pipe cleaner. No need to test on a menagerie of creatures with beady eyes that queried one's resolve. The liquid was pure and, more importantly, untraceable with a molecular structure similar to gamma hydroxybutyrate, without acrylate polymer nasties, capable of causing grievous bodily harm, but with a courteous tranquiliser to ease the pain. It wasn't entirely new. Not ground-breaking in any way. He'd had something similar at his disposal for quite some time for reasons only he knew—mad scientists tended to need little motive, or if they did, it began with eccentricity and ended in complex formulas designed to uphold diatribe.

Ricks tenderly folded in each corner of the paper with nimble fingers and ran a length of twine around the twisted orifice, forming a neat pear-shaped parcel like a bag of treats distributed at a kid's birthday. A dozen doses would be enough to bring an army to its knees. Less than half that would suffice Chiba's needs, and the cops could confidently pursue the next stage of their gambit, no matter how illogical it sounded. It was precious. A clear upgrade from their previous product. And it would kill in half the time without fanfare or a ripple of caution.

The chemist smiled wryly and turned his gaze to the closed office door where tactics were being drawn up, thrown out, and desperately revisited. Ricks liked the idea of being a hired gun, and he didn't mind pulling on the gloves and finding the solution—in fact, it was the reason he'd continued his studies. It presented the possibility of turning iron into gold. Brought him one step closer to his mentor Isaac Newton. Perhaps the next opportunity that was presented would be accepted voluntarily. But not with this lot. He didn't take too kindly to being held to ransom.

Happy to toast to a job well done elsewhere, far from the row of tainted tonics he had conjured, Casey Ricks removed his coat, threw it across the bench where the neat line of gifts resided, and turned on his heels. They—the academic temptress, the brute with a buzz cut, and their superior, who would be in need of a hip replacement before too long—knew where to find him, but with any luck, they wouldn't need to come knocking.

CASA DI VINCENZO

A handful of half-filled baggies, two sheets of acid, and a tightly fastened glass cylinder housing red and white capsules sat on the coffee table like the discarded remains of a junk-food dinner.

"That's all I had," Maslow said with his palms turned upward and his pockets turned out. "And Katie bought fuck all. I mean, she had a pretty high tolerance and could have cleaned me out had she wanted to." His voice was thin, and his shoulders encroached on his neck. He knew the meeting was an accusation and his defence needed to be irrefutably airtight. No holes, no leaks, no reason to be water boarded or executed. Maslow knew how Vincenzo fixed a problem.

He looked impeccable for somebody that spent most nights in the club, and any physical baggage had been discarded while running errands to places most feared to tread.

Cleo sat to his right, the chesterfield offering little comfort. She leaned forward as the heels of her knee-high boots bounced on the well-oiled floorboards. She needed to stretch, exhale the stress from her lungs, but it probably wasn't the right time to collapse into a downward dog pose. The hide of a polar bear lay before them as if to suggest that an even greater predator was in their midst. Neither had been present during Katie's final minutes, but they had definitely heard the pandemonium through social media. Snapping 'inappropriate selfies' was a movement that seemed to be gaining momentum. Sadistic narcissism came with the privilege of youth.

Nicky sat behind a sturdy redwood desk on a swivel chair fit for a high court judge and squeezed his finger tenderly where the ring once resided. He looked tired but still up for the fight, and he took comfort in the fear he could elicit by simply summoning the nocturnal creatures to his lair. He allowed a smirk to crease his face. Something had been taken from him, and nobody ever stole from Nicolai Vincenzo and lived to pen an apology.

"So, Anthony, you're telling me she took her business elsewhere?" Nicky grumbled. "That a no-good half-wit was offering her a better product for a better price?"

"No." Tony couldn't help but scoff. "Nobody has a better deal than us, Nicky, you know that." He shifted uneasily in his chair.

Cleo's eyes darted. She wasn't a user, nor a dealer, and she felt like plugging her ears.

"Then why the fuck would she go sniffing around a degenerate bagman for a hit?"

"That's what I can't get my head around. One minute, she was the Katie we all know and love, the next, she was sprawled in the alley being eaten alive."

"Eaten alive?" Nicky's raised his eyebrows. His back was hunched as if he were ready to pounce. He ran with a pack, but he wouldn't need them on this occasion.

"You know what this stuff does." Maslow raised his hands by way of apology.

"And Nadia. Could she have been holding?" Nicky was growing impatient.

"Nadia didn't do anything without Katie's consent," Cleo chimed in. "She never had the guts. Never had the inclination to be anything other than Katie's shadow."

A fuse sizzled beside Nicky's ear. Rage was a symptom of grief, but it was a feeling that never really left his side. "You must have an ID scan, a guest list, anything we can use to smoke this bastard out."

"We had hard drives, but the cops have already been through and cleared it all out," Cleo informed, knowing she was being less than helpful but hoping transparency would work in her favour. Anything to see the other side of the door.

"Cops?" Maslow turned to her. "It's hardly their domain," he quizzed.

It was time for Cleo to raise her palms. "Procedure, they said." She also wanted to add: *Shut up, dickhead.* "And you didn't ask for a warrant?" Something didn't smell right, but that had also been part of Nicky's cynical nature for as long as he could remember.

"I thought you would be happy that they were on the case," Cleo confessed.

"We take care of our own around here, Ms. Rodriguez." Nicky wasn't going to get anything out of these two, and he momentarily decided to holster his stick of dynamite. "This place of yours—Jove—surely, it has a lot of eyes on the floor?"

"We pride ourselves on our security," Cleo remarked.

"And they'd know if somebody new was preying on young girls?" Nicky screwed his hand into a tight ball and once again suppressed the need to break something.

"We have a staff briefing later today. You can rest assured that we'll take a statement from each member of our team."

"Well, if you don't mind, I think I'll attend this briefing, Cleo. I have a way of being able to jog memories, some say it's my greatest asset." Nicky Vincenzo wasn't asking.

"Of course," Cleo responded without hesitation, fearing the consequence of resistance. She rose to her feet, sensing the appointment had reached its natural conclusion.

"And as for you, Maslow." Nicky turned his attention to the hustler that looked like he could be reduced to a puddle of sweat at any time. "You are gonna sit here and eat your way through that stash to prove it's as good as you say."

Maslow's face contorted and turned to Cleo for support. She avoided eye contact and backed away, not wanting to be party to the proposed dinner date—she had enough suitors. Distance was now her only ally.

"But…" the shrinking dealer uttered in protest.

"And Dennis is gonna watch every mouthful," Nicky continued as a heavyset biker type stepped into the room on cue—his face tattoos more the product of prison boredom than pop stardom. "Just to ensure you don't leave the table before finishing your dinner."

"There's a dozen tabs of acid in that mess." Maslow trembled at the prospect.

"Well, we can't expect your customers to buy with confidence if you haven't sampled the product. You can be our very own sensory evaluator."

Dennis crossed the room, snatched the drugs from the table, and firmly grabbed Maslow by the arm. He resisted slightly but knew there was nowhere to run. It was either submit and brace for the trip that awaited or wear a bullet between the eyes. He was left with no option but to take his chances.

Cleo watched in disbelief as both men exited the room. She knew how it would end.

"Now, Rodriguez," Nicky cooed, grasping her attention like a schoolgirl that had somehow escaped a scolding. "If you don't mind, we have a meeting to attend."

SUBURBIA

It was going to be difficult to adjust to life without a car, but Elijah could safely assume that his license had been revoked and his vehicle impounded for the foreseeable future. That seemed the logical conclusion for failing to indicate while running pedestrians aground.

His trainers, although sold by a reputable sports brand, also didn't seem to be handling the terrain all that well. Frays in the fabric were growing apparent and the soles were practically wearing thin before his eyes. He had covered some distance throughout the day but definitely not enough to warrant a full combustion of footwear. Elijah had always thought shoes maketh the man, and he was beginning to feel like a failing gambler balancing on the brink of destitution. Card sharks were having their way.

He had avoided trains, and any form of public transport, for that matter, and as he stood on a crest and looked across the tiled rooftops of houses nestled closely together, like meek constructs seeking companionship in a mean world, he realised that he hadn't been back to the neighbourhood in which he was raised for at least a decade. He inhaled deeply through his nose and realised it still smelled the same. A smouldering chimney resembled an incinerator his father would indiscriminately feed before he left for good, and the jasmine wrestled with lavender for ascendency. It was pleasantly familiar. He had very few friends in the area save for Francis Köhler. Sure, there were some familiar faces from formative years who had become acquaintances on social networks, but Francis was a true rock. Not a weekly catch-up guy, more a 'happy to see ya when I see ya' type of friend.

Francis had never called him names, never accused him of what had happened with his mother, never been part of the 'in crowd.' He still lived with his parents, still doted on his model train set, but most importantly, he still had the ability to keep a secret. He didn't crave popularity and thus was happy to remain quiet even amid scandal and innuendo. Not one word escaped his mouth without lengthy consideration. He was the kind of guy that was rarely called upon in class, but when he was, he wouldn't be hurried into a hasty response. He was a thinker, and, in his mind, words should only be formed to represent optimal thoughts. There was too much verbal clutter already.

Not surprisingly, as an introvert, Francis had entered the world of IT—predominately remote assistance, handling connectivity queries and the like. As a result, and much to his pleasure, he didn't often leave the house. Computers had always been reliable, impartial, obedient; they simply became a cosy, semi-lucrative profession. He much preferred artificial intelligence over the human equivalent.

A warm orange glow emanated through the windows of each house. Dusk had arrived and a sense of security was being forged behind closed doors, and Elijah desperately craved a safe house, a fortified nest to lay low. Without Nathalie, Francis was his one and only chance.

The recognisable suburban streets were comforting, a supportive wink in a time of need. But it hadn't always been the case.

House fires made the news because they not only devastated families but they reminded communities that they were vulnerable, potential victims of what lay beyond the front door and the circuitry within. When Elijah lost his mother to an inferno that burned throughout the night, aspersions were cast. Not discreetly around dinner tables or shady bars, but openly, in his company. *Where was he that night? Why were matches found in his dresser? What prompted arguments before the blaze?* Strangely, he answered coolly and calmly, despite the crushing sorrow that ravaged his insides, which led to further allegations. He was the prime suspect and he was constantly under the scrutiny of the neighbourhood watch. Nothing was the same after that night. He became an orphan and a perceived criminal in the same breath, and at seventeen years of age, with little care for perception, it's difficult to elicit sympathy. He was old enough to care for himself, old enough to live with the guilt. Although he had a widely supported alibi, and no motive was ever established, he became the kid that inflamed his mum, burned her like a witch at the stake.

They say it takes a village to raise a child, but that same village can also tie you up and feed you to the vultures.

Elijah moved away, lived with an aunt, and the charred remains of the family home sat in ruins for years before the landlord bulldozed it and erected functional yet soulless units.

In the aftermath of the fire, like many postcodes, the area lost much of its charm. Community trust waned and newcomers didn't have time to stop for a chat. Kids no longer played on the street, and it was difficult to take pride in one's castle when investors handed out pieces of the pie with inflated price tags leaving little for curation and care.

But now, upon returning, Elijah felt an electricity in the air, a nostalgia that transported him to nights riding skateboards and racing home before dinner was served. Again, for a fleeting moment, he felt innocent and free and then he remembered why he had returned. This was his foxhole, and he was only too happy to keep his head down and his tail between his legs.

He found the place easily enough, save for a few wrong turns here and there. He hoped Francis would answer the door—he couldn't stand the possibility of his parents trying to place him and then arriving at the answer: the Firestarter.

Elijah lifted the brass knocker and pecked the heavy wood several times. It resonated through the house as if it were a vacant cavity, and he listened for movement. He stepped back so he wouldn't dominate the peephole and lingered in the shadows before an overhead globe blinked to life. The door creaked open and Elijah rolled up his sleeves as if posturing for confrontation. Francis' bespectacled face peered around the heavy wooden door. He hadn't changed a great deal. Tufts of a poorly manicured beard interrupted smooth skin and his hairline receded slightly, but it was clear that he was the same guy that had squinted through the camera lens for his yearbook photo all those moons ago. Voted most likely to find comfort in pyjama bottoms and supersized frozen Cokes.

"I'm not harvesting 'til Wednesday," he said through a yawn and lowered glasses as he pinched the bridge of his nose. "I don't know how many times I have to—"

"Francis," Elijah interrupted. "It's me, Eli." It had been a long time between drinks, and a lot could change while rotating the sun, including the recollection of an old friend.

Francis straightened his posture and focused his vision. "I said Wednesday," he stoutly reaffirmed before closing the door.

CHIHUAHUAS DRESSED AS DOBERMANS

The squadron of security guards lined the dance floor in military formation. Cleo and Vincenzo, along with two of his cronies whose brows were losing the battle against gravity, stood on an elevated podium generally reserved for dancers or louts that wanted to be seen above the crowd. A venue that opens its door around midnight is a wondrous thing in the daytime. It promises possibility in its dormancy. It's a drama club momentarily taking a break from the drama queens.

Although there were only eight staff members in attendance, and there were several hours before they officially clocked on, they were still fitted out from head to toe in black attire and identification tags. They were loyal workers, workers that had been threatened on countless occasions, but gave as good as they got. In their presence, Cleo commanded respect—this was clearly a weekly consultation—a dictator preaching to her obedient few and not just a pantomime served up to appease the Vincenzo clan. But rather than discussing capacity protocols, jammed toilet bowls, and punter indiscretions, as was the norm, the focus was solely on Katerina Vincenzo and her interactions the previous night.

"We've all read the news and we all here know Katie and Nadia," Cleo began. Her voice was firm, she was a boss in every sense of the word, but it seemed forced, as if a knife were being applied to her back. "We need to know their movements from when they entered to the time they left."

The employees adjusted their positions and looked at one another, searching for answers. Like any other night, the club had been busy, and it was hard to keep track of individuals, especially those with the energetic tenacity of Katie Vincenzo. There had been a few altercations, a few forced evictions, but nothing out of the norm, nothing to suggest foul play. Each guard remained silent as if pleading the fifth.

"Was she acting strangely when she arrived?" Cleo pressed.

"Define strangely?" a voice quizzed from the crowd.

"I mean, did she seem in good spirits?" Cleo had always thought of Katie as somewhat self-destructive, a party girl that rebelled against her father while out on his dime. She was spoiled in more ways than one.

"Katie was being Katie," a second voice added. "She was... lively." It was an observation but one that could have easily been perceived as accusatory.

"Did she spend time with Maslow?"

Again, the small crowd fell silent for fear of incriminating others. Maslow was more than a friend to most. He was their dealer too.

"Cleo," said the only woman present except for herself—the industry was still dominated by swinging dicks. "Don't we have cameras we can check? Katie does have a habit of covering a lot of territory, she moves between floors quite often." The woman almost immediately regretted speaking when she locked eyes with the men flanking her boss.

"This is true, and we pride ourselves on surveillance protocols, but the authorities..." Nicky stepped in front of Cleo before she could finish. He was tired of waiting in the wings, and he was tired of the absence of answers.

"The recordings are gone, that's all you need to know," Nicky said in a hushed tone.

It was enough to prick ears and send goose bumps rippling across hair follicles.

"I am sure many of you know who I am, and you know why I'm here. I need answers not murmurings of self-preservation."

They all knew exactly who he was, and *he* was the reason for any form of preservation.

"Now, I will ask once and only once: Did any of you see anybody strange, perhaps somebody new to the club whacking off in the shadows?"

Figures, frozen like Terracotta Warriors, darted their eyes every which way but straight ahead. Their job descriptions didn't include answering to known gangsters...or maybe they did.

Then a hand was raised, acknowledging the change of command. Nicky pointed like a teacher giving a student permission to speak. "There was one guy…"

"Spit it out," Nicky encouraged the only way he knew how.

"Baseball cap, high collar, nursed a drink for a long while. He was hanging around just outside Maslow's entourage. Looked like a tourist. I didn't pay him much mind."

Cleo's own mind raced back to the man she had encountered in the doorway. The Czechoslovakian. He fit the description. Except he had kind eyes. Not the kind of guy that would feed poison to young girls.

"And a woman," officer Number Seventy-Two declared. "There was a woman. Short black hair. Looked like she'd cut it herself. Wore a boiler suit like a mechanic, like she wanted to go unnoticed, which struck me as strange—everyone is vying for attention in a place like this. She sat in the corner and waved away any potential drinking buddies. She had her eye on something, but I couldn't say exactly what that was, though."

"Oh yeah, I saw her too. Attractive."

Nicky's eyes darted to the original voice, who seemed to be on the ball, a guard that would happily stare at a prized vase all day if that was the assignment. He was a sturdy fellow with a chin that could take a punch, knuckles that had thrown a few. He filled the uniform and then some. Number Fourteen. Nicky immediately warmed to him.

"I spoke to her briefly, asked if she was doing okay," Number Fourteen continued. "She had a strange accent, rhythmic, like her tongue was rolled. Possibly Scandinavian. Said she was waiting for her boyfriend, but I ain't seen no boyfriend."

Nicky turned to Cleo. He'd heard enough. "Rodriguez," he snapped. "Fucking ID scans, up-here-now. It seems your team is a sight more helpful than you and that dipshit, Maslow." He expected to have names and addresses by the end of the day.

Cleo briskly exited the room knowing she still had a lot to do if she were to claw her way clear of this shit show. They had little to go on, but it was enough to get them off her back. If she could present a head to be mounted, she could save her own.

"You and you—stay." Nicky threw a pointed finger at the chest of Numbers Fourteen and Seventy-Two and then stabbed a thumb towards the door. "The rest of you, out." And with that, class was dismissed.

CHEWING GECKO

Francis sat across from Elijah on a replica Eames nursing a cup of peppermint tea. The basement was tidier than Elijah remembered—in fact, the décor was streamlined, compartmentalised, and minimalist, preventing dust from coming to rest. It was notably Danish. Elijah had expected mounds of clothes, discarded books, a computer glowing in the corner like a living, breathing organism feeding on power and light. Francis had a thirteen-inch silver laptop. Closed and neatly stowed. It was understated, even if it was weaponised.

The door had crept open after Elijah called to his friend using his childhood nickname, Ghost. A reference that had tickled the folds of his ears and reminded him of sneaking in and out of mainframes that should have had better security.

Either it was the old Gatorbeug blower, Eli C, or somebody from 4chan had traced his handle. Thankfully, it was the former.

Upon entering, Elijah had told him the story—there was little time for pleasantries. He needed advice, words of comfort. He needed to purge.

"You ran people over in your car?" Francis quizzed, his face expressionless.

"Yes. Apparently. I—I can't really remember," Elijah stammered. This would be a deal breaker. Francis wouldn't dare house a known felon. He hadn't listened to anything beyond the grounds for his arrest.

"I didn't read anything about it in the news." Francis sipped his tea. "And I read a lot of fucking news. I'm a media monitor, for Christ's sake."

"They covered it up, kept it quiet. It was the catalyst for everything else that has gone down. I wish it had never happened."

"Kept it quiet? It doesn't sound like something you could keep quiet. There are victims, victims' families, rubberneckers. A smashed-up vehicle in the middle of the city. Any journalist worth their salt would be knee deep in this shit in no time."

"They're powerful. They get things done. They know how to silence people," Elijah explained, but it felt implausible in his mouth.

"Well, that sounds like a pretty big ball gag. I don't know any organisation, even government that could put that shit to bed."

"And the girl?" Elijah quizzed.

"That I *did* read about," Francis corroborated. "Toxicosis. Mass organ failure. Pretty ugly shit. Closed casket type stuff."

"I know. And this is what they want."

"You did that to her?"

"Yes. I mean, no. I couldn't. Somebody from the task force did, though." Elijah rubbed his palms together and felt like he was betraying trust. Exactly whose, he wasn't sure.

"I read about a guy that ate a gecko—a party trick—same thing happened to him. Rotted from the inside in a matter of hours."

"She didn't eat a fucking lizard, Francis. Her drink was spiked. She was poisoned. Poisoned by the people I work for."

"It makes sense." It was hard to tell if he was being flippant to provide friendly sustenance or he had simply spent too much time doom-scrolling.

"None of this makes sense." Elijah was exasperated. He leaned forward and placed his head in his hands as if the weight of the world was bearing down.

"Well, according to Oxford scholars, police officers are extremely likely to have psychopathic traits. And although psychopathy doesn't make a serial killer, a close correlation between the two can be drawn."

"What are you trying to say?"

"I'm saying that if you give a gun and a badge to somebody with the tendency to harbour disturbing thoughts, you're gonna have a few unexplained casualties on your hands. Hell, the Golden State Killer was a cop."

"And if that person is the head of a task force, a Doctor Caligari holding the keys to the medicine cabinet?"

"Well, then you're sitting on a pretty big fucking time bomb." Francis rattled a bottle of aspirin in his hand and threw back a measured dose like someone that had grown accustomed to nursing headaches.

FEEDING FRENZY

An illuminated red sphere amid parallel lines, indicating a geographical location, a target, blinked on a computer screen. Kelvin sat back and drew heavily on his cigarette—the tip burning bright in the moonlight that filtered through the blinds.

"He didn't get too far." He spoke as if it were a chore, as if syllables were rare and not to be wasted. "I thought he may be more…ambitious."

"Should we go?" Batal asked as he sat beneath the hue of a table lamp, rolling a tumbler of whiskey in his hands. He couldn't see the display, but he trusted K's instincts.

"When the time comes, we'll send a trainee."

"Are you sure that's a good idea, sir?"

"When he moves, we'll make an example of everyone he has come into contact with."

"Scorched Earth?" Batal liked the idea of complete devastation.

"When this is all said and done, he'll have nobody to turn to. They'll have to hire pallbearers for his funeral." Kelvin had a short fuse, but he was also happy to bide his time. Nothing good came to those that abandoned patience.

"And if he stays?"

"Well, then we flush him out. He's no good to us hiding in a cave. We need him on his feet, active, ready to fight another day."

"Why?" Batal questioned. "We have others."

"He needs to finish the job. Then we can feed him to the wolves. The cartels will want blood and we'll give it to them. Dead operatives buy us more time."

"I have a feeling he won't come quietly. He sees nothing noble about the cause."

"Unfortunately, young Elijah is now *our* property and we can use him in any way we see fit. Even if that means handing him over to those seeking redemption. An oil spill never goes unnoticed, my friend. The least we can do is offer a mop."

"A sacrifice?"

"You could say that, but I like to think of it as shuffling the deck. We just need to ensure we keep holding the aces." Kelvin extinguished the butt of his cigarette and turned back to the screen. The pulsating signal remained in place, content with its surrounds and resolutely oblivious to the omniscient voyeurs.

Kelvin knew the area well. He had combed it several times searching for talent. Cafés. Bars. Restaurants that served food to locals that claimed they hadn't tried better elsewhere. Every neighbourhood had prospective employees—those at a crossroads or a dead end who needed a purpose, a hint of incentive. That's not to say that all targets he identified became success stories, and small catches often led to landing bigger prizes. You just needed to know which bait to hook and which ones to feed to the gulls.

That's how Kelvin had built his task force. It was a simple recruitment strategy that required stamina and a keen eye. The assurance of a better life sealed the deal. He offered a seat in a travelling circus that knew no bounds, and the desperate and vulnerable clambered aboard. Those less willing were persuaded via other means, and Kelvin was adept at twisting arms to the breaking point.

"Do we know the whereabouts of his next of kin?" Kelvin turned his gaze away from the computer and back to his fidus Achates.

"It's taken care of," Batal said. "She's isolated. No lines in, no lines out."

"And the girl in the hospital?"

"Nadia Unsworth?"

Kelvin shook his head to suggest her name mattered not.

"Brain dead. On a machine. She isn't coming back."

It was music to Kelvin's ears, but he also felt the encore had played too long. A crescendo should never be drawn out longer than necessary.

Nevertheless, it would make further headlines when the plug was pulled, and that was something he could look forward to. Drugs were the enemy and that needed to be reinforced. Poor Nadia Uns-whatever was just another helpless victim.

PLOTTING AND SCHEMING IN MAMA'S BASEMENT

"Remember Jodi Nubrick?" Elijah asked as he flipped through a philosophy text by Bertrand Russell exploring epistemology.

"Remember?" Francis replied, comfortably seated among a mountain of cushions. "How could I forget?"

"And the time she overdosed at Steven Winslow's party? Took a cocktail of coke and weed and flu tablets."

"That was some scary shit."

"Scary, sure. But it didn't stop anyone taking their own gear that night, or any other night, for that matter."

The lights had grown dim and the two men seemed to be settling in for the night.

"I guess we were too dumb to know any better." Francis knew they had never been 'dumb'—both he and Elijah had always been at the top of the class. Street smart too. That was what happened when you were forced to grow up quickly.

"We thought we were invincible." Elijah placed the book down on the coffee table. "Yeah, we knew it could happen, but it was just gonna happen to somebody else."

"Optimism bias."

"That's right. And these cops, they don't get that. They think these kids will be scared into submission. That if they see their friends go down, they'll curl up beneath a blanket and go cold turkey."

"A lot of people are gonna have to die before that becomes a reality."

"A lot. And I think they're willing to go that far. In fact, I don't think it is about attacking the dealers, the money-makers. I think it's about sweeping the streets and applying a Band-Aid to a festering wound."

"You need to tell people about this. There's a community that feeds off this kinda stuff." Francis knew conspiracy theorists that had gained notoriety for less. Chemtrails. Dustification. Vaccines that triggered autism. Cell towers that spread viruses. It was all just the tip of a very fucked-up iceberg.

"If I pop my head up, it's gonna get knocked clean off," Elijah continued. "They are just waiting for me to trip up."

Both men fell silent for a moment. It wouldn't be the first time Elijah had tripped up, but the stakes were higher than they had ever been.

"Who's gonna listen anyway? I have a hard time believing all this shit is happening myself. I feel like I went to sleep after breaking up with Nathalie and woke up in another dimension."

Francis shrugged. "I believe you." It felt like a good time to stand and embrace, perhaps show his friend the door and bid him farewell, but he remained seated. There was more to be done. "Do you still have the drug? The gecko juice that ripped the heart out of those two girls?"

"Yeah. Why?" Elijah responded coyly.

"I know a guy." Francis sat up, suddenly excited by an epiphany. "A chemistry student. We could get him to reverse engineer it, see what's in it."

"And why would we do that?" Elijah failed to share his friend's enthusiasm. "The less we mess with this stuff, the better."

"If we know what's in it, we can make it. And if we make it, we can use it against them. Once we have the upper hand, we can make all kinds of demands."

"Stop saying 'we,' there's no 'we'—you're not involved. Let's keep it that way." Elijah didn't want to see anybody else get hurt, especially somebody close to him.

"If you get close enough, you can feed it back to them," Francis said soberly. "Be like that seal that chases the fucking shark to avoid being eaten." He was serious about most things and this was no different.

"Why don't I just storm the station with an Uzi and blow their heads off?" Elijah was taking it less seriously.

"Because you'd be arrested. And everyone would say, *Remember that guy, he was always the most likely to screw up*. They don't deserve that vindication." Francis took a sip of his tea. "And you'd probably miss anyway."

A wry smile swept across Elijah's face for the first time in a long time.

"Don't you want them to choke on the shit they've been dishing out?" Francis locked eyes with his friend. "You can watch that nasty shit turn them inside out."

Although he liked his friend's turn of phrase and the image it evoked, Elijah wasn't sure. What was being proposed flew in the face of the coping strategy he had decided upon. Untethered flight, as opposed to a bare-knuckle fight, seemed to offer a greater chance of being extricated from his assigned duty. He needed more icing on the donut.

"How do you know this guy?" Elijah asked.

"We dated for a bit. Just didn't work out." Francis was nonchalant and quite selective in his explanation.

"And why didn't it work out?" Elijah needed more.

"He is very good at what he does, and very committed. He wanted me to sample a few things. I wasn't comfortable with that."

"Sample?"

"Vitamins. Supplements. You know, nothing serious." Francis swept it aside.

"Sounds like you had your very own Theo Morell," Elijah scoffed.

"Nah, he's a good guy," Francis defended. "Just a little misunderstood."

Francis reached into his pocket and removed his wallet. He folded it open and located a creased business card and tossed it to Elijah, who peered down at the matte finish and embossed lettering.

"That's where you can find him. I'll call ahead." Francis rose to his feet and Elijah followed suit. He would need his coat, but if this ex-boyfriend was all that Francis had claimed, he wouldn't be needing the rolling pin.

"He'll be expecting you," Francis said as Eli turned to the door. "And take these." He threw Elijah a set of keys, which he caught and hugged to his chest. He gave his friend a look of thanks, but there was no need for goodbyes. They would be reunited again. Someday.

LASTING IMPRESSIONS

The club was still hours away from re-opening, and in the offices where books were occasionally cooked, all four faces stared down at a grainy black-and-white image as if they were opening a gift on Christmas morning. Digital photography had come a long way, but it still had its limitations.

"You're sure that's him? Patrick Svoboda?" Nicky demanded. He hated computers and preferred to avoid them where possible. Simply put, they reinforced what he already knew: he was getting old and losing touch. But when they worked in his favour, he marvelled at their ability to impart wisdom, and envied those that could wrangle their inner workings.

Cleo and the security guards nodded their heads in unison. Although the blacks bled and the colouring was absent, it was undeniably the man Rodriguez had obligingly granted entry. Unlike many of the other male patrons, his headshot wasn't trying to win accolades from modelling agencies, but his boyish good looks were still irrefutably photogenic.

"And last night was the first time he'd ever caught your eye?" Nicky was curious and he wanted all the intel he could harangue before rushing out the door. It was one thing to have the target confirmed, another to know if an army awaited.

"First time." One spoke for all.

"And he didn't seem to be working for anyone? No contact, no associates I need to know about?"

"He was alone," Cleo said assertively. All eyes turned in her direction: *How could she be sure?* "We spoke, briefly, as he entered. It was convivial."

"You spoke to this cunt?" Nicky incredulously seethed through clenched teeth.

"I was screening him, trying to get a gauge on his character," Cleo retorted. She could hear the hostile rattle of the snake in her company, and she needed to put some distance between herself and his fangs. "The name was familiar, but the face wasn't."

"And did he say anything about murdering my fucking daughter?"

"No." Cleo shuddered.

"What?" Nicky craned his neck towards Cleo's lips as she reared back defensively.

"Look, I'm sorry, Nicolai." A tear ran down her cheek. "We run a good place here."

Nicky turned back to the screen. "Now show me the other one. The bitch you saw."

"Do you want to take down the address?" one of the security guards asked.

"I have the fucking address," Nicky hissed.

The guard read the room and quickly proceeded to scan through the pixelated images, gliding the computer's mouse across the desk to reveal those in attendance the previous night. Most were young, not long out of school, and their IDs mostly took the form of probationary licenses or student cards.

"Stop," the second guard instructed calmly. He was a big guy, and big guys were accustomed to getting their way without having to raise their voices.

A comparatively older woman appeared on the display. Mid-to late-twenties, striking, black semicircles beneath her eyes, the low resolution chasing away any blemishes, apart from a beauty spot just above her top lip. A pair of crescent-moon earrings hung like Christmas ornaments. Here was a woman that could have comfortably stepped into an Ingmar Bergman film. Her hair had been cropped messily, and her pursed lips curtailed any signs of vibrancy. She looked bored, annoyed, as if she would never be content.

"That's her." A finger pointed.

"Vanessa Haden," the controlling guard read, noting her malaise.

"She doesn't look Scandinavian," Cleo noted, gathering herself.

"It doesn't fucking matter what she looks like. If it's her, it's her," Nicky concluded.

"It's her," Number Seventy-Two emphasised. He was adamant and that was enough.

Nicky stepped backward, away from the glow of the screen, away from the staff that had aided his investigation. He sunk back into the shadows of the control room where he was flanked by his associates—two wrecking balls that swung at the discretion of one man.

"Vanessa Haden and Patrick Svoboda," Nicky sang. "A couple of dirty rats that killed my daughter under your roof, under your watch. A couple of dirty rats that you aided and abetted by turning a blind fucking eye."

"Nicky, we co-operated," Cleo pleaded. "We turned them over…"

"Do you know what happens to a maid after she has cleaned a crime scene, Cleo?" Nicky continued. Somebody somewhere was celebrating a birthday. Accepting a marriage proposal. Somebody was having a screaming orgasm. But right then, right there, the depths of despair had opened wide.

No response was forthcoming. The answer was clear, and it burned in his eyes. He knew no other way and he made no apologies. If he didn't do what had to be done, he ran the very real risk of vacating his throne, and he wasn't willing to do that just yet.

Nicolai Vincenzo stepped out of the room, leaving behind a tableau he knew all too well, and as he crossed the unoccupied dance floor, the overhead lights throwing his shadow in all directions across the parquetry, a rain of deafening gunshots provided a prelude to that which awaited his daughter's tormentors. He had made a promise to Katie, and he would make good on those parting words.

PART IV:

A MARKETPLACE FOR POACHERS

PHARMING CLONES

It was late and the university car park was empty. Elijah had never attended such an institution, and he admired the carefully manicured lawns and the paved walkways that led to limitless possibilities. Under the soft light of Victorian garden lamps, he couldn't help but think what fate may have awaited if he'd been afforded access to one of the many doors that dotted the establishment. The authorities didn't tend to intrude on the lives of the educated, the highly esteemed, and they most definitely did not resort to coercion to get them into doing their bidding. He was vulnerable because he was nobody, but his actions had enticed their searchlight. He wasn't without blame.

Francis had agreed to stay home on the condition that Elijah borrowed his car to visit Casey Ricks, soon to be associate professor, master of alchemy. Francis was dead set on his plan to manufacture the product and put it in the mouths of those that had caused all the calamity in the first place. He was an avid fan of Greek mythology and he had always harboured a desire to be aboard the Trojan horse. This was one way to play out his fantasy. He liked bugs in the system, especially when he was responsible for their dissemination.

Francis had called ahead without outlining the finer details; he had simply suggested that a friend needed a hand with a composition query. Subterfuge was the order of the day. Ricks, although busy, worked late, so it wasn't a problem. His laboratory was always open, and he was only too happy to assist a former lover.

Elijah had bid his friend farewell with a firm handshake and had vowed to return the keys when the job was done. He wished they had been reunited under better circumstances, but he was grateful for the advice, even more appreciative of the loan of his car, even if it was a beaten-up, old Datsun with a smashed headlight (and not the DeLorean he was hoping for).

Elijah made his way across the campus without encountering another soul. The air was thick with fog, and he hoped it would mask his footsteps and hide his whereabouts from those that cared to enquire. At a building that looked much like all the others, he leaned his finger into an intercom and was welcomed almost immediately by the deactivation of an electronic clasp on the glass door. The signage had led him to the right department. He seized the handle, disappeared out of sight, and scaled the stairs two at a time.

The professor was waiting for him at the door and ushered Elijah warmly into the workroom, unaware of the covert nature of their meeting. Ricks took a seat on a stool, the wood worn smooth by years of use, while Elijah leaned on a benchtop, careful not disrupt the stationed apparatuses. Ricks was young for somebody cast as an 'expert,' and his features were buoyant as if a sense of vitality seeped from his pores. His hair was thick, his eyes burned brightly, and he had a positive aura which was almost condescending in the company of his guest. He was the kind of mentor a student would like to share a beer with. If he'd had a long day, he didn't show it.

"So, this equation…" Ricks cut to the chase.

Elijah felt sick with fatigue. It felt like he hadn't eaten or rested properly for days, and here he was about to confide in a complete stranger, a stranger that could push a panic button and have him handed back over to those he was trying to outrun. He felt for his neck. The tracking device was still there. Concern was as multilayered as the Earth itself.

"What I'm about to tell you probably wouldn't meet the approval of the college board," Elijah ventured.

"I'm guided by ethics, Elijah, but not compelled by them," Ricks said coldly. He was a man that seemed to value progress above all else, and Elijah suddenly understood why Francis had suggested a visit. He, no doubt, had thumbs in various pies.

"I have been prescribed a drug which is intended to do harm, to kill the user." The words sprung forth from Elijah's mouth like soldiers on the front line, ready to detonate an IED, ready to die for a cause. It was unnerving, to the say the least.

"And why would somebody prescribe you such a thing?"

"Because they want me to poison those that operate outside of the law."

"Criminals?"

"I wouldn't call them that."

"And what would you like me to do about it? Flush it down the toilet? Feed it to a passel of piglets?" Ricks didn't like his time wasted and the clock was ticking.

"Francis said you may be able to tell me what's in it?" Elijah queried, uncertain if he was pushing this newfound friendship too far.

"I could do that." Ricks didn't lack any confidence. "And then what?"

"We could make it." It sounded silly, harebrained. Francis had given him a bum steer.

"You know what's wrong with this world, Elijah?" Ricks paused but the question was clearly rhetorical. "There are too many fucking guns. Everyone is clambering over each other to arm themselves. If we have a problem, the answer is always guns. There's always a new threat, a new enemy, and we all line up to take a shot at the target. People live with crosshair vision, and you want me to help you to distribute more weapons, more ways to die?"

"These people—"

"Ahhh, people," Ricks interrupted, "now there's the real problem."

Casey Ricks reached beneath his desk, moved a few boxes, shuffled a few pages, and returned to his upright position holding a rat, a healthy brown rat that sniffed at the air and blinked heavily, adjusting to the light. It sat precariously on a perch created by his thumb and index finger, and he nursed it like a newborn.

"Meet Hitomi," Ricks introduced, holding the rodent aloft for appreciative eyes.

He then placed it into a shoebox sitting on the floor between the two men.

"I can't decode and synthesise your drug, Elijah, not in the time we have."

Elijah's face dropped. He had been sold on the prospect, no matter how ludicrous it sounded. A light had sparked and now it was all but diffused.

"My guess is that it's a grey death—a fentanyl-laced heroin. Cheap, dirty. Lazy. Made by assholes for assholes," Ricks continued. "But I do have something that will prove equally effective. In other ways."

Elijah's eyebrows and spirits lifted.

Ricks produced a syringe from a drawer, flicked the vial to awaken its contents, and squirted a teasing amount of liquid from the nip to extract any bubbles. Elijah was familiar with preventing air embolisms from his time spent with insulin injections.

"This formula is possibly ten times more lethal than anything else I've ever held in my hands." He was beginning to look and sound like a mad scientist, and Elijah couldn't help but wonder what kind of web he had walked into. "Think of it as pancuronium bromide, potassium chloride, and sodium thiopental with a dash of secret herbs and spices. Death isn't always instant, but it is inescapable."

"You made this?" Elijah asked.

Ricks swiftly bent down and injected the needle into the rat, the plunger releasing the clear contents into tissue running parallel with its spinal cord.

"I did," Ricks responded proudly.

"But why?"

"I grew up in Dharavi. Do you know it?"

"It's a slum, isn't it?"

"Yes. In Mumbai. One of the world's biggest. As soon as I could read, I wanted to make something of myself. But it meant I had to leave my community, my people. I vowed I would return with something that would make a difference."

"And this is what you came up with?" Elijah gestured towards the juiced-up rodent.

"Euthanasia is now widely accepted, Elijah. Everybody should have the right to end their suffering in a humane way. Unfortunately, though, it is still an esoteric concept."

"You're bringing death prematurely to the masses. I know some people that would be happy to fund your work." Elijah's moral compass was being tested again.

"We all die, my friend." The phrase rolled off Ricks's tongue as if it were a mantra he had become accustomed to reciting.

Elijah stared into the distance. Since the passing of his mother, not a day had slipped by without death making headlines in the forefront of his mind. He took comfort in the fact he hadn't been in a position to end or preserve her life. One day she was there, the next she wasn't. Simple.

"There is a supreme being within us all, Elijah, and we should have agency to flick the switch at a time of our choosing. Even the Dalits of my homeland deserve that."

"Dalits?" Elijah wasn't familiar with the reference.

"The outcastes," Ricks clarified. "Some of whom crave an escape, a fresh start."

The notion of 'reincarnation' bounced around in Elijah's head like a pinball, before he continued: "And this has been cleared? By your superiors."

Ricks grinned and turned his attention to the rat. Elijah followed suit and noticed minor convulsions that grew more rapid, more paralysing. In no time, the movements ceased, the rat stiffened, and all life was abandoned.

Ricks swivelled in his chair and began to scribble notes across a pad. He recorded his observations in a messy, almost-indecipherable scrawl.

"You didn't need to do that." Elijah wasn't accustomed to such acts of cruelty. He tapped at the shoebox with his foot, hoping to rouse the animal. Nothing. Hitomi was gone.

Ricks crossed his t's and dotted his i's and dropped the pen. He then reached for an unlabelled vial on a shelf high above his head, stowed as if it were a precious liquor. He used a second syringe to penetrate the seal and extricated five millilitres of the turquoise-tinged fluid.

Again, he drove the nib into the rat's neck.

"When you are doing the kind of work I am," Ricks said, leaning back in his chair, "you don't have superiors."

Elijah broke his gaze and stared back down at the creature which trembled slightly, twisted and turned, and quickly found its feet. Blinking swiftly, it returned to catching scents on its whiskers and investigating the corners of the box as if nothing had ever happened.

"You paralysed it?" Elijah quizzed incredulously.

"Oh no, it was definitely a goner. Hitomi visited the Otherside."

"But how?"

"The question isn't so much how, but why?" Ricks theorised.

"Then why?"

"Because we can," Ricks responded. "All human endeavour is to prove that we can, that we have control of our destiny and nothing predetermines what we can and can't do. Why else send a man into space?"

"To discover what's out there? To see beyond our little blue dot," Elijah protested.

"Nobody gives a fuck about the landmass of Saturn's moons."

"That's it?" Elijah was standing on the edge of a landmark discovery, and he couldn't believe that he was being met with flippancy and existential riddles.

"It works easily as well ingested orally," Ricks noted. "You can try it if you like. But I should warn you, I haven't yet entered human trials."

"Is that why things ended with Fran?" Elijah accused.

Ricks didn't bite. Instead, he picked up the rat and allowed it to squirm a little in his grasp. "That's the third time Hitomi has been reanimated, bounces back every time. She'd have some great stories to tell."

"About your negligence?"

Ricks bristled. "It's how it works, Elijah. Vaccines don't just arrive on a silver platter. Cures are unpleasant, until they're not. And remember, you came to me."

"Why are you showing me this?" Elijah quizzed.

"You don't strike me as a killer. With this, you'll be able to rattle a few cages. Restore some of the power that has been taken from you. My people call it Swarāj."

Both men fell silent. Elijah had fallen down a rabbit hole, and everything seemed to be getting stranger and stranger, and he was beginning to have a tough time distinguishing what was real and what wasn't. What was right and what was downright deranged.

"So"—Ricks clapped his hands and broke the stillness—"how many vials should I put you down for? Consider it a donation for conducting the clinical trials." Scruples had all but been abandoned.

Elijah considered his options. They weren't exactly jostling for position, and this was a way to choose life over the trail of death that lay in his wake. He had already signed off on his soul in the presence of Munro and Yates, and another contract appeared inconsequential. Elijah held out his open palm like a child accepting candy. He would worry about the side effects of his decision, and the unlikely partnership, later.

PUTTING A FACE TO THE FACE

Through a passenger-side window wound halfway down offering a skewed view of reality, Nicolai Vincenzo gazed upon an abandoned residence that sat between ominous warehouses like a tugboat at a convention for ships. Its orifices had been boarded up with splintered slats of wood and its walls spray-painted by local gangbangers looking to populate the area with their tags and slogans. It was a turf war, and those who doused the most decorative art won. The yard was also home to a fierce battle between weeds and discarded trash. It had been a long time since it had housed anything of importance.

"Sure this was the place, boss?" the driver asked, leaning across to admire the view.

"Well, it doesn't fucking look like it, does it?" Nicky wasn't in the mood for conversation. He had already spent long enough in Limo's company, and he was tired of his face and his voice. Due to his appearance and demeanour, he had been nicknamed after a variety of bovine—a dirty big French bull, to be precise—and Nicky would have been happy to cut him loose and put him out to pasture. But there was still a job to be done.

"Fake IDs?"

"It would appear so. Both of 'em. Should have known there'd just be ruins in this wasteland." Nicky's mind was like a Rolodex, and beneath the surface, the pages were flipping as if caught in a gale. "There are plenty of skeletons buried in this neighbourhood. I dug most of 'em myself."

"What the fuck is going on, Nicky?" The confusion was shared.

"That's what I would like to know. But what I do know is those IDs were better than most of the counterfeits I've come across. Whoever put them together knew what they were doing."

"The Ballard Brothers?" Limo offered.

"What the fuck would those amateurs know about forgery?" Nicky was annoyed by the mere suggestion. "Nah, this was pro."

A few names came to mind, and if they didn't know anything, they would be encouraged to give up more names. It was a game of pass-the-parcel before the truth was revealed. Visits would be paid soon enough.

A car rounded a corner in the distance and headed their way, its headlights illuminating the vacant street stained with tyre marks and chewed rubber.

"Now, who do we have here?" Nicky pondered aloud as he squinted his beady peepers to focus on the make, the model, and the identity of the driver.

"Not sure, but there's three figures. Two up front, one in the back." Limo had a keen eye. Both men felt for their revolvers as it drew nearer.

The car pulled into the driveway of the staked-out address and shut off its engine. Nicky and his accomplice had gone unnoticed, in all likelihood mistaken for a forsaken vehicle. Just another stolen motor left to rust.

Two men exited the car before helping a young woman from the back seat and escorted her to the front door. A welcoming porch light didn't spring to life, but one of the men was able to effortlessly remove a chain and padlock and all three disappeared behind a makeshift door.

"Was that her?" Limo asked, still acclimatising to the darkness.

"Who the fuck else would be turning up here in the middle of the night?" Nicky projected an air of certainty.

"And the two guys?"

"Probably a hookup. Miserable bastards from the clubs, no doubt." Nicky knew the type, hell, he'd probably been one—guys that didn't know when to go home, never knew when the party was over.

"Something doesn't feel right, boss. It could be a trap. You know, an ambush."

"Come on," Nicky said as he swung open the door and jumped from the car. "We get in and we get out, but nobody comes out with us—nobody."

A light shone from deep within the building. Nicky and his sidekick crept down a long, dark hallway with their guns clutched to their chests, pointed skyward. A false step would give up their guerrilla tactics and probably end with chins blown clean off. Water ran from a leak in the ceiling and pooled on the floor. At regular intervals, a corroded shopping trolley or rotten wooden pallet needed to be quietly negotiated. A shoe rack full of footwear provided evidence of life, along with murmurings of a cordial conversation, which could be heard in the distance. Cutlery cluttered and a television audibly came to life. Electricity in such a place seemed dubious, profoundly dangerous. The unannounced visitors made their way forward as if exploring a cave's tunnel. When they made it to the clearing, they stood for a moment and observed the domesticated scene before them: dinner prepared in a humming microwave, red wine poured at a dining table, and three heads bathing in the glow of an idiot box broadcasting the daily news. The sink was full of dishes as if a family called the place home. It was warm, pleasant, and in stark contrast to the decrepit surrounds.

"See anything you like?" Nicky said over his raised gun and the noise of each appliance.

All three occupants jumped from their seated position and instinctively backed up. These were not the lions he had expected, not the street hoods that would spray bullets in the face of any intrusion.

"Cosy place you've got here," Nicky mused as his eyes scanned the surrounds.

"Who the fuck are you?" one of the men heaved.

The gun recoiled in Nicky's hand before the sound of the shot was fully appreciated. A plughole appeared on the wrinkled forehead of the vocal resident, and shards of skull and plods of brain matter painted the wall. He was dead before he hit the ground.

A piercing scream shook the windows and contorted faces. It was the type that was bloodcurdling, involuntary, and would have alerted the neighbours had there been any. It was a Foley artist's wet dream.

"I'll be the quizmaster, shall I," Nicky said as he inspected his weapon. "Too many voices tend to confuse the answers."

The woman had instinctively raised her arms like a cactus in the desert, and the man was slightly crouched, the blast still echoing in his ears. Both were frozen stiff as if an icy blizzard had blown into the room.

"So, in the words of our deceased friend, who are you?" Nicky punctuated.

"I'm Detective Yates and this is Vanessa."

"Nathalie," Nathalie corrected.

"Detective, hey?" Nicky raised his eyebrows and glanced at Limo before turning his attention to the body sprawled on the cracked linoleum. "And this guy?"

"Detective Munro."

Nathalie digested their names—she had only known them as Elijah's interrogators.

"And why exactly are two cops and a young lady boarded up in shithole like this?"

"It's a private residence," Yates blurted.

"Doesn't look too fucking private to me. At least, not now."

"We're a protection unit." It was a lie, but it was the company line. Cops often masqueraded under the guise of 'serve and protect,' and this was no exception.

"And you're doing a stand-up job," Nicky replied sarcastically, his scales bristling.

"How did you find us here?"

"It doesn't matter how we found you, the question is why we're here."

Yates was having difficulty joining the dots. He and Nathalie had just returned from administering a lethal dose—the target was another small-time drug user, but big enough to send a message—and they had most definitely not been tailed from the club. It wasn't supposed to go down like this, they were supposed to remain anonymous, inflict death from afar like a drone pilot dropping missiles over the Shabwa Province in Yemen. There was a distinct kill chain, a clear exit strategy, and this was not part of the plan. Somebody had fucked up.

"Then why are you here?" Yates summonsed his voice.

"Because less than twenty-four hours ago, my daughter was murdered." Nicky spoke clearly, although tinges of denial coloured his words.

"That has nothing to do with us."

"On the contrary, you stupid fuck, it has everything to do with you." Vincenzo spat on the floor in disgust before continuing: "And Vanessa here may be able to shed some light on exactly what happened." Nicky turned his attention to Nathalie, who was silently weighing up the inevitability of the situation. She had made so many wrong decisions and this was the natural conclusion. "Where were you last night, Vanessa?"

Disco balls were a thing of the past, much like confetti and streamers and circumspection. Now it was all piercing lasers, timed rotations, and strobes that gave the impression that there was a short-circuit in the mainframe. The nightclub scene, however, had not deteriorated, and passages between partygoers were hard to come up—the trek to the bar was like hiking through thick terrain, and the pandemics that had so recently kept them at arm's length seemed like a distant memory. It really was a sight to behold, and as Nathalie stared up at the heights above, she felt like an ill-fitting pop rivet that threatened to bring the whole thing crashing down.

Somewhere, up there, Elijah was engaged in a high-stakes game of hide-and-seek and she had been given similar instructions. Stay out of sight. Don't invite attention. Pick up the slack if necessary. She was the second shooter—'coverage,' Kelvin had called it—if, and only if, the first post lost its nerve or the equipment misfired.

Nathalie knew she was being tested. They wanted to know where her allegiance lay. They wanted to know if she had the mettle. But, perhaps more importantly, they wanted to know if her camouflage would extent to such foreign surrounds.

A figure brushed Nathalie's shoulder, and then another bumped her from the other side. She spun with the force, and two hands reached out to steady her momentum. The man before her seemed to offer familiarity but failed to spark any form of recognition. He was cut from stone and looked as if he'd been born in the suit he wore.

"Thanks." Nathalie found her voice but had a tough time hearing it herself.

The man pulled her closer, his hands gripping her upper arms firmly.

"Your boyfriend is about to do something stupid," he said calmly, as if the impeding noise would pale in the presence of his voice. He was freshly shaved, and his skin smelled like pines trees, his breath: peppermint. It was a welcome respite from the fog of sweat and cheap perfume.

Kelvin had eyes on every inch of the club, and nothing happened without his knowing.

"Stupid?" Nathalie wasn't surprised but she needed clarification.

"Let's just say he has failed to meet his obligations, and we both know the boss won't let him walk if you don't clean up the mess." The man maintained a measured tone as if he were automated. He was aware of a glitch but was unable to fully compute the consequences in an emotional manner. There was an obstacle that needed to be overcome, and that's all that mattered. Disobedience was not an option. Failing to meet the mission's objectives not a consideration. Pragmatic, some call it. Rational. Nathalie just thought it matched his hardened exterior. Dogs of war didn't need to feel.

"Is there a mark?" Nathalie, too, was beginning to sound ruthless.

"She's headed our way." The man tilted his head to suggest she was advancing quickly from Nathalie's blind spot. Like most prey, she had no idea of the ambush that awaited.

Nathalie took a deep breath, closed her eyes, and let the air fill her lungs. Although she wanted to float away, she knew what had to be done. She slowly exhaled, relaxed her neck muscles, and gradually let sight return.

And that's when Nathalie saw her. Youthful, euphoric, and untethered like a kite cut from its string. The young lady skipped by and melted into the panorama as if she were destined for the canvas that had been presented. Nathalie understood why Elijah hadn't gone through with it. There was no such thing as the perfect crime, even in the name of social revolution. Nothing noble about killing something so beautiful. She shot a glance towards her acquaintance, who had pushed himself up against a wall, comfortably flanked by two illuminated exits. He narrowed his eyes and nodded, again confirming the target.

Nathalie felt for the vial and considered the potential combinations. If it was to be last drinks, it may as well be something indulgent, something that offered affection—even a Molotov cocktail deserved to be fastidiously poured and lovingly served. She turned to the bar, swept her hair from her face, and made a peace sign with her fingers.

"Two mimosas, please," she yelled over the colliding frequencies, before adding: "With prosecco." Cheap bubbles would do the job and there was no need to be too sentimental; after all, she was still holding down a hospitality wage.

"Did you fucken hear me? Where were you last night?" Nicky repeated.

Nathalie's tongue sat like a stunned fish, hoping to be released or put on ice in a hurry. Fear coursed through her body like she had never known, and she felt like jelly, capable of melting into the floor at any time.

"If you wanna talk, you talk to me. She has nothing to do with this," Yates intervened.

"You were at the club last night," Nicky continued unabated, still holding the woman's gaze. "You preyed on my little girl, Katerina. Katerina Vincenzo."

A piercing sound struck Yates, and his head spun. He now knew who he was dealing with and he knew there was no easy way out. A fist tightened its grip around his heart.

"I didn't…" Nathalie trembled.

"Oh, but you did," Nicky explained. "Whatever you gave her punched a hole straight through her insides. Made a real mess. Doctors pronounced her dead on arrival." There would be time to grieve, but at that instant, the graphic details fed Nicky's anger.

The image hung in the air like dust particles, and Nathalie felt short of breath, a wave of panic crashing through her veins.

"Who is Patrick Svoboda?" Nicky asked.

"She doesn't know." Yates spoke out of turn again.

"Is that true?"

Nathalie fought the growing nausea.

"Because if it is, I don't need you," Nicky continued.

"She's not the one you're looking for. This is a misunderstanding." Yates was growing hysterical. He had never been on the receiving end, had always been the one pointing fingers, making allegations, and poking his catch of the day.

Nicky tilted his head and Limo crossed the room. In a fluent movement, he tossed a chair aside, dried his hands on his shirt before he grasped Yates by the throat—his grip crushing his oesophagus like a plum—and plunged a large blade into his abdomen. It was brutal, it was inescapable, it was unbridled hostility, and it was straight from the manual.

Yates folded in half and was repeatedly peppered with blows, the knife striking bone and piercing kidneys. Blood immediately stained his shirt and spilled to the floor. Unlike his partner, his death would be slow and painful.

Limo wiped the sharpened steel on his own shirt and stepped back across the room as if he'd done it a thousand times before and neither took pleasure nor distress from the act.

"So, do you know Svoboda?" Nicky cooed.

Nathalie dared not look down at the blood that had begun to seep into her boots. Raptures of anxiety coursed through her body, and with little to no control, she allowed her head to nod as if it were spring loaded, as if everything she held dear fizzed and crackled like an interrupted transmission.

SET YOUR WATCH, NOT YOUR TRAPS

The only way that Elijah would pick up the scent of his associates on the Spikies task force was if they came to him, and so he returned home and took a seat in his most comfortable armchair—the type that grandfathers reserve for themselves and grow intolerant of those that hover too closely. He would just have to wait for the sheriff and his posse to ride into town.

Naturally, they had already paid him a visit, and although the place hadn't been turned upside down, they had messily been looking for something.

Thankfully, Doug was safely oblivious in his modest aquarium—more a glass receptacle, really—and, better yet, they hadn't located his phone which he had taped to the underside of his bed frame. He knew they would be tracing it, but they hadn't been able to zero in on its exact location. Again, he placed a hand to the swollen lump on his neck. Had the implant been transmitting a signal or was it all just a ruse? A ploy to keep him in line. No matter, it had to be removed. Sure, he wanted to be found, but he wanted to keep an arm's length between himself and Kelvin, and that could only be done if he remained in the shadows. One step behind yet always ahead. But first, he had to contend with the arrival of sleep, a welcome visitor amid the chaos and exhaustion.

Elijah pulled open a kitchen drawer and noted the implements at his disposal. He took a butter knife and ran it across the back of his hand. It hardly made an impression. He then turned his attention to a serrated steak knife, examined its tip, and pressed it into his palm. A red dot of blood appeared almost immediately. It would do the job. He gleaned a bottle of vodka from an overhead cupboard, took a swig, and turned to his reflection in the stainless-steel fridge. The face that stared back looked like a mutated version of himself, and for a moment, he failed to recognise the person staring back. The eyes were cold, and a heaviness rested over his features. Only days ago, he had been relatively carefree, excited by the prospect of a new day, and now he was about to cut a hole in his neck to remove a government-approved tracking device, trapped in a game of kill or be killed.

Elijah applied the knife to his skin and made a neat incision from his earlobe towards the base of his hairline. But that's all it was: *neat*. It wasn't deep. It wasn't wide. And there was no way he could get his fingers within the split to prise out the buried treasure. He tried again, more haphazardly this time around. Again, it made little progress. He would need to enter vertically, like a flagpole rocketing into a patch of dirt. The blade would have to plunge directly into the tissue, that was the only way that excavation could commence properly.

Elijah placed the knife in position and willed himself to dig deep.

The first cut is always the deepest.

Through gritted teeth and eyes tightly shut, he pummelled the base of the handle like a near-empty sauce bottle. When he felt resistance—like carving stone fruit—he rifled through the drawers again and found a pair of tweezers that he used to place garnish on some of his more fanciful dinners. His mind suddenly raced back to his and Nathalie's second-year anniversary. Elijah had burned the fish terribly—a black carcass on a bed of green vegetables—but he had still taken the time to carefully place the herbs and edible flowers. He had tried to salvage the lost cause, and Nathalie had adored him for it. They ordered pizzas and made love on the couch that night. It was messy, it was intoxicating, it was one of his happiest memories—it was just a shame that it seemed so long ago.

The tweezers entered the wound like the beak of a bird feeding its young and vigilantly navigated their way to the implant.

When contact was made, Elijah pinched the callipers and brought his revelation to the surface. He held it aloft for inspection and discovered a delicate pill wedged between the clasped metal. He placed it on the counter for a closer look. The red-and-white enclosure was partly transparent, and the contents appeared dark and dense. It was larger than he expected, a little bigger than a Brussel sprout but much smoother to the touch.

Under Elijah's perplexed gaze, a crack began to form in the gelatine shell and the casing shivered before a leg kicked free of the confines. A second breakage occurred—a fault line giving way to a sinkhole—and an eye peered out accompanied by a deafening squawk.

Elijah awoke with a fright as his telephone screeched to life. He really needed to change that ringtone. Through a cold sweat, he fumbled it into his grasp and answered sheepishly, clouded by both sleep and the prospect of bad news.

"Hello," he croaked, fearful that a poison dart may spit from the earpiece.

"Eli," the voice sprinted urgently down the line.

"Nathalie?" Elijah sat upright and wiped his face to make sure he wasn't still dreaming. There were no remnants of eggshell scattered across the blankets.

"Where are you?" Nathalie asked.

"Where am I?" Elijah mirrored the question with a startled inflection.

"I need to see you."

Elijah crossed the room and peered through the curtains onto the street beyond. It was still night. "I'm not sure right now is a good time, Nat." There were no strange vehicles parked on the curb, no prying eyes. A sense of normality permeated, and all was peaceful, which was a welcome change.

"I *really* need to see you," Nathalie reiterated.

"Where were you when I needed you?" Elijah didn't want to sound annoyed, but he did. "Do you know what I've been going through?"

"I do," Nathalie said emphatically.

"From the minute you walked out, shit has gone from bad to worse," Elijah continued.

"I know." She didn't have time for conversation or to listen to his sob story.

"How could you possibly know? You've probably been holed up with Tina or Beck, or that guy that always comes into work, Kelv…" A lightbulb went off in his head, and Elijah froze. *No*, he thought, *it couldn't be*. Now wasn't the time to be haunted by thoughts of betrayal or jealousy.

"Listen. We just need to talk."

"Well, I'm here." Elijah shook off his discontent, it was silly, unfounded, and he looked around the room like a prisoner waiting for visiting hours to begin.

"Where's here?" She was growing impatient.

"At home. Our home."

"I'm on my way," Nathalie hurriedly signed off.

"Nat, wait," Elijah blurted.

"What?"

"I don't know. It could be dangerous. There are these people…"

"I know, Elijah," Nathalie repeated soberly. She only ever called him Elijah when he was in trouble.

PYRRHIC VICTORY

The streetlights and neon signs blurred past as the car sped along the empty city streets. Nicky sat alongside Nathalie in the rear passenger seats—their shoulders rubbing, his hand locked around her forearm—as Limo guided the missile at speeds well exceeding the legal limit. She handed over her mobile, and without considering its worth, he tossed it from the open window. This part of the world would be waking up soon, but at that hour, there were few cars and even fewer pedestrians in sight. Nobody would need to dodge the projectile, and it wouldn't be reported for quite some time. It was the quiet before alarm clocks and warmed engines spelt an end to the temporary armistice.

Nathalie watched the shopfronts glide by and wondered what would happen if those behind closed doors knew of her predicament. Would they bother raising the alarm, possibly rendering assistance themselves, or would the lure of a little more shut-eye prove too persuasive?An average life, her previous life, seemed much more enticing than the one she currently led. She wished that she was curled up beside Eli in the bed they had shared. She wished she hadn't stormed out, tired of his apathy, his unwillingness to strive for more.

And she wished that she had never met Kelvin—an older man that had swept her off her feet with poise and sophistication, grace and wisdom. He was the one that had suggested the *experiment*, and, with Nathalie's help, Elijah was the last piece of the puzzle.

The Victorian two-storey estate stood on a five-acreage block an hour out of town. It was all heavy doors, long halls, and brown stone adorned with artefacts from all corners of the globe. It must have been a feat of economic management to own such a property and be well travelled—or it was the product of inheritance and rich bloodlines. Nevertheless, however the foundations were laid and whatever the title read, it all seemed too much for one man.

Nathalie stood admiring a shiny contraption that featured eight steel balls rotating around a central globe. It was a model of the solar system, and as Nathalie watched over it, she felt light-headed and small. The room was positioned between two archways, and it was neither a foyer nor a dining room, more an observatory built around the mechanical centrepiece. She was accustomed to her modest abode, and the prestige was overwhelming.

"We can thank Copernicus for understanding our place in the universe," Kelvin said as he entered the room holding two glasses of generously poured shiraz. He handed one to his guest, who accepted it graciously. "Life is dependent on push-and-pull relationships."

Kelvin placed a finger on one of the arms connected to the orbiting spheres. It fell motionless before he allowed the clockwork engineering to continue unabated. "Sounds simple but nothing ever is."

Nathalie took a sip from the bulbous wine glass without removing her eyes from the machine. She had once seen an automaton that scribbled notes across a page, but it was just a plaything and didn't evoke shifting tides of emotion or a sense of vulnerability.

She wanted to ask Kelvin about the existence of God, the possibility of heaven and hell, but she already knew his answer. Nathalie had been raised by religious parents but had never shared their views and denounced the Church at a young age. Faith was for those who had nothing; it was a lighthouse designed to guide those who feared the jagged rocks and couldn't see their way free of the fog. It was for those who feared being alone. But now, for some reason, the presence of a higher being seemed comforting. It seemed like an easier option to relinquish control, to be a spectator.

"Hypnotic, isn't it?" Kelvin said, snapping his fingers. Nathalie lurched and broke her stare. Time had momentarily become stagnant, and she nodded sheepishly to gather her bearings. "It's an orrery."

Nathalie took another sip and let her eyes wander around the room. It was grandiose, even regal, but nothing was as impressive or as captivating as the functional science experiment. She was in the heart of the building.

A fireplace crackled in an adjacent room, crying to be stoked.

"Shall we take a seat?" Kelvin tipped his head towards the warmer confines, and Nathalie followed his gesture.

Flames licked at the hearth and the overhead lights were dimmed to their lowest threshold. It was cosy, perhaps a little too much so, and as Nathalie sunk into the leather sofa, she felt the wine rush to her head. She had never been a big drinker, but it was unlike her to suddenly feel sleepy. Some date.

Kelvin sat across from her on a matching one-seater with his legs folded as if he were about to give Nathalie a psych evaluation.

"Do you like it here?" he asked. "My place, is it what you expected?"

"It's beautiful," Nathalie replied. "I knew it would be."

"Oh?" Kelvin sat upright as if one of his favourite subjects had been broached.

"The way you dress, the way you speak, it is very…taken care of."

"That is very kind of you."

"Back home, I would say *utstrålning*." Nathalie was trying eagerly to impress this man, and she wasn't entirely sure why.

"Your partner, Elijah." Kelvin paused. "Does he speak your language?"

"Sometimes. A little." Nathalie lied. Kelvin had spoken of Elijah at the café, but she hadn't thought conversation would turn to him so quickly, so abruptly.

He shook a bottle of aspirin, removed two pills, and threw them back without lubrication. Nathalie thought about the combination of medication and alcohol, but he was a grown man and could make his own decisions.

"Someday I would like to share this place with somebody." Kelvin changed the melody and it was exactly what Nathalie wanted to hear. She had made poor decisions in the past and she didn't want to proceed down the wrong path again. Good men were so hard to come by and she felt her biological clock was racing. She wasn't desperate but Kelvin offered a ray of hope, and every day he stepped into her workplace, her heart fluttered, her thoughts ran rampant like wild roe deer.

"His mother died, didn't she?" Again, he reverted back to his favourite subject. He was at ease in his castle and everything at his fingertips was malleable.

Nathalie nodded. It was something Elijah didn't like to speak about so she wouldn't do it on his behalf.

"Must have been tough," Kelvin prompted.

"He adjusted," Nathalie said defensively, impatiently. It wasn't turning out to be the romantic tryst she had been expecting. When invited to visit, she thought it was for dinner, maybe an opportunity to flirt a little. She didn't want a divide to form between the two of them—Nathalie was still strangely enamoured with the man before her—and she was willing to consummate their relationship if, and only if, he was willing to drop his guard. "But yes, it was not easy," she concurred.

At that moment, a bell rang through the house like those that swing in clock towers on the hour, every hour, of every day.

"That will be work," Kelvin said as he rose to his feet and crossed the room. He leaned down and tenderly kissed Nathalie on the lips, bridging the divide and sending the deer into a frenzy. After a satisfying moment, he withdrew and refilled her glass as if he knew all the levers to pull. He turned and exited the room, promising only to be a minute.

Nathalie ran a finger across her cheeks to even her complexion and swept her hair to the side. It had been a while since she had been given any affection and she wanted to look nice.

The room was what a designer might call rustic, and the wood-panelled walls featured framed pictures of wildlife, along with a bull's skull, tribal masks, and other paraphernalia that could be classified as culturally insensitive. It wasn't to Nathalie's liking, but at least Kelvin had good taste in clothes and aftershave and women.

As she glanced around the room and made herself comfortable, curt murmurings could be heard from the foyer. It sounded like a parcel being delivered and accepted.

"This is Yumi," Kelvin said as he appeared in the archway with a female acquaintance wearing an affable smile. Nathalie immediately sized her up. Both women were roughly the same age, or so she thought, and shared similar dimensions. But Yumi enviably radiated a soft glow—the type of radiance that came with an undeviating yoghurt, grain, and green leaf diet and benefitted from robust exercise—all of which was complemented by a collared ivory dress that would work for a business lunch or while on safari. She would no doubt appreciate the colonialist's treasure trove. Nathalie forced a smile.

Kelvin was holding a slim manila folder and again excused himself to file it away.

Yumi shimmied into the room, slung her trench coat over a statuette, conceitedly took a sip from Kelvin's wine glass, and stood before the fireplace. She really was in good shape, and the amber tones created a halo effect around her body.

"I've heard so much about you," Yumi said in an attempt at flattery.

Nathalie smiled and remained silent. She couldn't return the acknowledgment, and she wasn't interested in what those discussions had been about.

"I am sorry to burst in like this." Yumi warmed her hands by rubbing them together. She sensed animosity and feared being held in such regard. "Business. Sometimes I wish we could just throw it in a dumpster and set it alight." Yumi paused and realised it was something she had done quite frequently. Not that she'd ever admit it.

Nathalie rolled up her sleeves and tugged at the neck of her sweater as if the flames had begun to burn a little brighter. It was her turn to talk, to ask about the weather, the nature of her relationship with Kelvin, but she curled her lips inward and counted the seconds until their company became a crowd. It had been hard enough accepting the invitation to the house, and Nathalie wasn't in the mood to extend her chivalry further. In many ways, it seemed to compound her deceit of Eli. Here she was drinking expensive wine, comparing garments, and fraternising with strangers while he was at his station trying to earn a meagre living. She also didn't trust the woman before her. Her presence at such a late hour was an invasion of privacy, and it seemed she was only present to set her sights on the new plaything. She was being judged, objectified, and Nathalie shied away from the scrutiny. The best course of action was to avoid all unnecessary banter as well as eye contact. After all, the last thing she wanted to do was promote the possibility of a friendly dalliance and the willingness to raise a flag on common ground.

Yumi noticed that Nathalie's eyes had fallen upon a framed portrait of a lion sitting in long grass, its mane blowing in the wind, chin stained by an earlier kill.

"Do you know why a lion clamps its jaws down on the jugular?" She turned towards the black-and-white image and ran her hand across its dusty frame.

"To kill their prey quickly?" Nathalie wasn't in the mood for trivia, but she would play Yumi's game.

"Yeah. You could say they're considerate." Yumi flicked the particles in the air, indicating the place was in need of a maid's touch "Not all predators have that compassion."

"We mostly worry about ticks in Sweden. And moose."

"How well do you know Kelvin?" Just like her boss, Yumi had a habit of changing tact.

"Well enough."

A vacuum had sucked the air from the room, and Nathalie recoiled and sat upright. Was she being tested? Was this woman possessive? Or was she doing Kelvin's bidding like a couple of kids in the schoolyard? *He likes you, do you like him?*

"And the age gap?" The inquisition continued.

"It's not important." Nathalie spoke the truth. It wasn't important to her; in fact, she had hardly given it a thought. She had a loving father and she didn't need a replacement.

"He sure is phlegmatic," Yumi conceded and Nathalie shrugged—she had no idea what that meant, and she didn't want or need a translation. "He is going to offer you a job."

"What?"

"Don't worry. He likes you," Yumi cooed. "It's in the best interests of everybody. Even Elijah."

"Elijah?" Nathalie's heart raced. How did she know about Elijah? And why was his name on everyone's lips?

"He likes him too," Yumi added as if he'd been included on the king's honour roll.

Footsteps could be heard treading the staircase, and Kelvin's shadow loomed large before he entered the room, having stowed the folder safely under lock and key.

"Sorry, where were we?" His eyes were saucers and he had clearly freshened up in more ways than one.

Yumi reached for her coat. "I was just—"

"You—you were about to offer me a job," Nathalie interrupted while casting a scowl.

Kelvin turned his gaze from Nathalie to Yumi, who was now rooted to the floor—she had some explaining to do—and his face grew discernibly sterner. What was left of the air in the room fanned the flames. He turned to the bottle of wine and calmly topped up his glass.

Kelvin had explained it was for the greater good, a revolutionary approach to ridding the streets of peddlers and pushers, but she felt used, betrayed, chewed on, and spat out, and she had thrown Eli to the wild dogs—hungry canines that didn't care if he lived or rotted alongside those he was blackmailed to erase. Sure, Elijah could have taken better care of her, could have considered parenthood, and he could have shelved the cards for a day or two, but he didn't deserve to become the face of a heavily tainted organisation. And now she was leading a fucking *varulv* to his doorstep.

Their fate was now in the hands of others, and any thoughts of an early retirement from being stuck in deep shit were now on hold.

Nicky leaned closer, his stale breath wafting across Nathalie's cheek as he spoke: "Who do you work for?" He paused to moisten his lips. "Who wanted my Katie dead?"

Nathalie recoiled, refusing to take her eyes from the passing vista. Urban streets really did take on new life before the break of dawn. They appeared rejuvenated. Momentarily free of neglect and harm. In a matter of hours, the rising sun and human contact would put paid to that. The atmosphere would once again be soured.

"This is bigger than you." Nathalie found her voice.

"Princess." Nicky sat back as if to gain stature. He was unshaven and growing more reptilian as each moment passed. "There are very few things in this world bigger than me." He spoke slowly, thoughtfully. "Friday-night football. Presidential elections. A tsunami off the fucking coast. But not a couple of kids playing with a batch of bad pills."

Through the glass, Nathalie noticed the people sleeping rough, their bodies pressed like stomped bugs to the hard concrete of the sidewalks. A succession of wrong turns, hard luck, and never being given a chance. To many, they were street trash, vermin guilty of vagrancy, an eyesore responsible for their own failings. But Nathalie knew they were victims of society—always at the mercy of those trying to get ahead. The system had been broken long ago.

"The wheels they are already in motion," Nathalie responded distantly.

Nicky scoffed. "Yeah." He craned his neck to see the illuminated speedometer on the dashboard. "I'd say they're doing about sixty miles an hour."

Nathalie turned her head, finally acknowledging Nicky's presence. Her azure eyes were ablaze, her expression shaped by a stiff upper lip. "You're not the only bad guy in this story."

At that moment, Nathalie saw Limo pull harshly on the steering wheel, and before she could feel the car swerve or hear the tyres squeal, a second vehicle erupted into the driver's side panels like a whale hell-bent on dismantling the hull of a ship. The car lost contact with the road and tumbled on its side, the floor repeatedly exchanging places with the ceiling, as if caught in a rolling barrel.

Darkness blended with shards of light, and pebbles of broken glass became suspended in midair. Nathalie's seat belt cut deep into her torso, but she felt no pain as she braced for each additional kiss of the tarmac. Her body heaved with each compression, and the reverberation was reminiscent of a can kicked along an alleyway.

When the car finally did come to rest, its acrobatics stunted by a light post, all three occupants of the vehicle hung upside down—two of them unconscious. Nathalie had a metallic taste in her mouth and blood had spread across her face from a sizeable cut on her chin, but, otherwise, she was fine. Nicky and Limo, having taken the brunt of the blow, weren't so lucky, and Nathalie noticed that they dangled limply, bones broken and protruding and failing organs triggering convulsions.

A sense of tranquillity descended. Nathalie reached across and relieved Nicky of his handgun—he wouldn't be needing it—and shakily fumbled with her seat belt socket. She pushed her open palm against the floor, groaned noisily, and, with all her remaining strength, unclasped the one thing that had kept her alive. She fell to the crumpled roof of the car and dragged herself out the window. The street was still quiet except for the purr of the battering ram—a black Camaro with a smashed front end. An airbag had been activated, but it now hung over the steering wheel like a deflated bubble of gum. Batal was standing beside the ride, unscathed, with a shotgun in his grasp. It could have been an elephant gun, but in his hands, it looked like a child's toy.

Without a second thought, Nathalie turned on her heels and ran down the middle of the street—she wasn't sticking around to meet the man on the end of the pump action. Pain sliced through her body, but it was something she'd deal with later. She had seen enough. Right now, she had to put as much distance between herself and these warring worlds and get to Elijah. The clouds had burst, and they needed to devise a way to survive the deluge.

Batal placed two bullets in the chamber and pointed the barrel in Nathalie's direction. The gun was light in his hands, and he held it lovingly with a relaxed grasp. He had a shot, a clear line of sight, she wouldn't even feel it as the projectiles ripped through her chest. But Kelvin's words echoed in his mind: "Kill the girl, but only if it's necessary," and Batal wasn't one to disregard an order. He lowered the weapon and made his way to the upturned auto lying battered and beaten like a failed prototype piloted by a pair of crash test dummies. The orders to dispense with Nicolai Vincenzo and his associates were very different, and, after the execution of Yates and Munro, things had gotten personal.

He bent down and blasted the shotgun into the driver's window, obliterating the target from point-blank range, the interior immediately taking on the appearance of a blocked nasal cavity. He then pumped the shotgun, discarding the empty shell, and preparing the second, and repeated the dose for Nicky, who was more than likely already dead.

Batal took one last glance down the street. Nathalie was almost out of sight, and the gunman silently applauded her tenacity—she was as beat up as both vehicles but still held her head high—she would have made a good soldier. He knew, however, that she could only run so far before she sipped from the wrong cup.

WHEN THERE IS NOTHING LEFT TO BURN, SET YOURSELF ON FIRE

Elijah's tongue cautiously ran along his teeth, curiously checking for damage inflicted by bluestone-sized fists on his final night at the casino. A night that seemed like a very distant memory. Some wobbled, others were cracked and chipped. It was a problem for another day, but one that would no doubt prove expensive.

It had been nice to hear from Nathalie, and her need to talk gave Elijah hope. He wasn't in this alone. She had seemed clear-headed, a little insistent, but that was her way. He often put it down to the language barrier—Nat had to be economical with her words, and it was sometimes difficult to relay emotion when speaking in a foreign tongue. Although her English was of the highest order.

Elijah leaned back in his chair and pointed the remote control at the television—the distraction would ward off the prospect of any more restless sleep, and if he had to wait, he may as well zone out and fill his head with useless infotainment.

The picture that greeted him featured flames spewing from a first-floor window, a team of firefighters blasting their hoses from the ground below surrounded by onlookers—students and lecturers that resided on campus. A journalist appeared and spoke of a missing member of the college community, feared lost in the inferno. The scene then cut to a shot of a suburban home billowing black smoke, an orange glow lashing through broken windows. The journalist continued by stating the residents had no chance. Francis and his mother were likely asphyxiated before the blaze destroyed the family home. According to the chyron, both fires were being treated as suspicious. Connected. Deliberately lit. Arson was suspected.

Elijah leapt from his seat and again ran to the window. Sunlight was peeking over the roofs of nearby houses. Mist hung low, safe for now from the gentle breeze that rustled the trees. They had been aware of his whereabouts and were now eradicating all known acquaintances. The message was being received loud and clear. It was time to hand himself in. Acknowledge defeat with his head held low and his wrists held flaccidly for cuffs. The noose had been hung, and he was being prepped for the gallows if he didn't abide.

And then Nathalie appeared. Face bloodied. Clothes torn. A limp accompanying each step. It was a miserable scene and one that didn't seem entirely out of place.

Nathalie staggered to the door. Elijah greeted her. He had so many questions, it was difficult to decipher which one to lead with. Instead, he embraced her with a warmth he had rarely known. She was hurt and he felt responsible.

"We—we need to leave," Nathalie stammered as she leaned into Elijah's grasp.

"There's nowhere—"

"It doesn't matter where," Nathalie interrupted. "We can't stay here."

"This is our home," Elijah protested, trying to muster a sense of nobility.

"They will be here soon."

"Who will?" Elijah asked but he knew the answer. Nathalie knew more than he did, and he had to trust her instincts. A tear ran down his face. How had things gotten so out of hand? "We could go to the police?"

Nathalie broke his embrace and stepped back. Her face said it all. A combination of castigation and bewilderment. "*Sluta.*" It was a Swedish term she had never quite relinquished, and Elijah had grown accustomed to it.

"How much do you know?"

Nathalie's mournful expression said it all. A burden of responsibility weighed heavily. His suspicions were confirmed.

"How? Why?" Elijah had so many questions that he knew may never be answered.

"I know about your assignment. I know about the people who put you up to it."

"Kelvin?"

Nathalie nodded as she held Elijah's gaze. A tear blossomed and she bit her lip.

Although he wanted to press further, he knew it wasn't the time.

"I think these people are rogue, they're operating outside of the law," Elijah explained. "It's covert. There's no way this shit is authorised."

"And if the cops hear us out, then what? They throw us in a cell and let us rot. There's no—how do you say—cavalry, Eli."

"And what do you propose?" Elijah was happy to surrender control. He was tired and had never been able to defeat Nathalie in an argument anyway.

Nathalie showed him the gun she had taken from Nicky Vincenzo.

"Where did you get that?" Elijah felt like a blind man looking for a light switch. His curiosity was exasperating and pointless.

"It doesn't matter where I got it. It matters that I have it,"

Nathalie responded. She cradled the weapon like it was the child she'd never had.

"I don't even know you anymore," Elijah said, only half jokingly. "Do you know how to use it?" He made a silent pact to never again be surprised by anything.

Nathalie clocked the slide, exposing the muzzle, and readied the handgun like she had seen one too many heist films. "I think so."

"Okay. Now what?"

"We turn tables." Nathalie's voice declared that she had never been more serious in her entire life, and her eyes confirmed it.

STRAYS

Yumi Chiba rolled a pair of raven-coloured stockings over her toned calves beneath the soft glow of a vintage Italian arc lamp. Her blouse had been buttoned haphazardly and strands of hair fell from randomly placed pins, but she maintained an air of finesse and, despite the circumstances, a sense of control.

The hour was late, or early, depending on one's relationship with the clock, and she felt guilty that Batal was still prowling the night, doing much of the heavy lifting. She was even more concerned about Elijah and the damage that may be inflicted on a company asset.

She paused and considered what the day ahead may offer. She didn't like unpredictable, but in the current climate, nothing could be forecast.

"Do you think we chose the right kid?" Chiba said as she tilted her head upward.

Kelvin, sitting upright between crumpled sheets, a trio of sevens tattooed on his inner bicep, and reading from a stapled document, reluctantly lowered a pair of circular framed eyeglasses and pondered the question. Shirtless, and clearly postcoital, he looked as manicured as he did in a blazer and tie. "The right kid?" he repeated. He wasn't in the mood for chitchat.

"Our screening could have been flawed. There's a chance the treatment won't take."

"We have never failed in the past." Kelvin ran his hand across a fine stubble that had begun to sprout from his jawline.

"But it's not often we have a runaway. Somebody that doesn't want to play by our rules." Chiba didn't want to sound alarmist, she was simply trying to solve a riddle aloud.

"There are ways to convince young Elijah, Yumi. If he wants to remain a living, breathing, contributing member of society, then I'm sure we'll be able to twist his arm."

"And if he continues to stray?"

"Well, then the flock will proceed without him. We are very good at making people disappear, Yumi, especially those that won't elicit a search party."

A malt-tinged Burmese cat with a leather-brown nose leapt onto the bed and nestled beside its owner. It was clearly time for the lights to be lowered.

Chiba looped an earring through her lobe and slid into a pair of chic stilettoes. "Maybe the flock should be entrusted to devour its own. Test the limitations of their loyalty."

"They've already been briefed." Kelvin tossed the pages aside and placed a hand on the squinting feline, who purred appreciatively under the touch. "When the time comes, they will know what needs to be done. We have no reason to question their commitment."

Yumi Chiba rose to her feet and placed a spaghetti-strapped handbag over her shoulder. She had only just rolled from the bed but already looked like somebody groomed for exclusive abodes and a night on the town.

"It appears we have no shortage of contingencies," she said as she corrected her hair and reapplied a delicate layer of lipstick with the aid of a wall mirror. "I just hope it doesn't come to that." Chiba turned and made her way to the open door without a parting kiss or even a final glance. She had fallen for Kelvin's silver tongue, his authority, and she was already beginning to regret the after-hours rendezvous. She was accustomed to working long hours in this man's company, but this was a new development, and it was one that had left a sour taste in her mouth. Her own bed now awaited, and she would need all the sleep she could muster.

Kelvin looked down at the smug feline that rested by his side. He was again alone, but he took solace in the fact that he had an army that would follow his every command, even if it meant he prevailed as the last man standing. In his mind, it was a father's right to kill a son as long as the father benefitted, even prospered, from the act. Sure, the castle may tumble, and the soldiers may fall, but he would always have the means and motive to rebuild and recruit.

KNOW WHEN TO FOLD 'EM

Most weekends were busy at the casino, and that day was no exception. The carnival atmosphere was in full swing, and Elijah and Nathalie stared unimpressed at the bulbs that never dimmed and the oversized projections that were lost in the bleak morning light. They had seen it all countless times before, and it had lost its lustre long ago. A hologram of a gyrating Jennifer Lopez welcomed the masses with a rendition of "Waiting for Tonight." Although it was still the a.m., and heads needed a respite, the net had been cast. An invitation promising good times before bank accounts were drained. A momentary escape before the realisation that debt was a persistent burden and not easily discarded in a gaming lounge.

Not too far along the promenade, a troupe of fire-breathers spat gasoline into the air and basked in the glow of their creation. A group of young men whooped and hollered, excited about the company they had kept into the wee hours of the morning. And a cluster of teenagers loitered, pining to be adults but not wanting to grow up. The sun was beginning to push through the clouds, and all manner of creatures had come out to play. It was a sideshow to the main event, and that event never slept.

Elijah knew where the Bulgarians would be stationed—twin pillars manning the main entrance, trying to hold back the tide, seeing off those that prided themselves on all-nighters. Fortunately, he knew of alternative access points and could avoid the scrutiny and heavy-handedness of bouncers, which he knew all too well.

Nathalie was mostly silent and absentmindedly fell in step with Elijah—happy for him to take the lead. This was his world, and she was blissfully unaware of its machinations.

As they entered and advanced across mind-boggling patterned carpet and past busy chip-stacked tables, the former croupier nodded and grinned at acquaintances, but nobody looked twice or attempted to heed his progress. The control room, however, would soon acknowledge his presence and surveillance cameras would be hastily redirected. The eyes of the behemoth would turn to them, and that's exactly what the pair wanted.

Elijah and Nathalie stepped into an empty elevator and hit the button for a floor just below the penthouse suites. There was a gaming room reserved for the casino's most important clients, those that liked to spend big and could afford to take a loss, even expected it. At that time of day, and at such lofty heights, it would be unoccupied—invitees, with newly acquired entourages, would arrive later in the evening after they had shown their lucrative hands among the masses. Winners never went unnoticed.

Elijah stood facing the sealed doors, his posture surprisingly straight given the amount of rest he had procured. Nathalie happily slumped in the corner—her wounds had been cleaned, but abrasions and bruises were still apparent. She had been cracked but was far from broken. She had a fighter's mentality and there were more rounds to endure.

"There's something I need to tell you," Nathalie said, her voice smaller than either of them anticipated.

"You know they killed my friend," Elijah responded, his mind elsewhere. Confessions could wait. "He had nothing to do with this and yet they still fucked him over. And for what reason? To send me a message? To get me to chant their slogans?" He shook his head, lost in thought.

Nathalie had so much to tell Elijah. She wanted to rewind the tape to the beginning and fix it all. But she knew it wasn't the time. They had to finish the game before they reviewed the video. "Where are we going?" she asked instead.

The elevator came to rest, and the doors slid open. Elijah stepped out and pulled a metal accordion-style gate aside. On the other side was a chandeliered ballroom lined with bronze statues and expensive-looking paintings—the type with frames that could empty your pockets and often found their way into permanent collections. At the centre of the room sat a golden roulette wheel flanked by two additional tables—one for poker, one for backgammon. The carpet was only a little more pleasant than the floors below.

Three neatly dressed dealers, readying or packing down their stations, stiffened at the sight of the visitors and grew even more startled at the sight of Nathalie's raised gun. A guard busying himself in the corner, who had initially gone unnoticed, reached for his holster that hung beneath a proud gut. It had been a long time since he'd been active in any capacity.

"Not a good move," Nathalie warned as she turned the muzzle in his direction.

All hands across the room were suddenly raised. No need for a warning shot, although Nathalie was itching to squeeze the trigger.

"Your shift is over," Elijah announced to the captive audience. "If you could please vacate the room in an orderly fashion, we would greatly appreciate it."

Without needing further encouragement, the casino staff, not wanting to take a bullet to the back, quickly sidestepped towards the exit. A parade of crabs longing to make it to the shoreline and be left alone.

"And don't bother sounding the alarm," Elijah continued in a cordial tone. "The authorities are already on their way." No defiant deed ever went unnoticed in the palace built on broken dreams.

The elevator arrived, and the crème of the crop entrusted with catering to the rich, mostly CEOs, crime bosses, mining magnates, barons, and blessed shareholders and heirs, who hadn't worked a day in their lives, disappeared behind the sealed doors, the guard offering one final stink eye to protest his emasculation.

Elijah hurriedly dragged two chairs to the centre of the room. He turned them towards the door and took a seat. Nathalie was reluctant to follow suit.

"Elijah, why are we here?" He had remained aloof during the ride over.

"Where else could we go, Nat? They will kill anyone we contact." Elijah knew it sounded crazy, but crazy had become a reality. "Don't you understand? These people are above the law and they're not afraid to take down whoever gets in their way."

"And when they get here?"

"We negotiate our release."

"Negotiate?" Nathalie quizzed in disbelief. "We will not walk from here."

"I don't plan to, Nathalie," Elijah stated cryptically. He rose to his feet and began to prepare himself a drink in the corner of the room. "It all began here. I don't remember much of anything after the Bulgarians beat me down. Near on strangled the life out of me."

"That's what I would like to—"

"I have a drug," Elijah announced.

"A drug?"

"Something that's not approved by the FDA."

"And what do you propose? We throw it at them?"

"No. You're gonna feed it to me." Elijah had never been more serious, and Nathalie was shocked by both the revelation and the conviction.

"Have you lost your fucking mind? Feed it to you? I've seen how the spikes work, Elijah. It's suicide."

"That's what we want them to think, Nat. The only way we get out of this alive is if they think I am dead. I want it to end here."

"Elijah, you will be dead. Properly, no-reverse dead." Nathalie fumbled with her words. She wanted to plead but also shake the stupidity from his thoughts.

"That's where you're wrong, Nat. My formula is an antidote. It brings you back."

"From the dead?" Nathalie couldn't believe her ears.

"I know it sounds ridiculous, but it's true. You inject me with the poison. I enter a period of stasis. And then you bring me back." Elijah presented the plan clinically. From the moment Nathalie had arrived on his doorstep, he knew that they could work together to dig their way out of the hole they had fallen into. Ricks had presented him with an opportunity, and he had to take it. Hitomi had proven it was possible.

"And what if no, what if it doesn't work?" Nathalie wasn't buying any of it.

"It will. But we have to do it now." Elijah returned to his seat and dropped his whiskey-filled tumbler to the ground. The carpet did its best to absorb it, but a damp stain appeared almost immediately. He then reached into his pocket and produced a leather satchel. He unzipped it and showed Nathalie two vials: the venom and the anti-venom. "I'm going to inject this one." He held up one with a red seal. "And then you are gonna give me this when they leave." He pointed to the second glass cylinder.

"How?" Nathalie asked like a concerned student on the eve of an exam.

"There will be a syringe in my pocket. Once it enters my bloodstream, I'll regain consciousness," Elijah reassured her.

"I'm not sure I can do," Nathalie said as emotion welled in her eyes. "I have the gun. We can use the gun." She raised the pistol as if it had become an extension of her arm.

"If you shoot, then they shoot, and they have bigger guns with more bullets."

Nathalie lowered the weapon.

"Please trust me." Elijah took her hands. "I know I've been a screw-up in the past, but I can get us out of this." He nodded calmly to put Nat at ease, and after a deep exhalation, she returned the gesture. "But promise me," he continued, "only resuscitate me when it's safe to do so, when you are clear."

"Resuscitate?" Nathalie asked. It was an important term to get lost in translation.

"You know, give me life," Elijah reassured. "Just like the insulin, you know how it works." The game of 'doctors and nurses' was not a foreign concept to them both.

Nathalie leapt forward and embraced him, and this time, Elijah returned the gesture. It had been a long time since they had felt so close. Against all odds, maybe something could blossom in the barren landscape in which they found themselves. Spring lay on the horizon—they just had to endure the depths of winter.

"Well, here goes nothing." Elijah broke the seal of the canister, tilted his head back, and emptied the contents down his throat. The taste was surprisingly pleasant—better than some expensive gin he'd sampled—but before he had a moment to saviour it, the chandeliers spun, the taste of bile lubricated his tongue, and he was on the floor.

His body convulsed and his eyes darted behind close lids. He thought of Hitomi, he thought of his mother, he thought of pills rolling like dice into open mouths that resembled portals, and then he was enveloped by darkness.

Nathalie didn't know whether to call for help or prematurely commence the rescue mission, but she sat obediently, Elijah's words echoing in her ears: "Only when you are clear." His body then became motionless, his soul disappearing down a rabbit hole, and all Nathalie could do was consider how deep the warren ran.

ONE TICKET TO THE PICTURE SHOW

The steering wheel had a mind of its own, turning haphazardly one way and then the other. Clenched fists held on for grim life, while ears were pinned back by the prevailing gravity. A sharp pain shot down both forearms from the tension. A dragon slayer trying to outlast the beast. Elijah took his eyes off the road for a moment to peer down at his feet, which seemed suspended, well clear of the pedals. His head then tilted fiercely upright, the straps tightening around his skull.

The bodies appeared again, more frequent than before, slapping against the windscreen like bugs in the Outback. Elijah couldn't look away, a pair of metal callipers clamping his eyes open, a brace preventing sideways movement. His hands and feet were buckled to a barber's chair in a warehouse that hadn't been seen before nor since.

The corners of the frame disappeared, and the film texture softened. His chair reverberated with the barrage, his ears bristling with every thud and muted scream. Mass carnage on an unimaginable scale and no cinder blocks parked on sidewalks to cease the mayhem.

A city reduced to a battlefield.

Dashcam footage from the Nice attack, where revellers celebrating Bastille Day were reduced to nothing more than roadkill, played over and over—a persistent loop to accompany a spiralling descent. Even when the vision juxtaposed with street surveillance and clearly depicted a truck careening down the busy esplanade from an onlooker's perspective, Elijah failed to acknowledge that he wasn't in control.

With a headful of drugs and no means of escape, his reality was the vehicle's cockpit and he was responsible for the unfolding destruction.

The Pharmacist stood with Kelvin in the shadows, monitoring the proceedings. "How long do you think this will go on?" she asked her superior.

"As long as it takes, Chiba," Kelvin muttered. Elijah's well-being was clearly not a point of concern. "We need him to believe. To think that he did those horrible things. Enraged by the monotony of his nine-to-five, Nathalie's abandonment, his mother's death. He needs to be beaten into submission. And then he will be driven by guilt."

Chiba made a note on her clipboard. It added up on paper.

"Do you know how the Children of Islamic State are desensitised?"

Chiba shrugged her shoulders, the corners of her mouth turning downward to meet the gesture. Middle Eastern affairs were not her forte.

"They play football with severed heads," Kelvin continued. "Brutality is normalised. They are taught that they serve a greater purpose—death is but a gateway—and when they are unleashed, they know only one enemy, one course of action." He looked off into the distance away from the shard of light forming rapidly moving images. "Hitlerjugend, Saddam's Lion Cubs, that Benghazi mob, they went through the same thing, and we saw the success of those campaigns. Sometimes we need to learn from the worst to perform at our best. Even if it doesn't make it into the textbooks."

"This will not teach him to hate the targets," Chiba offered.

"No, but it will muddy his conscience. And we will offer salvation. A way to redeem himself." Kelvin was confident in the lure of forgiveness. "Spikies depends on it."

"And what happens if his penchant for violence is redirected towards those that introduced it in the first place?" Chiba asked.

"That's why we have B," Kelvin stated without hesitation. "He is one of our finest examples. He knows his purpose. His training is the gold standard of what can be achieved."

Chiba peered across at the projector like Bandura inspecting his Bobo dolls. What reels had previously been unspooled? What training sessions had taken place in that exact building? Some questions were best left unanswered.

YOU CAN ONLY BE KILLED ONCE, TWICE IF YOU'RE LUCKY

On the inside, it was difficult to determine the time of day. There were no clocks, no windows, and very few entries that led directly to the outside world. It was an ecosystem that existed beyond time and space. The sounds of hyperactive slot machines and coins cascading into metal drawers falsely aroused feelings associated with celebration, and everybody wanted a slice of the cake. It was *Super Mario* for adults, but nobody ever collected nearly as many gold coins.

Batal strode through the casino trailed by the two Bulgarians— Varna and Plovdiv. Although not directly involved in the Spikies task force, it would be remiss, even foolish, for casino management not to co-operate fully with the authorities, maybe even throw them a bone or two along the way. Yes, Nathalie had brought Elijah to Kelvin's attention, but it was the Balkan twins that had handed him over on a silver platter. After they had knocked him free of any logical thought, they had, upon very clear instruction, driven him to a secluded warehouse. The whole time whispering words of reassurance and details to fill the voids of his floundering cognisance—the poor guy even thought he was behind the wheel riding off into the sunset in complete control of the situation. He was like Don Quixote without a sidekick and the stunning vistas de la Mancha.

The floor manager, wearing an overpriced suit and a sour expression, met the three heavyset men at the doors of the elevator. The load capacity was sure to be tested.

"They're upstairs. Rearranging furniture. Waving fucking guns around," the weekend supervisor briefed.

"Both of them?" Batal quizzed irritably as if he had better things to do.

"Did you not hear me? They have guns in the high roller's lounge. That room is reserved for our most valued clients." The man's moustache was pencil thin, and it wiggled to life with each syllable he spoke.

"Was anybody hurt?"

"Listen," the manager continued, "because you don't seem to be hearing me. When we handed this dead shit over to you, we didn't expect that he'd be back on our doorstep, splashing around in blue chips, or whatever the fuck he is doing up there. We have a business to run, and that room, shall we say, can be very lucrative."

Batal turned his full attention to the man for the first time. "There's an arrangement. Do I need to remind you of that?"

"We are fully aware of—"

"Good." The elevator doors parted. "Then get out of our way so we can clean this mess up." Batal spoke in a calm and measured fashion, and it was clear he could inflict harm in much the same way. He did carry a badge, however, and he had to be discerning in a public space, or at least make it look like provocation.

The moustache sat motionless as the glorified maître d' diverted his gaze and stepped aside. He was well out of his weight division.

Batal peeled back the gate and surveyed the room. It really was quite impressive. Nathalie was knelt beside Elijah, who was still sprawled across the floor. Tears stained her cheeks.

"He's dead," she screamed across the room. "You did this."

In her stooped position, she looked frail, deflated, the lone survivor of a merciless hurricane. The last few days had taken their toll. But Batal also knew she couldn't be trusted.

"It wasn't meant to end like this," she continued. "Kelvin said it was an easy job."

"Where's the gun?" Batal asked before being drawn farther into the room.

"The gun?" Nathalie reached down, picked it up, and threw it across the room. "You can have the gun. Too many people have died already."

The weapon came to rest well out of Nathalie's grasp. Batal felt a little more at ease, but then again, he never felt uneasy. He made his way towards Elijah's body and kicked at his shoe. There was no response. No reflex. No sign of life. But also, strangely, no sign of a fatal blow.

"How?" Batal would have to file a report, and he needed the facts.

"He took *your* poison." Nathalie gestured to the empty glass, which was duly noted and filed under 'evidence.' "He said that he wanted out, that this was the only way."

The hulking man crouched beside Elijah and felt for a pulse. Still nothing. He was gone. In many ways, Batal knew it was a mistake to hire civilians. They were fragile, unpredictable, and this categorically proved his theory. Kelvin would have to take note.

"Why did you run?"

"What?" Nathalie croaked as her diaphragm heaved with emotion.

"Why did you run?" Batal repeated, rising to a standing position. He could squash her like a bug, stomp on her head until there was nothing left to identify. The thought crossed his mind. It would be as easy as pissing in the shower.

"I thought you were going to kill me," she confessed.

"And why would I do that?"

"Because that's what you do," Nathalie sobbed. "That's why Kelvin kept you close."

Batal's expression didn't change. He turned and moved back towards the exit. "Grab your things," he said over his shoulder, "we're leaving. You have a date with the boss."

Nathalie quickly produced a syringe from behind her back, which she had prepared only moments earlier, and stuck it into Elijah's neck like she was seeking vengeance through the use of a voodoo doll. The liquid leapt forth and the vein bulged, greedily drinking it up. She kissed his cheek for good luck and then scrambled across the floor towards the discarded weapon.

"The gun stays," Batal said as he turned to face her.

Nathalie froze.

She really had no intention of squeezing off rounds, but she liked the feeling of holding the smoothly sculpted steel in her hand. She looked up to meet Batal's cold stare, his hands clenched by his side.

"It really would be a shame to make a mess of this room," he said blankly.

Nathalie stood gracefully, ran the back of her hand across her face, and smoothed her clothing. She had seen firsthand Batal's bloodlust, and she wasn't about to give him a reason. She followed his lead and stepped into the waiting elevator.

At that moment, Elijah's foot twitched and his body stiffened. His eyeballs quivered behind closed lids. But nobody noticed as the doors pursed tightly and the cramped box speedily descended— Nathalie holding her breath amid the mass of flesh all the way to the ground floor.

A FIRE INSIDE

Smoke billowed from an upstairs window, flames leaping from some-where deep in the house, maliciously claiming responsibility for the destruction. Neighbours watched from the street below, mouths agape, fingers pointing out shapes in the plumes, phones recording. Curi-ous, not overly concerned, except those that lived in close proximity and could foresee the orange tongues jumping containment lines. A warmth swept across the faces of those in attendance, and the glow had all the hallmarks of a Guy Fawkes festival or a witch-burning cer-emony. Shame nobody brought marshmallows, but the hues made for good selfies.

Elijah watched, rooted to the spot, as an emergency worker yelled questions in his direction. Later, he would learn that a candle was left alight. An accelerant was found along with a bottle of pills.

His mother didn't stand a chance. She was probably already dead when the fire took her body. Peaceful. Transcendent. A chariot riding steadily away from the turmoil. A numb yet dignified cessation of bodily function that did not suppress the flight of the soul.

He wanted to take the firefighter's twin-sided axe, smash in the door, douse the flames, and drag his mother to safety. But instead, he just watched, wondering if her bed offered comfort in her final moments or simply combusted in a final act of betrayal.

He had never dreamed of being a hero. It wasn't in his nature. But if it had been, the moment was lost. Possibly forever.

Elijah sat bolt upright, his eyes bulging, arms as heavy as lead. He ripped the syringe from his neck and placed it in his pocket with the other pharmaceutical paraphernalia.

The room was as he had left it, minus Nathalie, minus the anticipation of guests. He staggered to his feet. Although his head was full of mothballs, he felt better than he had for quite some time. His conscience was clear, so, too, his outlook, and he now held a strong hand with a pair of aces up his sleeve.

It felt good to be a dead man.

But he foolishly hadn't banked on them taking Nat and he also knew they'd be back to bag and tag him. Probably dispose of him in a shallow hole on the outskirts of town, along with all the other lowlifes they had made disappear over the years.

Elijah reached down to grab the gun and a sharp pain shot down his back. There were some side effects to death, and he clutched his rib cage as if he'd been collected by a baseball bat. After all this was said and done, a massage would be in order.

He gratefully wedged the shooter into his waistband. It was a gift and it would be thoughtless not to accept the offering. He peered around the suite and admired the prestige. Every fitting was majestic. Every stitch woven with care. How he would love to stay and play a few hands, slide the cards across unblemished felt one last time, but, alas, time was of the essence and he had already used up his free life, another gift from beyond the grave.

For a moment, he considered exiting the same way they had arrived until the thought of crossing paths with the Bulgarians stopped him in his tracks. Surveillance was strict and he would need to be smart, otherwise it had all been for nothing.

He moved quickly to the back of the room, behind the roulette centrepiece, and began to run his fingers along the seam of the wall. Rooms of such calibre were renowned for having dumbwaiters to deposit the money to vaults below, extracted from bottomless pockets and those commonly guilty of schadenfreude. Losses were swept aside, while eyes remained glued to the Nikkei Index, and devoured into the belly of the beast. Astronomical sums that needed to be held under lock and key not like the peanuts thrown around by chimpanzees downstairs.

The wallpaper was adhered neatly without peeling, and as Elijah trailed straight lines, the elevator whirred into action—the digital numbers offering a countdown as it neared his lofty location. He frantically tried edges with his nails. Knocked on sections to find a hollow point. The numbers continued to click over. In mere moments, he would have company in the form of the men that had thrown him into this mouth of madness. Two brutes who enjoyed nothing more than punching things.

A bronze statue caught Elijah's eye. A plump cherub reaching for an unseen floating feather. A leg raised as if in dance. A loincloth hanging precariously. He pulled down on the arm as if playing the slots, and a vent popped open, revealing a compartment not much larger than a fan forced oven. Without delay, Elijah raced for the opening, crumpled into the tight confines, and jammed the shutter closed just as the elevator sprung open and coughed up its cargo.

Through the metal Venetian grill, he watched as the Bulgarians scratched their heads, searched the room, and argued like two slobs trying to locate a television controller. Their *aylyak* had been abandoned. They weren't accustomed to letting a prized fish off the hook, and they cursed in both English and their native Slavic tongue.

It was days like these that prevented hair regrowth.

Elijah ejected the magazine from the gun. It was full. Sixteen shots plus one in the chamber. Enough to do some damage. He poked the nine millimetres through the fake vent, took aim, and fired two shots in quick succession. The gun recoiled fiercely in his grasp as the racing bullets dug deep into the adjacent wall.

Both guards collapsed to the floor and took cover as best they could.

Elijah considered advancing. He didn't want to engage in a shootout. It was possibly now or never to take the advantage while his targets were on the back foot. But then again, he was concealed, an invisible threat, a sniper in the thick of the wilderness. He could wait.

Elijah knew they wouldn't call for backup and he knew they wouldn't retreat. It simply wasn't in their nature. They wouldn't take being fired upon lying down, and that's what he was counting on.

"Do you know how to use that thing?" a voice eventually rose from beyond an upturned gaming table.

In response, Elijah fired a shot in their direction.

The bullet blasted a hole in the padded perimeter of the soft green baize. It was a clear answer and one that didn't reveal his whereabouts.

"When children play with gun, gun always—"

Elijah fired another shot. He wasn't in the mood for a parable. This time, he was much closer to the Bulg's eye and an exhalation of relief emanated from behind the barricade.

Perspiration was beginning to drip from Elijah's brow, but he knew they would be sweating even more. Their shield was merely timber, not marble, and he would hit the sweet spot soon enough. He was well on his way to a flush, but he would happily take a pair.

NATHALIE, PART II

Promises. He had a way of constructing them and gently releasing them into the atmosphere like origami caught in a zephyr. He hit all the right notes, and many fell prey to his tune. A Pied Piper. A milkshake duck. And the waitress from Gothenburg hadn't been immune. At first, it had been a warm smile and a wink of the eye. Then came the courteous introduction, the handshake that held on a little longer than necessary—his slender fingers strong and well manicured, his greeting pitch perfect, and his grasp of *Svenska* honourable.

Each new visit to the café brought with it a heightened sense of emotion. Excitement, joy, fulfilment. He spoke of running away, settling down, seeking comfort and security. Everything that Nathalie held dear. He was well heeled and spoke with an eloquent tongue—a way with words she'd never encountered before. She didn't fall for him because of his chequebook or the fact that he was a big deal around town. Not for his benevolent tips or his unwavering etiquette. She fell for his charm, his potency, the escape he offered, and the life he promised. She fell for the idea of being the centre of the universe, admired like a constellation forever burning bright. And it all turned out to be a lie. She should have known it was too good to be true. Fairy-tale endings were just that: fairy tales. A bedtime story read to convince children that all is right and proper in the world. That good things happen to good people. But they don't. Good things happen to horrible people, and the rest go on reading co-ordinates from confused moral compasses. The glass is half empty, and cracks just keep on appearing.

Nathalie should have known that something wasn't right. His interest in Elijah was fanatical, insatiable, and he wanted to know everything.

Where does he work? Does he have a particular skill set? Hobbies? Is he emotionally stable? Insomnia, anxiety, things of that ilk? Who are his friends? Does he have family? Is he one to fight or flee?

He ate up every new piece of information, taking mental notes like a tailor sizing up a client for a bespoke suit, and every answer yielded a ticked box. He was particularly enthused to hear that Elijah had very few acquaintances, no known family, and his sleight of hand was cause for celebration. Oh, and the fact that he was apathetic to the world around him almost drew applause. He was the perfect candidate, and unbeknown to Nathalie or Elijah, he was about to be elected.

Nathalie was the gatekeeper, and she had indolently let the fox enter the chicken coup without protest. And now the feathers were strewn as far as the eye could see.

"You said that you would take care of him," Nathalie pleaded as Batal pushed her into a leather ottoman. Her mind was elsewhere.

The office was dark, shrouded in only glimmers of sunlight bouncing off adjacent buildings, entering through immaculately polished floor-to-ceiling windows. It wouldn't have been out of place for an owl to be perched in the corner, a hyena chained to the leg of the desk. But instead, Chiba stood over Kelvin's shoulder like she often did. Much like a butler waiting to be called upon.

"We didn't expect him to go rogue," Kelvin said as if he were already tired of the exchange. "Our profiling—built on many of *your* commendations—suggested that he would do the job without resistance."

"And you were supposed to be his welfare officer, his one phone call." Nathalie directed her ire towards Chiba. "Six p.m. or whatever the fuck you called yourself. And you were never there. I knew from the moment I met you that you couldn't be trusted."

Chiba dropped her head in embarrassment.

"You had me. Why did you need him as well?"

"You were never meant to be on the front line," Kelvin explained. "Your role was simply to observe and react. And to that end, you performed honourably—you did exactly what was asked of you."

"And now you have blood on your hands," Nathalie accused.

"We have taken known drug dealers off the streets. Decommissioned key players. Punched a hole in the network. Do you know how many lives that will save?"

"And Elijah? What was he?"

"He used his car to kill innocent civilians," Chiba meekly accused.

"But he didn't," Nathalie snapped back. "We both know that you brainwashed him. Made him think that he was bad, that he owed you something."

"He died thinking he had, that's all that matters," Kelvin confessed, growing agitated.

"And you can't dig for gold without clearing a few trees, Nathalie."

"So, it's about money?"

"Through our efforts, we are creating a business opportunity," Kelvin confessed. "And, yes, at some stage, we would like to pick up the slack in distribution."

"*Glupskhet*," Nathalie remarked in her native tongue.

Kelvin was the only one to understand but it mattered little.

"You may not agree with our methods, but sometimes it's just best to howl with the wolves, run with the pack."

"Do you care? Did you ever really care? About Elijah? About those cops that didn't get to say goodbye to their families? About me?" Nathalie gestured to the window through more tears. "Or do you just like to throw bombs and look the other way?"

"I am good at what I do, Nathalie," Kelvin responded. "I play people like mandolins, or fiddles, sometimes timpani drums. And they do what I ask of them. They are grateful for the attention. But when they fall out of tune, or their spark fades, I need to trade them in. Get shiny new ones." Kelvin waved his hands briefly like a maestro before his orchestra. "It's a waste, I know. But it's a necessary cycle. Any composer will tell you that."

Chiba gritted her teeth. Nathalie's stomach dropped.

"And what does that make me?" she asked. "A mandolin?"

"It makes you, my darling, an unsculpted piece of wood, and nothing more." Punctuating Kelvin's statement, Batal stepped forward, placed a plastic bag over Nathalie's head, and tightened his hands around her neck, emphatically sealing the opening.

She immediately gasped for air but only managed to suck in a mouthful of the transparent hood. The hot air consumed her face, and her moist eyes burned as if rubbed with sandpaper. She saw red, a result of capillaries bursting around her irises, and fireworks exploded in her mind, synapses overwhelmed and short-circuiting amid the panic.

She wrestled with the oversized hands, but they were clamped securely, steadfast in their want to drain life. She kicked and screamed and flailed her arms, but it was all to no avail. It was like she had been grasped by a giant octopus and was being dragged to the seafloor. The heaving mass too much to overcome. The lack of oxygen making her head spin.

And with her arms now limp and eyes pointed to the heavens, Nathalie took her last breath. She considered the last word she had learnt—'resuscitate'—and pictured Elijah, in his bow tie, his vest, sporting a cheeky grin and a forgiving glint in his eyes, standing at his station, dealing her a final hand.

IN DEFIANCE OF GYNOCENTRISM

Nathalie fell to the floor with a soft thud. There was no mess and the disposal of the body would be easy. Batal stepped back and flexed his fingers to regain circulation. There was no menace in his eyes, no remorse nor satisfaction. Nothing. He was a killer by design. A grizzly bear always looking for its next meal. He raised his head and locked eyes with Kelvin, who sat unmoved by the scene before him.

"Such a shame we couldn't keep her on," Kelvin mused. "She was good at the hunt."

"Nobody ever suspects an attractive woman," Batal added as he turned his line of vision to Chiba. It was an accusation intended for the dead and the living. "They get away with murder." He rolled his head in a circular motion to loosen the muscles in his neck.

"We're gonna need fresh blood," Kelvin thought aloud.

"Would you like me to prep the viewing space?" Batal queried ever reliably.

"No. I want you and Chiba to do the interrogation when they come in. Push them. Make sure they know the game and the rules." Kelvin took an emery board from a drawer and ran it across the tips of his nails as if sharpening his claws. "Hell, show them an obituary that will go to print if they step out of line. Something short that points out how pathetic their lives have been."

"The Bulgarians?" Chiba asked as she ran a pen across a notepad.

"Give them a call. See if they have any *replacements*. A loner. No ties. Low self-esteem. Somebody impressionable. They can administer the drugs, set the projections."

"Do they know the dosage? The subject could fall into psychosis."

"You're the fucking pharmacist, Chiba. Read them the label."

"And what should we do with Munro and Yates?" Chiba wanted all loose ends accounted for, and she was only too happy to change tact to avoid Kelvin's wrath.

"Let them rot," Kelvin said categorically. "By the time their bones are discovered, we'll claim no knowledge of their undertakings. Cold case investigators will link it to Nicolai Vincenzo, but we don't need to enter the frame. That's a tedious file at best."

Kelvin made his way across to the lofty windows and peered down onto the streets below. Hordes of revellers paraded into the mid-afternoon sun, treading the footpaths like busy ants fixated on reaching new destinations, new experiences, new levels of intoxication and enlightenment. They were thankful for the hours of illumination and would hold down the fort as best they could into the night until the rays of light returned.

"We mustn't forget that there is still a job to do," he continued. "Spikies was established to rid this world of vermin—vermin that carry a plague—and until we have cleansed these streets, really scrubbed them clean, we cannot rest. Users, dealers, a kid experimenting for the very first time, nobody can elude our grasp."

Chiba had stopped taking notes, and Batal was transfixed by an expression of peace that had fallen upon Nathalie's appearance.

It reminded him of another life, one that treated guilt and innocence in much the same way. A shovel full of dirt would never bury those faces, and the inevitable composition always infected his arteries, thickening his blood and his resolve. Embalmed by misery.

Kelvin turned to face his colleagues, which quickly snapped them both back into reality. "Now call those fucking Bulgarians and bring me somebody we can use."

NIGHT FEVER

"Waist…thirty-one! Thigh…twenty-three! Inseam…thirty-three!" an eager tailor hollered, like the host of an anatomy-themed game of bingo, as he ran a tape measure intimately around a young man's sculpted torso.

An unseen data entrant took notes silently, vigilantly, like a good assistant should, all the while admiring the handsome visitor. Handsome visitors were about the only thing that made the job worthwhile.

The fastidious worker took pins from his mouth and inserted them into the fabric, ensuring the amendments would be accurately bespoke. He was a surveyor of the human form and he took his job seriously; it was a lifelong passion. The fresh-faced fellow knew his dimensions, but he liked the pomp and fuss, he liked the royal treatment.

The appointment-only boutique was of the highest order, and finely crafted suits were draped on hangers as if they were museum showpieces, worthy of an admission fee. The heavy oak panels stunk of cachet and cigar smoke, and the conditions of entry were strict—a heavy wad of cash, the desire to pony up, and the ability to wear the merchandise well were all distinct advantages.

"Special occasion?" the hunched tailor queried. He was clearly in the twilight of his career and would have happily traded places with the client—although the years had treated him kindly, one more shot at the high life was a delightful prospect.

The customer adjusted the cuffs of his shirt to ensure his oversized wristwatch didn't go unnoticed and then placed a mint in his mouth. Freshness could not be underestimated.

"Business or pleasure?" the seamster continued.

Chit-chat was part of the service, and engagement was integral to the customisation of a garment. It built confidence and rapport, which were both essential to the new relationship—one that may flourish if given the right nutrients. The tailor was of quick wit and also well read, and he craved the opportunity to tackle various topics.

"I'm sure the nightlife warmly embraces a man of your stature."

Compliments didn't hurt either. The mirror never lied, but the tailor sure could. Not that he had to on this occasion. The guest's shoulders were broad, his jawline square, and his closely cropped hair accentuated his glacial blue eyes. He looked two parts militant, one part assiduous gardener, and he poured into the 50L perfectly.

Although he rarely smiled and seemed lost in a thousand-yard stare, he was the type of guy any woman would like to show off to her friends. He was an enigma.

A phone vibrated from the inner lining of the man's jacket, and he turned away from the cowering storeman who was busying himself with the neat crease of trouser hems.

He raised a finger to demand silence—shot a hardened glare suggesting that a lack of adherence could be bad for one's health—and answered the mobile without uttering a word.

A considered voice shuffled down the line, and as he absorbed the information, his eyes grew even more piercing and his superficial temporal veins bulged.

"Move the body? Now?" the man repeated as he looked down at his new threads.

A wave of disappointment washed over his face.

The instructions continued. It wasn't a polite to-and-fro. Not a congenial conversation between two equal peers. He wasn't being asked, he was being told.

"And tonight, do we proceed as planned?" the man quizzed. Following orders was non-negotiable, but it would be a shame not to step out in the new get-up.

He nodded and his expression relaxed—his pupils returning to their former circumference. He had been appeased.

The phone was again pocketed. He swivelled almost robotically and made his way towards the storeman, who was meekly pretending he hadn't heard a thing while stowing expensive items in unlocked compartments behind the counter.

"I'll take it now," he said as he offered a platinum credit card.

The final amendments had yet to be made, but it seemed time was now of the essence. What had been done would suffice.

The tailor accepted the plastic payment and scanned the embossed lettering.

"This is you?" he asked with a tinge of vocal fry in his voice. It wasn't an indictment; it was a genuine point of interest.

"Would you like me to spell it?" The response was stern, and it was clear that the young man found common courtesy banal, a sign of vulnerability.

"Oh no," the older gentleman ushered. "That's fine. It's just not a common name, but I've come across it a few times in recent weeks. Always reminds me of 'svelte,' and, of course, we love that word around here." He knew he was rambling, and a feeling of dread hung in the air. He swallowed hard and offered a strained grin.

Anxiously, he then processed the payment and handed the card back to its rightful owner. All was in order. Hurried fashion had never been a trait of the business, but that's exactly what was on show. Closing time couldn't come fast enough.

The man across the desk smirked ever so slightly. Power came from watching others disintegrate and he was positively radiant. He had nothing to add, and his expression again suggested that the time for civility was over. Wearing what he had purchased, as well as a pair of leather gloves which he pulled over his hands, he turned and made his way to the door.

The night was young and there was still much to be done. The task force demanded it.

FIXING HOLES

Bullet holes littered the poker table, while a number of stray shots had poked gouges in the wall beyond. The ugly, bald-headed moles, however, had yet to raise their flags or their heavy frames. They hadn't offered a counter shot or uttered a triumphant phrase from *Боят настана*.

Elijah had neglected to count his discharges, but based on the weight, the clip was now surely half empty, and although his whereabouts had yet to be detected, the trajectory led to no other place than the vent. He was a furtive hunter in a ghillie suit, but the vegetation was fast disappearing around him.

The casino would be filling up with both serious punters and those out for a flutter—all hoping to roll their luck to an inflated bank account. In either case, there would be kings for a day and those that fled to the highest possible vantage points and threw themselves into dark depths below. A return ticket to paradise for some, a one-way exodus to damnation for others.

Elijah took aim at the chandelier and fired, hoping to send it crashing towards his assailants. It was feat a more accomplished marksman could execute. Somebody more familiar with clay pigeons and silhouettes clipped to automated lines in shooting galleries.

Not surprisingly, he missed.

It was like landing a dart in a bull's-eye, a golf ball in a tin cup with a three-iron, and the only other time Elijah had fired a weapon was as a child, at cans, with slugs. He had missed every time on that occasion too.

An incomprehensible slur came from behind the upturned table. It was more than likely a taunt, a threat, a verbal attack to arouse a response, but Elijah held his tongue. If it were a truce, an offer of cease-fire, he would have considered it, but he knew they were up for the fight and could wait all night before the idea of olive branches even entered their minds.

That's when a phone started to ring.

A polyphonic version of "La Macarena," or some other generic shit designed to encourage uncoordinated buffoons onto dance floors, disrupted the airwaves. Every mindless bleat was both nostalgic and cringeworthy. At first, Elijah thought the sound was wafting from overhead speakers—the casino wasn't renowned for its eclecticism—but when he heard a set of sausage fingers rifling through linen pockets, he knew the source. It was now or never. He had to take action, or he would be dealing with a battalion before he had time to drop the dumbwaiter. There was a score to settle, and it was time to throw a Hail Mary.

Elijah kicked out the ventilation grill and, while doing so, heard a digital beep of acceptance: the phone had been answered.

"The kid, the kid is alive," a voice urgently cried out.

It was a revelation Elijah had wanted to avoid and his cloak of invisibility was immediately discarded. He raced towards the toppled table and barrelled into it with his shoulder—a firefighter trying to clear a door, a convict trying to crash through a cell wall. The mobile phone dislodged from the guard's grip and slid across the floor as both brothers became pinned to the floor.

Again, the verbal leak ricocheted around the room: "The kid is alive," but this time it was joined by a chorus of obscenities—some recognisable, others not. They had an impressive arsenal of terms and phrases. It was a gymnastics routine for the tongue.

Elijah climbed onto the upturned plank of wood, the legs pointing skyward like ships' masts, and, like a pirate on the high seas, rapidly fired a succession of shots into the restrained men before they had a chance to prise themselves free. A commendable headshot made light work of Varna, or Plovdiv, only a mother could tell.

"You invite the pack," the surviving brother coughed as he grimaced under the load pressed against his chest. A splattering of blood covered his face like an ode to abstract expressionism. Elijah tilted his head and admired his work. It seemed they shared everything, and death would be no different.

The peppering of bullets was swift and accurate, and it was the least Eli could do. He may not have earned a call up to become a firing squad member, but he was starting to warm to his newfound skill with a firearm. Thankfully, the unruly and less-than-desirable carpet concealed the blossoming pool of blood, and Elijah didn't have to dwell too long on the damage that had been inflicted or the cost of the clean-up. The room would be ready for punters in no time.

He diverted his attention to the illuminated mobile phone. The line was still active and whoever was on the other end was still listening.

Elijah crept nearer as if it were a stick of dynamite, not wanting to turn his gaze for fear of the fuse catching alight and reducing all to ash. Perhaps even springing to life and attacking him—the dream of the tracking device's metamorphosis was still vivid.

Drawing closer, he noted Yumi Chiba's name splayed across the screen accompanied by a phosphorescent backlight.

He picked up the handpiece with trepidation—the gun in his other hand seemed less likely to cause harm—and placed it to his head. Deep breathing could be heard but no words leapt forth. For a moment, it felt like time had stopped. That feeling you get when you have either won or lost it all. The air grows thick, sound falls flat, and nothing else exists except the space between your ears—and that space strains within a vice-like grip, an invisible hand kneading suspended matter.

"Chiba?" Elijah found his voice. There was no point pretending to hide when the spotlight had been shone in his eyes.

A muffled sound, and then silence, was the only response. Fleetingly, Elijah thought the line had gone dead, and then he realised a palm had been pressed against the phone.

"Chiba," Elijah insisted, "I need your help." Elijah spoke to the hand as if it would find compassion, as if it would have the answers. It did not.

Another stifled noise stumbled forward, then the sound of parting lips, followed by three simple words: "Where are you?"

"Are you going to help me?"

"We can help each other," Chiba said in a hushed tone. She was clearly trying to keep the conversation out of somebody's range, and Elijah knew exactly who that somebody was.

"I need protection. I need a safe house."

"Tell me where you are, and I'll come and get you."

"I can't trust you. I can't trust any of you." Elijah didn't want to become hysterical, but he hadn't planned on the call. He hadn't planned too far ahead at all.

"We can help." Chiba spoke pragmatically.

"How? How could you possibly help me?" Elijah urged. "You got me into this shit in the first place."

"It wasn't just me, Elijah. Everybody, even Nathalie, thought you were a good candidate to join the team," Chiba complimented.

"Team? It wasn't a team. It was a bunch of cops with lunatic ideas," Elijah shot back. He was starting to think that his time was better spent running, but past evidence would suggest that was ill advised.

"Come in. We can debrief." Chiba liked straight lines. Clear plans. Simple solutions.

And containment was her intended course of action.

"Where's Nat?" Elijah quizzed, throwing the conversation off course.

Chiba hesitated. Either due to the question or a disturbance in the room. "She's fine. She's here," she lied.

"And Kelvin? Batal?" Elijah wanted the full picture.

"They're here too."

It was Elijah's turn to hesitate. It was a full fucking reunion and the only thing missing was the guest of honour. "Do you know the diner on the Mountain Highway?"

"I know a few," Chiba responded.

"The one near the Greenwich turn off," Elijah added.

"Great coffee."

"I'll be there in an hour." Elijah paused. "Maybe longer, depending on traffic."

"I'll save us a booth," Chiba affirmed.

Elijah shut off the phone and threw it across the room. He turned to the already bloated corpses he had left in his wake—their screwed-up faces suggested they were disappointed to be meeting their maker so soon—and he bent over to pat them down. As well as some loose change and a packet of cigarettes—maybe it was time to start smoking—he found a quarter-ounce bag of coke and held it aloft.

"Lucky you didn't get spiked," he muttered as he slid it into his own pocket. He glanced around the room and noted the stacks of chips—mostly high denominations. Rumour had it there was a one-hundred-thousand-dollar chip to be played. Pirate's treasure, hexagonal in shape. Elijah decided against trying to locate its whereabouts. Adding murder to the rap sheet was enough for one day. And, anyway, he had a bus to catch.

PASSENGERS

By the time Elijah arrived at the bus shelter, he was feeling two sheets to the wind and not at all himself. Not surprising given the veritable smorgasbord of illicit candy he had consumed over the preceding days. He stared down at the pebbles of broken glass that littered the footpath, which so often accompanied a bus stop, and wondered if he had created the mess.

Elijah had never been fond of public transport, but under his new persona, he was warming to its scheduled dependability, and, with any luck, he'd never find himself behind a steering wheel again. But as the vehicle approached, he felt hesitant about climbing aboard. Its sheer size was foreboding, and the grill took on a menacing snarl as it loomed larger.

The doors swung open as it pulled into the curb, and a mass of people spewed forth as if faucets had been loosened. Elijah stepped aside, waited patiently until the stream evaporated, and as he entered, the driver tipped his hat as if to acknowledge the squall that had been kicked up by the cocktail of drugs in his system.

Elijah pushed on and navigated the centre aisle like a tightrope artist, carefully eyeing each incremental step. Walking the line, he passed a number of weary travellers with their heads hung low, commuters that were knee deep in an arduous trek, battling their own demons, who didn't want to be disrupted. He could sympathise.

Elijah fell into a seat towards the rear and tilted his head back, pointing his chin to the sky, compressing his fatigued neck muscles. Perhaps Chiba could prescribe something for the pain. Consumption bred consumption. At the very least, a hot bath would never again be taken for granted.

The purr and slight vibration of the engine were comforting for some, but it triggered a cramp in the stomach and a clattering of teeth for others.

Elijah's vision blurred, shadows lurked in the periphery, and a fog descended over the bus. The overhead lights swirled, inducing nausea, and he had to swallow hard to keep the rising tide at bay. The mobile compartment had an ecosystem unto itself, and it was growing inclement, oppressive. His stop was well off in the distance, and to pass the time, he would have to clench his jaw, allow thoughts to chase distraction, and recite what needed to be said. The last thing he wanted was to leave the door ajar for panic and cause a scene. And if a brown paper bag was to be offered, he'd accept it appreciatively.

A man to his left placed a cigarette in his mouth and cupped a light to ignite its tip.

"I'm not sure that's a good idea," Elijah said from within a bubble that had formed around him. "There's no ventilation in this thing." The air was growing thick, and Elijah breathed deeply to regulate his temperature.

"Don't you have a better...whatchamacallit?" the man said through pursed lips. He raised his head and Elijah immediately recognised him. He wore a stained singlet two sizes too small, along with round-framed sunglasses, and sported matted locks that hadn't seen a comb for days. It was Cindy, Cindy Lee from the garden rave. "Don't you have a better cause?" he clarified. His fingers were yellow and his face a bluish hue.

Elijah's thoughts did somersaults. Had Cindy died that day? Had he even taken that detour? His superiors had never mentioned it.

"He's a self-righteous asshole," a man standing to his right said. He swayed with each movement of the bus and wore a dirty tee with a sheet wrapped around his waist. It was Daniel Burson. "All I wanted was a drink, this guy a cigarette, and look what we got...a one-way ticket."

"If you wanted to fuck me, you just had to ask," a female voice leapt from the back seat.

Elijah turned to find two young girls: Katie and her protégé, still dressed for a night out, their lipstick smeared, mascara bleeding, faces slightly contorted. One held his gaze while the other exhaled heavily on the window and drew a heart in the vapour with her finger.

Elijah closed his eyes and saw only red specks against a black backdrop.

"Did you ever manage to learn your name?" Cleo Rodriguez said from the row of seats ahead, her eye peering through the divide. Her black leather jacket was peppered with holes, and smoke escaped her mouth as she spoke. "Patrick the Jackal seems more fitting."

"Patrick the Jackal, I like it," Daniel Burson agreed.

"She is the cat's mother. She is not a jackal."

Burson let out a howl that caught the driver's ear and was met with a disapproving glare in the oversized rearview mirror. Elijah looked away and caught his reflection. He was alone but his mind was a crowded house.

"Cleo, why did you put this dumbshit on the guest list?" Katie screeched as she cast daggers at the man hollering in the aisle. Eli was thrown back into the throng.

"He's with Maslow," Cleo responded.

Elijah cast his eyes down the walkway and saw the outline of another man, his features blurred as if his image had been captured, and permanently affected, by a slow shutter speed.

Elijah squeezed his eyes shut again, and a searing pain struck his brain like a lightning bolt. What the fuck had Ricks put in this shit? Mescaline? Bath salts?

"This isn't my doing," Casey Ricks said from behind him. His charred body had taken a place beside Katie and Francis, who looked equally cooked. "You created this mess."

"Fran?" Elijah sought a comforting word from his friend, but none was forthcoming. Fran simply turned towards the window to watch the street pass by. Elijah followed his eyeline, and amid the jets of colour that shone from the concrete landscape, he noticed Munro and Yates standing on the sidewalk, two thugs, likely crims, standing between them. None looked too impressed.

"Bye, Daddy," Katie said in a childlike voice as she waved at the passing faces.

A rat scurried beneath Elijah's feet. Then another. And another. He lifted his feet and placed them on the seat beside him as if the floor had turned to lava.

"Not the trip you were expecting?" Cindy Lee was having a hard time sparking a flame. "Just keep your eye on the light, not on the dark."

"What light?"

"The one in your pocket."

"The one you've always followed."

"And that'll help?"

They all began nodding. First Cindy, then Maslow and Burson, Cleo, the crowd in the back row. It was contagious.

"She, it gave us life, it brought us together."

"You want me to drink the poison? You want me to join you deadbeats?"

"You don't want to disappoint your mother." Cindy raised his hand and pointed.

Elijah craned his neck and saw a woman sitting alone towards the front of the bus. Even without seeing her face, he knew it was his her. Hooped earrings. Hair that had spent an evening in curlers. A long neck attached to a wafer-thin figure. He hadn't been afforded the opportunity to say goodbye nor an open casket at the funeral—it was for the best—but he didn't need to remember her in a way that wasn't befitting her beauty. A beauty that would forever endure in his mind. That version riding the bus shared her likeness, but it wasn't his mother. He squeezed his eyes shut, the specks returned, and he sat back.

"They've had you on their radar a lot longer than you think," Cleo said. "You think you have free will, but it's all just a lie."

"You're all just ghosts," Elijah countered. He knew he was hallucinating; he knew it was all a manifestation of the war inside his head, but he was fast growing tired of it.

"We're all *your* ghosts. You brought us here."

"This is your dollhouse, She." Cindy Lee had a way of getting under his skin, and Elijah considered whether he'd ever maintained a close friend. They were both now drenched in perspiration, and a smell hung in the air like discarded garbage and unrefrigerated meat.

"Can anyone else see these fucking rats?" Katie now also had her legs raised, which hiked up her skirt and left little to the imagination.

"Just guinea pigs." That was the smudge, Maslow. There was a mouth in their somewhere, not that anyone was listening.

"I'm not going to rot with the rest of you." Elijah's voice cracked a little.

"If only it were that easy." Burson was more likeable when he was howling.

"We can't just leave." It was the first thing that Katie's friend had said, but it struck Elijah between the eyes. Were they really here to stay? Was this his punishment? Was the bus carrying him forth into a spiral of insanity? Had he died back there in the gaming room?

He wanted to scream. He wanted to pull the emergency exit and return to his normal way of life which entailed dealing with drunken punters and bickering with Nathalie, but always making up in the best way possible between crumpled sheets. He wanted to punch Maslow in the face and watch bugs crawl from his skull. Extinguish the cigarette in Cindy's eye and watch him self-combust. But instead, he pulled his knees to his chest and began to rock back and forth. He scrunched his eyes closed and tried to clear his mind by entering a cavernous vortex, a cone of solitude. Sleep was the cousin of death, and Elijah was only too happy to facilitate a family reunion. *There's no place like home. There's no place like home. There's no place like home.*

A hand cupped Elijah's shoulder and shook him firmly. He blinked back into consciousness and saw Nathalie standing over him, the light beyond giving her face a pleasant, almost angelic aura. She had cut her hair.

"It's time to wake up." Her voice sounded gravelly, deeper than expected.

Elijah blinked again and gathered his bearings, and suddenly realised that he wasn't being awoken by Nathalie but rather the man that had doffed his hat and chartered the freight.

Elijah scrambled upright and scanned his surrounds. They were stationary, the engine had been cut, and apart from the driver, the bus was empty. Thankfully, the bus was empty, and no longer a vessel to carry the damned to their final destination.

"It's the last stop, kid," the driver said cautiously, not wanting to poke a dishevelled and confused traveller who was experiencing psychosis and a serious comedown.

The window offered a view onto a world absent of high-rise buildings and busy footpaths, and the roadhouse was framed by dead trees and dull grey skies. It was a miserable afternoon, and it was the perfect place for a rendezvous for two parts of the Spikies fraternity.

It may not have been the last stop, but it was a good place to start. Every end had to have a beginning.

PART V:

LIES, BETRAYAL, AND OTHER ACTS OF FOREPLAY

JUST DESSERT

The diner was like most on the outskirts of town. Soap-streaked windows, along with oversized letters, dominated the front to entice weary travellers and fugitives in need of a rest stop. Trucks and run-down vehicles dotted the car park. Upon entering, the sizzle of the hot plate was the warmest greeting you could expect to receive, and the coffee smelled like it had been brewing from the previous week. Steaks and pancakes were the specialty of the house, and steaks and pancakes were usually ordered, unless you were feeling especially adventurous and asked for Bratwurst on crusty bread with mustard and fried onions. No bells. No whistles. The cook didn't wipe his sweat and the waitresses didn't give a little extra for tips. The cogs of the machine fit perfectly, and everything ran just fine.

When Elijah stepped from the bus, he immediately locked eyes on the sleek BMW X4 parked as if it were gracing a showroom. Chiba had arrived early, and Elijah hoped she hadn't brought her entourage.

A bell hanging over the door chimed as the weathered figure entered the roadhouse. Chiba raised a hand, and true to her word, she had reserved a booth in the corner with a view of the easily forgettable asphalt. And even more meritoriously: she was alone.

Chiba wore a brown tweed suit and wouldn't have looked out of place at a horse race or a turf party for a league of gentlemen. Elijah felt underdressed; in fact, he couldn't remember the last time he had changed his clothes. Frayed skinny jeans, a tightly buttoned collar, and leather boots with relaxed laces had become his suit of armour.

Both attendees looked equally exhausted.

The smell of burnt meat hung in the air along with the smoke it produced. Elijah dropped his head and made his way past the other diners who were hungrily devouring their lunch, or engaged in vigorous conversation, and slipped into the cushioned cubicle.

"Are you alone?" Elijah asked the woman across the table, requiring confirmation.

"I said I would be," Chiba ruminated. "And you, are you alone?"

"I think you know I am. You made sure of that."

"We made it very clear that you shouldn't run."

Elijah dropped his head and folded his hands before continuing: "You also made it clear that I ran over a bunch of people. That I committed mass murder."

"And who is to say that you didn't?" Chiba maintained her poker face.

Elijah raised his head and met the woman's steely gaze. She must have been nearly forty, but time had treated her well. "I saw some shit."

"You had a dream?"

"More a memory," Elijah said with clarity. "And I wasn't driving."

Chiba fidgeted and reached for a menu. "Well, I wouldn't know about that. Just fata morgana probably." She took a pair of thick-rimmed spectacles from her pocket and placed them on the bridge of her nose. "My branch specialises in health and well-being and not the criminal exploits of my subjects."

"And that's the thing…I'm not a criminal."

"Well…" Chiba glanced the diner's offerings.

"I was beaten and brainwashed and put through the wringer."

"You signed the deal, Elijah. In most books, that is a confession." Chiba settled on her decision. "I think I'll just have a sundae."

"The terms were false. I was innocent."

"I don't think anyone is ever innocent, Mister Caulfield. Especially you."

Elijah shook his head. He was trying to hold it together. Trying to avoid flying into a rage or turning into a blubbering mess. He had been branded as guilty his entire life, and the label wasn't easily peeled away.

"Where's Nathalie?"

The question hung in the air for a moment…

"Can I take your order?" A middle-aged waitress appeared at the table, a notepad draped over the elastic of her skirt and a pot of percolated coffee at the ready. A pencil held her hair in place, but it was rarely touched. Years of taking orders had sharpened her recitation skills, and, helpfully, the menu was flimsy at best. Her name tag read: *Molly*.

"I'll take a chocolate sundae and just a cup of your finest," Chiba requested.

"And you?" The waitress turned a greasy eyeball in Elijah's direction.

"Just a coffee."

Molly filled two cups with deep, dark liquid and left the pair to continue their conversation. Most of the customers valued their privacy.

"You need to forget about Nathalie. She's with Kelvin now."

"But is she safe?"

"*Your* safety is my priority, Elijah," Chiba reiterated.

Elijah suddenly knew something was wrong. Square shapes were trying to fit into circular holes, and something just didn't add up.

"You spoke to her?" Elijah pushed.

"Would you please excuse me." Chiba stood without answering the question. "I need to use the bathroom. As you know, it's been a long day."

Elijah raised his hands and let the woman go without protest. He clearly wasn't going to get a straight answer, and he sure as hell wasn't going to get a sympathetic ear. It was another dead end, and Elijah was getting used to them.

Chiba was avoiding the question, and that could only mean one thing…

Nathalie had arrived with the gun. She was frightened of these people. They were no longer happily united. There had been a rift and Nat had seen something she wasn't supposed to—or maybe she had just backflipped, a completely understandable manoeuvre given the circumstances. In any case, it seemed unlikely that she was still sleeping with the enemy.

Elijah felt for the vial in his pocket. It was still there. The final dose. One last spike.

He took it from his pocket, glanced around the restaurant, and, pretending to reach for the sugar, poured the contents into Chiba's coffee. There was no need to stir it as it sunk into the murky depths and no need to feign that all was business as usual—nobody raised their eyes or cared for his business at all.

There were heavy rain clouds on the horizon, and the dappled light cut the landscape into searing shapes. Elijah reflected on not rushing into the burning building on that fateful day. He hadn't been part of the rescue party on that occasion, but now he was resigned to wielding the axe himself. He was the last stand and he would go down swinging.

"So, did you think it over?" Chiba reappeared at the table without warning, just as quickly as she had left.

"Think what over?" Elijah blurted much too quickly like a game show contestant wrestling with their timing. He didn't know where to look, but his eyes kept coming to rest on Chiba's cup and saucer.

"Coming in." Chiba dabbed her face with a handkerchief before placing it into her top pocket. She looked fresher, energised, a return to her former self.

"And if I don't?" Elijah knew the answer, but he needed to hear it from Chiba.

"They are the police, Elijah. They can get things done, make people disappear."

"And you?"

"I'm off the clock," Chiba said with a wry smile as she reached for her coffee.

Elijah zeroed in on every movement as she took a sip. Every line around her mouth came into focus. Her jugular seemed to heave against the buttoned collar as she swallowed. And as she lowered the cup, she seemed to bristle with distain. Something within knew it couldn't be undone. It was irreversible.

"Not quite what it used to be," Chiba said as her face soured slightly. A glimpse, perhaps, at what was to come. "But it sure as hell still beats the shit they used to serve up in Shibuya. Coffee in a can was my best bet back home."

"Tell me, do they know I'm alive?" Elijah repositioned himself as the centre of attention, an old croupier's ploy to ensure gamblers didn't spend too long considering their immediate vicinity or prioritising thoughts.

"No. You're something of a miracle. I think they'll be happy to see you." Chiba had forgotten about the coffee.

"Is my secret safe with you?"

"No, it is not." Again, she wiped her lips.

Elijah sat silently for a moment examining the Pharmacist's face. *What would happen when the drugs hit the sweet spot? Would it be painful? Would she split open like an overstuffed hessian sack? Would she be granted death before her insides bubbled and boiled?*

"You know my hands are bound."

"And the Bulgarians?" Elijah asked, relaxing his scrutiny.

"They were responsible for finding another —"

"Another subject to go along with your project?"

"You could say that." Chiba shrugged and took another mouthful.

"And they were to be taken to view the footage?" Elijah quizzed knowingly.

Chiba fell silent. "Kelvin still believes that to be true." She shook her head in an attempt to relinquish the taste from her mouth. "But, of course, you put paid to that."

"Where is the warehouse, Yumi? Where do you take them?"

Chiba sighed. "All new members of the team are taken to the Ninth Dock. It's isolated. But if you come back in, you'll save everyone the effort."

"Did you ever sit for them?"

"No," Chiba said vehemently.

"So, you do this by choice?" Elijah prodded.

"I'm part of the police force, Elijah, I do whatever they ask of me."

They let the idea hang in the air for a moment. In many ways, they had both been victims of authority, manipulated to trust those that propagate the best interests of others but who had an agenda entirely their own.

Elijah took the gifted eyedropper from his pocket and placed it on the table. "I'm not gonna need this anymore." He flicked it into motion, and they both watched as it rotated before coming to rest in Chiba's direction like a game of 'spin the bottle,' like her number had come up.

"There ain't no topping left for the ice cream, honey," Molly said as she again appeared at the head of the table.

"What?" Chiba failed to compute the message from the kitchen.

"There's-no-chocolate-for-the-sundae," the waitress reinforced phonetically as if speaking to a foreign child. "Would you like fudge, maybe blue heaven?"

"What flavour is blue heaven?" Elijah quizzed.

"It's blue." Molly's patience was wearing thin.

"It's okay, we were just leaving," Chiba said as she slid across the pleather seat.

"So, no sundae?"

"The coffee was more than enough," Chiba answered facetiously as she rose to her feet and married buttons with adjacent slits in her waistcoat.

"Okay. Suit yourself." The waitress hastily turned on her heels and scurried away to relay the cancelled order.

Chiba threw a crumpled note onto the table and shrugged a heavy fur coat over her shoulders. It was hard to imagine that she ever looked anything less than camera-ready.

"We're leaving, yes?" she repeated, this time in Elijah's direction. It was framed as a question, but its recipient knew it was a demand.

"Do I have a choice?" Elijah planted his palms on the table and pushed himself upright. He would go. He needed to confront the man that had masterminded all the bullshit, needed to watch what the drug did to Chiba. But most importantly, he needed to see Nathalie.

An eighteen-wheeler road train raced by as Elijah and Chiba crossed the car park, the driver offering a smile as the two figures braved the cold weather. Elijah nodded in response. It felt like vindication, positive reinforcement. A spectre that offered a hint of truth. He was at peace with choosing to administer the drug. It was murder in the first degree, but it was also a necessary evil. An act that would defend against further deaths. A Valkyrie. A bullet with angel wings.

Chiba pinched the bridge of her nose, squinted tightly, and steadied herself against the compact luxury vehicle.

"Are you okay?" Elijah asked as he swung open the passenger-side door.

"Yes. It's just this constant pursuit." She grimaced. "This old feline just isn't cut out for it anymore."

"Well, you can stop chasing." Elijah ducked his head and stepped into the car.

"Yes, I guess I can." Chiba followed suit.

The snug black leather immediately warmed Elijah, and as Chiba turned the key in the ignition, he felt like a child that had wandered too close to the precipice and had fallen into an underbelly seething with predators, those that hunt for sport and turn their backs on the carnage they create. It was only now that he felt like he was starting to assert some autonomy, some control. He was finally raging against a system that had always kept so many beneath the tread of its boot.

"Do you know how many people die at the hands of police each year in the US alone?"

"Should I?" Chiba asked as she pulled onto the freeway, the steering wheel effortlessly sliding through her gloved grip. She had a lot of numbers colliding in her head, and it was sometimes difficult to keep track of the most relevant.

"Over a thousand." Elijah didn't know the exact figure, but he knew it was over a thousand too high. "And in ninety-nine percent of those cases, no charges are laid against the killers. Nobody is held responsible."

"You're not going to start chanting 'defund the police,' are you?" Chiba banged out each syllable on the steering wheel.

"It just seems like an abuse of power, don't you think?" Elijah took his eyes off the passing scenery and turned to Chiba. Perhaps she could repent, or at least admit there was a problem with police methodology, before she became guilty of driving under the influence.

"Have you heard the song 'Livin' Thing' by ELO?" Chiba asked. It wasn't the response Elijah expected.

"Of course. My mum always played it too loudly when I was a kid."

"So, then you'd know that a lot of listeners believe it's anti-abortion. Pro-life. That to terminate a foetus is a terrible thing to do." Chiba found the melody.

"And is that what it's about?" Elijah asked.

"No. It's about a bad paella on a Spanish holiday." Chiba activated the windscreen wipers to combat the first signs of rain.

"I fail to see the connection between the lyrics of a song and the actions of some trigger-happy cops." Elijah turned back to the blurred edges of the road and the slowly passing outlines of mountains in the distance.

"How about this," Chiba continued. "In modern retellings of almost all fairy tales, we forget to mention the antagonistic nature of the titular characters. We almost always forget that the story of Jack and the Beanstalk is about grand larceny. Even Goldilocks is guilty of breaking and entering."

"Why are you telling me this?" Elijah felt Chiba was trivialising the truth.

"Because you should know as well as anyone that there are always two sides to the story. It just depends on which news you're reading. The devil is in the details we're denied."

"So, George Floyd wasn't the victim of police brutality? Breonna Taylor wasn't shot five times in her own apartment?" Frustration was combining with uncertainty. Had he administered enough? Perhaps the dose was a dud.

"You don't need to test my empathy, Elijah. I know the difference between murder and wanton endangerment." She would have made a good lawyer. In fact, anything Yumi Chiba turned her attention towards would have received high praise.

"I wish I had evidence of that," Elijah said. He had given her a chance, the opportunity to condemn breaches of humanity, but she had failed to take it. When the time came, Chiba would not be awarded an honourable discharge.

"You know, you're something of an anomaly," Chiba said while changing lanes.

"How so?" Elijah played his part, much like he had in that interrogation room, which felt like weeks, even months, ago.

"We've never had a Spiker go rogue," Chiba continued. "You're the first one to offer any form of opposition."

"Spiker?" Elijah didn't remove his eyes from the passing terrain. Frost blanketing the grassy fields. Ice clinging to wire fences. There wasn't a car for miles. "I like that."

"Yeah, you've definitely become a thorn in Kelvin's side."

"I like that even more."

"He's not somebody you want to piss off, Elijah." Chiba loosened her seat belt. She felt short of breath within its tight restraint. She flipped a vent to ward off the rising temperature.

"Tell me, how many are on the books? How many just like me?" Elijah again turned to face the driver, who still appeared assertive, alluring, and sanguine, even given the situation.

"Let's just say, you're not the first and you won't…" Chiba coughed before she could finish her sentence and a chunk of bloody mucus struck the windshield. It looked like half-chewed gristle, a discarded, over-ripe cherry…and it was just the beginning.

Chiba concealed another cough before she lurched forward and reflux reduced her throat muscles to mere bystanders—a stream of vomit leaping unabated from somewhere deep within. It was like an eruption from a hydrant. Coca-Cola meeting Mentos. And the constant flow threatened to reduce Chiba to a deflated bag of skin.

The car skidded before bunny hopping, and then sped up again, the accelerator pedal responding to shuffling feet that danced a merry jig.

Finally, the faucet was screwed tight, or the reservoir ran dry, and Chiba slumped in her seat, her head falling forward as if she had been slung over a coat hanger. Steaming serves of goulash pooled at her feet and in her lap, and the dash was doused in the crimson excrement.

Elijah leaned across, placed a hand on the steering wheel, and carefully glided the car into the gravel lining the asphalt. The BMW came to a neat rest and Elijah pulled the handbrake. Still, there wasn't another vehicle in sight.

Elijah located a faint pulse—the cop had some fight in her—but it wouldn't be long before her light was completely extinguished. Her suit had been reduced to a less-than-absorbent mop, and Elijah swallowed heavily against his own reflux. He had to act fast, and although he didn't want to have anything to do with what remained, Elijah steeled himself, reached into the damp breast pocket, and took her mobile phone.

He held it in front of Chiba's slumped head, gained access via face recognition, and tapped and swiped and quickly located Kelvin's number. Not wanting to initiate further conversation, he sent out a clear, concise, and expressionless message: *Meet at the docks.*

He had to restrain from adding an emoji.

Reception was weak and the battery was low, but the text reached its intended target without interference, ticked boxes visually indicating as much.

In no time, a reply soared through the airwaves and landed on the screen: *Okay.*

Just as he suspected, the overseer didn't want to miss a beat and he would drop everything for front row seats to the torture and subsequent fracture of a new candidate—another head for the wall. FOMO affected all generations.

Elijah had even less time due to Kelvin's enthusiasm, and he hurriedly dragged the lifeless body into the shotgun position and scurried around to the driver's side to assume the controls. He had to get back in the saddle if he liked it or not. The lines were open and quickly needed to be severed. He had to be fearless. He had to be ruthless. He had to be everything he'd only recently discovered.

He wiped the windscreen with his sleeve—the consistency resembling dog food cooked in thick gravy—and cleared a line of sight. He placed the vehicle into gear and eased it back onto the road. Again, there was no traffic to speak of, and Elijah prayed that it would stay that way as he turned back towards the city.

RANK AND FILE

Batal carried a zipped body bag over his shoulder and loaded it into the trunk of a parked car, the mass within folding unnaturally and coming to rest without a sign of struggle. He turned, scooped another from the tarmac, and dropped it into the darkened confines, on top of the other. It was as if he were loading bags of cement and the suspension strained under the mass. He never got tired of the heavy lifting, and it reminded him of piling branches and building bonfires when he was a young boy. Before the deployment. Before the clouds turned red. Before the rage muscled its way in.

"We need to leave." Kelvin's voice echoed down the alleyway.

Batal wasn't expecting company at the rear exit of the precinct and as he swivelled, he tightly balled his fists before realising it was his boss. He wouldn't have to add to the cargo.

"Fresh blood?" he asked.

"Chiba is meeting us at the docks. We can observe, step in if necessary." Kelvin appeared enthused, spritely, as if he'd taken his own elixir. The job kept him young.

"And these two?" Batal waved a large hand at the bulging sacks.

"Since when do you ask questions?"

Batal shrugged. "My chiropractor may need to know where to send the invoice."

Kelvin smirked. "Sometimes failings need to be aborted. Call it quality control."

"They got names?"

"Not that I know of," Kelvin replied. "If you really must know, one got mixed up with some questionable local identities after shopping our product around." He craned his neck to see beyond Batal's large frame. "And the other was supposed to be an accomplice to our friend, Elijah Caulfield. We thought we may need him to sell our story. We took him out when we thought things were under control. Seems we may have been a little…hasty." Kelvin knew it helped build morale to give the students some of the answers. "In either case, it's beneath your pay scale."

"And what have we got waiting at the warehouse?"

It was Kelvin's turn to shrug. "Bring an extra body bag."

Batal turned and rearranged the stowed corpses to ensure there was room for one more and firmly closed the lid on the rear of the car.

"In fact," Kelvin added, "bring two."

Batal twisted back towards Kelvin with a quizzical expression. There was always a clear game plan, but Kelvin was thinking on his feet and he hadn't drawn this one up.

"We can't afford to have any more failures. And this one is again on Chiba."

"Again?"

"She was entrusted to keep Elijah in line, and look how that ended." Kelvin didn't need to explain himself, but it was sometimes best to point out where the lines on a map led. "That fucking punk had so much potential and has been nothing but an unnecessary distraction. We should be well ahead of where we currently stand. That's on Yumi."

"We've got others racking up the numbers."

"I have no qualms with their output. All else are fair game."

"We can only dig the graves so deep before somebody trips on the remains."

"Yumi has nobody," Kelvin said. His recruitment tactics were scrupulous.

"She has always stood with us. Believed in the work." Batal knew the value of holding one's tongue, but he also knew the importance of standing his ground. Although he would never defy Kelvin, he was willing to test his iron will. It benefitted the task force's endurance, it's long-term success.

"If we have to continue to turn the soil with blood to ensure a favourable harvest, then so be it." Kelvin approached the parked vehicle and stood eye to eye with his most loyal employee. "Tell me, Batal. What would you do if a lamb was born with a curved spine and bent limbs?" Like many others, it was a test—and Kelvin had a way of evoking strong imagery.

"I'd snap its neck," Batal said without hesitation.

"Of course you would. It's the right thing to do and you're a good man." Kelvin knew the power of a compliment, and he placed his hand on Batal's shoulder. "A mercy kill," he continued. "And that's what we do. If something is defective, we take care of it and replace it with something shiny and new."

Batal nodded his head. He understood. If Chiba wasn't getting the desired results, then somebody else would. A broken part in the machine could not be tolerated.

Kelvin wiped at a blemish on the car's paint job with his sleeve before making his way around to the driver's side. "Now pass me the keys. I'm driving."

CAPTAIN OF INDUSTRY

Chiba hadn't lied. The Ninth Dock was extremely isolated, and seemingly long abandoned. There wasn't a soul in sight, and the only signs that anyone had ever been there was the warehouse itself and the crude tags created by spray cans that patterned its walls. If it were the Wild West, tumbleweeds would have blown past and a stray coyote may have solemnly looked for its next meal. Instead, it was a monochromatic scene of heavy steel and wrought iron, once a feat of solid engineering but now forgotten due to the rise of more technically advanced shipping stations in more accessible locations.

Elijah parked the car at the rear of the building where the edge of the wharf met the water. He then dragged two large dumpsters across to conceal its whereabouts—the buckled wheels making the task more arduous than it needed to be.

Although Kelvin was expecting to meet Chiba, the state of the car's interior may have raised some concerns, and Elijah didn't want to encourage prying eyes or those easily agitated arriving on high alert. He was still dead in their minds and he wanted to keep it that way.

He made his way to the side door and found that it was chained and deadlocked. Whatever took place inside clearly wasn't for inquisitive eyes either. Curiosity here could lead to something much worse than death. Elijah stepped back to take the whole building in. It was the size of an aircraft hangar and looked much like a beached blue whale. At its highest point, parts of its spine and ribs were exposed, decaying in the sunlight and the salty breeze.

It was condemned and derelict, fit for demolition, but it wasn't worth the labour or the nitroglycerine. Plus, it had been recommissioned by the state, and they weren't in a hurry to step aside and allow gentrification to roll into the neighbourhood. Not when they had a flourishing indoctrination enterprise on their hands.

Elijah noted a frosted window, its protective wire mesh pulled back like an open tin of sardines. That was his way in. He took a rock, bounced it in his palm to acclimate to the weight, and launched it like a kid at a carnival knocking down rigged milk bottles. The projectile broke right on through to the other side, and large shards of glass came crashing down, reverberating around the dock, but, due to the desolation, for Elijah's ears only.

Proud with his efforts, he scaled an empty gasoline drum, cleared the remnants from the frame with his sullied sleeve, and made his way through the opening into the darkened innards of the beast.

The lilac hues of dusk seeped into the warehouse, and Elijah immediately became aware of the large projection screen, an antique Koken chair with much-loved maroon leather and bronze finishings, and a pre-loaded sixteen-millimetre film projector. In another setting, it would have appeared charming, quaint, a hipster's paradise, but in the current surrounds, it was nothing but macabre, much like a backyard abortion clinic or Guantánamo Bay electrotherapy, perhaps a Moscow prison tattoo parlour.

After some initial uncertainty, he was relieved to find he was in the right place.

Out of habit, he triple-tapped his pockets. The handgun was still close by his side, but the number of shots at his disposal was running worryingly low. He had to make every shot count. Elijah made his way to the centre of the open space and ran the frames of the celluloid through his fingers. There were no less than three hundred feet, and the dust had not yet settled on the frozen images which he noticed mostly contained tableaus of carnage and destruction. Bricks from once-erect buildings lay scattered across barren ground as uniformed soldiers stood over cowering civilians. Bodies were pulled from the rubble, and heavy artillery accompanied the arrival of a well-resourced cavalry. Women had hijabs forcibly removed and men were instructed to stand in line with trousers pulled down around their ankles, all the while cradling hysterical children. It was a warzone, an unforgiving landscape where death was more likely than three meals a day, and it was difficult to accurately determine who were the good guys: the occupied or the occupiers.

The verité-style reel reflected a recently recorded event, and although there was no synchronised sound, Elijah could hear every scream, every demand made at gunpoint. He turned away and noticed other film canisters, each labelled with masking tape and black ink. The private collection included: *Iraq 2003, Norway 2011, The Tokyo Trials, New Zealand 2019, USA 2017, 2019, 2020,* and the blood-soaked narrative personally selected for Elijah: *France 2016.* The terror had been converted from first-person digital sources and used to brainwash, traumatise, and ensure obedience. It was a basic act of desensitisation while rewarding submission to primal instinct, and it was the perfect way to train a killer.

Whoever took a seat transformed into Pavlov's fucking canines, but they weren't salivating at the prospect of dog biscuits, rather regulated chaos and the loss of human life.

A small medicine cabinet sat beside the reclining chair, and Elijah knew at once that it housed concoctions that promoted conditioning, dosages that eased subjects into a situation where they believed they were responsible for the events unfolding upon the screen. They became the perpetrators before the lens, and their manipulated state meant they never had a foothold to argue the case.

Elijah cast his mind back to the interrogation room. He had been apathetic, willing to accept his fate. He had committed the crime because he had been told as much. At the time, he had remembered nothing of the screened footage. Nothing of the Pharmacist or the Anaesthetist or their fucking chemistry kit. The images of pedestrians fleeing and colliding with his vehicle had been absorbed in his stupor and solidified as memories, and the cops swatted at him like a piñata until he finally broke.

He had been fed a motive and there was no exculpatory evidence to speak of. His reality had been carefully torn down and reconstructed without his knowledge or empathetic reasoning.

Gravel shifted beneath car tyres and Elijah was awoken from his contemplation. He hurriedly fiddled with a timer on the projector in order for it to activate automatically and disappeared into the corners of darkness. Company had arrived, and it was time to confront his demons.

FISHING WITH JONAH

The broken window went unnoticed as Kelvin and Batal stepped from their own government-issued Bentley like a wily, old sheriff and his personal heavy riding into town. The scent of fish was in their air, but neither bothered to sniff the breeze. Instead, they made a beeline for the shackled door.

"She's not here yet?" Batal questioned as he wrestled with the chains.

Kelvin shrugged. New subjects brought with them new promise, and he would happily wait all day if necessary. And anyway, he felt more in control when arriving at the party early.

The door swung open, and the remaining sunlight cut a wedge into the heart of the building. It brought back fond memories for some. Mixed emotions for others.

"It gives us time to prepare," Kelvin said as he stepped past Batal into the warehouse. "There can be no shortcuts. We have to follow procedure without fault." It was a message for them both and something that would be reiterated to Chiba. Kelvin was cognisant of past mistakes, and for a task force working under a cloud of secrecy, he could ill afford their practices spilling onto the streets.

"Yates and Munro were weak. They loosened their grip when they should have been squeezing tighter," Kelvin elucidated as they strode meaningfully across the dusty concrete. "A subject must be reduced to nothing. They should be thankful for the opportunity when it is presented."

When they arrived at the centrepiece, Kelvin checked the film stock and then the cabinet of refrigerated supplies while Batal pulled on the restraints and tested the sturdiness of the chair. He noted tears in the fabric where subjects had clawed at the armrests and dried bloodstains on the floor nearby.

"The saddle is all in order," he concluded.

Without warning, the filmstrip then began feeding through the projector, and a flickering light punched through dusty particles, painting a numerical countdown and then unclassified footage across the suspended linen.

Startled, both men took a step back and raised their hands— each one indicating to the other that they weren't responsible for triggering the machinery. Well, not deliberately anyway.

"Welcome to the picture show, assholes," Elijah announced as he stepped from the shadows. "You've joined us just in time for the final act." It was unrehearsed, but it had a gunslinger's vibe which coordinated nicely with his raised weapon and dishevelled demeanour.

"Careful, kid," Batal warned, "do you know how to use that thing?"

Elijah racked the slide on the Glock. "It's funny what you learn on the job."

"Bite your tongue, B," Kelvin said, holding Elijah's gaze. "He hasn't earned your conversation, and words from beyond the grave have no place here."

Elijah knew it was only a slight tongue-lashing, but for some reason, it was biting, like he had disappointed a parent.

"And by the time this is over, he will have blown a hole through his foot," Kelvin ridiculed further.

"Your Soviet scouts may claim otherwise," Elijah countered, "if they could still speak."

The sound of the shuttle engaging the film's sprockets filled the air like a model train sprinting across an assembled circuit.

"Why did you do this?" Elijah asked. He still needed answers, a sense of closure.

"We just wound the key. You executed the rest, Elijah."

"You never even read me my rights." Again, his mind drifted to that initial meeting.

"We gave you a purpose," Kelvin declared. "Before us, you were nothing."

"Get in the chair," Elijah blurted as he waved the gun in Batal's direction. "I want to see how you do it."

Batal's eyes darted from Elijah to Kelvin and then back again. "It's—"

"I would appreciate if you did it quietly," Elijah interjected.

Batal sighed, dropped his hands, and lowered his body into the chair. A gun could be persuasive. Even muskets that took several minutes to load had greatly aided imperialist tyrants for centuries.

"Now you." Elijah turned the weapon towards Kelvin. "Strap him in."

Kelvin didn't resist, and he moved methodically to secure his loyal operative. He began with the waist belt and then the ankles, sliding the prongs into comfortable notches.

"Tightly," Elijah encouraged. "Just like all the other monkeys you've sent into space."

Kelvin then bound Batal's wrists to the shredded armrests, but not before the two men locked eyes and a pocket pistol was slid into his possession. No bigger than a smartphone, it wasn't a wise choice for an armed robbery, but under the circumstances, it could still do some damage. Kelvin concealed it in his palm and stepped back behind the morbid throne.

"And the gag," Elijah demanded.

Kelvin obliged and placed the ball gag in Batal's open mouth but not before pocketing the weapon. He pulled the tightening strap fiercely, almost gleefully.

Batal struggled under the pressure, but it was in vain. He was securely fastened.

"What's your plan?" Kelvin asked as he stepped to the side of the chair. "Are you going to reprogram a man that has experienced war? Witnessed the brutal slaying of innocent women and children, raped by those that masqueraded as saviours?"

"Did he witness it firsthand?" Elijah countered, his arm growing weary with the gun in his hand. "Or through a helmet cam, a chest recording? A citizen journalist?"

"What does it matter?" Kelvin hissed, losing patience.

"He didn't choose to be this animal." Elijah waved the gun as if he were directing the straightening of a picture on the wall. "Now inject him."

"What?"

"Take the syringes from the cabinet and empty every last drop into his arm."

Kelvin reluctantly bent down and removed a small medical kit from the cupboard. He placed it on the benchtop, and, from within, he produced two large hypodermic needles. A taste of the liquid fountained from the nib, and Kelvin looked towards the captive turned captor for reaffirmation. Elijah nodded.

Batal kicked and squirmed in the shackles as the sedative plunged into his bloodstream.

"All of it," Elijah beckoned.

"You'll kill him," Kelvin screeched as he held the lethal dose in place.

"On the contrary, you may just set him free."

And then Batal stopped flailing. His eyes rolled back in his head and foam bubbled from the corners of his mouth. His torso jerked in raptures as if something were burrowing beneath the skin, and the syringe stood upright in the crook of his elbow as if he were a pin cushion. And then he fell still like a fish that had been removed from the ocean for far too long.

Kelvin's clothing was soaked through with sweat, and it was the first time Elijah had seen him short of breath or out of his depth.

"He was a member of the team, Elijah," he said calmly through heaving exhaustion, "just like you. Remember. You signed the fucking contract."

"I will never be like him or like you," Elijah accused, rage erupting like volcanic ash.

Kelvin straightened his posture and inhaled deeply. "You know there's no way out of this, don't you?" He took two steps towards Elijah. "They'll come looking for you. Others that see virtue in what we do."

Elijah steeled himself, the gun beckoning him to fire at will.

Kelvin advanced further. "The orders will be clear, and, trust me, they know how to follow orders. Our best and brightest—"

"It's a shame you won't be around to see it all go down," Elijah interrupted as he braced for the gun's recoil. He was tired of social niceties.

Deafeningly, the bullet jumped from its barrier, followed a straight course, and made an incision in Kelvin's right ear before blasting a hole through the far wall. A scream of pure hostility roared from Kelvin's lungs, and before Elijah was able to disengage the next chambered projectile, he was onto him like a defensive linebacker—a shoulder connecting with Elijah's jaw like a battering ram—sending both men and the gun sprawling to the floor.

Pinning Elijah's arms to the ground with his knees, Kelvin began raining down blows, his knuckles hungry for blood, his tongue hanging loose like a wolf free of its sheep's clothing.

"We should have been united," Kelvin shouted as bone struck bone. Elijah's head bounced back after each swift jab like a speedball with a stiff joint, bruises appearing almost instantaneously. "A common cause. That's all we asked."

After a while, Elijah fell limp and Kelvin leapt up, stepped back and admired the damage he had done. It was like appreciating a gallery piece, considering the artist's method, their motivation. He straightened his suit and brushed at stains that flecked the lapels. Most of the blood was not his own, but his ear had been reduced to a deep-red mound of gnawed flesh. He picked up the gun that had inflicted the damage and discarded his own clownish miniature.

Elijah rose to a slouched position and spat blood from his mouth. One eye was now almost completely closed over and his lip had ballooned in size.

"I know the conditions weren't great, but we could've renegotiated," Kelvin stated like a reasonable man retracing steps in order to understand how he had arrived at such a juncture. "Altered a few things. Given you back certain liberties." He waved the gun as if it were free to make its own choices.

"You kill people for a living," Elijah wailed, a string of scarlet saliva seeping from his mouth. He was now seemingly trapped in Plato's cave—only shadows apparent in his proximity, an exit unfathomable.

"That's right I do, and I get paid handsomely," Kelvin declared. "You are so preoccupied with heroes and villains. It's all the same, Elijah. What matters is the plan."

"Succeed at all costs?" Elijah drooled as a wave of nausea crashed through his frontal lobe. "It's a simple formula."

"If the plan is right and the outcome is achieved, everything else is superfluous."

"And Nathalie, is she superfluous?" Elijah raised his head and strained to focus his vision. The dark was chasing away the final remains of the day.

"Nathalie shared our principles. But her cover was blown and she got spooked, and I'm afraid to say, there's no room for vulnerability in this line of work," Kelvin ruminated before continuing: "That's why you were such a promising candidate. After your mother's death, we thought you had shed all those arbitrary shortcomings like empathy and fear and compassion. I know Nathalie sure as hell never felt any warmth from you."

"Did she tell you I beat her?"

"No. I added that to your file. It helps with justifying our selection process."

"Where is she?" Elijah screamed. It was the last thing he needed to know.

"Don't you want to hear about your mother?" Kelvin fed on torment, and he didn't want to miss an opportunity to inflict further pain.

"My mother is dead," Elijah said softly.

"Why do you think accelerant was used? Why do you think they found sleeping pills in her system? It's not a coincidence that the investigation was neatly wrapped in a matter of days."

"My mother was unwell." Elijah imagined her luminous granite headstone and the flowers that always laid scattered around his mother's grave. Each petal representing the days she had been gone. He had only recently stopped visiting.

"Yes, she was, and probably suicidal too. We just expedited the process." Kelvin drew breath as if the confession was tedious yet essential. "We knew sparking the match would lead you to us. Trauma is the best recruitment tool we have."

All the emergency workers that were present that day took on a sinister appearance in Elijah's mind. Had they been there to help or simply hide evidence that outed the perp in their midst? Did they rush to rescue or know all along that it was futile? He had always questioned why she hadn't left a note, not said her goodbyes. But he knew single parenthood never sat well and she wanted Elijah to have a fresh start without the negative influence she would bring.

Elijah would not, could not, believe Kelvin's bullshit any longer. And, if by chance Kelvin had been responsible all those years ago, he knew a special place in hell awaited.

"My mother chose her path." Memory was all Elijah had left and he wouldn't allow it to be rewritten.

"Perhaps you can ask her yourself. I'd be more than happy to reunite the two of you." Kelvin raised the gun like a marksman challenged to a dual and lined up his target. "Do send my regards…"

An explosion rang out through the building like a canon trying to ward off an advancing fleet, an army that needed to be curtailed. Elijah gritted his teeth and clamped his eyes shut. The storm had arrived, and he feared what had been brought with it.

A hole the size of a football appeared where Kelvin's stomach had been just moments ago, and he collapsed without a yelp into a smouldering heap.

He was dead before he hit the ground.

From just within the doorway, the source of the blast appeared in the shape of a slumped silhouette. Arduously, it limped closer, as if only one heel remained, and a slender form manifested. It was Chiba, and she was brandishing a twin-barrel rifle that would have put even the mightiest big buck to sleep. She wasn't looking so hot, but remarkably she was still alive after coughing up what looked like most of her vital organs. *Huelga a la japonesa.*

"You've got some heart, Yumi, I give you that," Elijah said through a squinted gaze as Chiba sidled up beside Kelvin's corpse, which she kindly prodded with the weapon.

Not surprisingly, he was still dead.

On closer inspection, Chiba really was in terrible shape—drawing parallels with the walking dead—and it was apparent that she was incurring overdue fees on borrowed time.

"He had it coming," Chiba slurred, her speech resembling post-stroke tremors. She crumpled into a seated position beside her old boss. "What did I miss?"

"Well, you made a good ol' mess in your car," Elijah offered; it was a good a place to start as any.

"You drugged me?" The Pharmacist knew the score, but it was still framed like a question rather than a bitter accusation.

"I did," Elijah confessed. "When you were in the toilet." Death's door would soon be answered, and Elijah figured she had a right to know.

"Serves me right for dropping my guard." Chiba was resigned to her fate.

The projector continued to dart heinous images across the screen, but Chiba paid it no mind. Her reality was now contained behind closed eyes, a cave of her own.

"Yumi," Elijah said as he wiped his face and gathered his own thoughts. "I need to ask you one thing?"

A groan heaved in response. It wasn't much but it was something.

"Nathalie, do you know where she is?" He may have received an ass kicking, but it wasn't enough to derail the plan.

"Huh," Chiba responded as if she didn't understand the punchline to a joke.

"I need to know where Nathalie is." Elijah pulled himself upright.

"Why?"

"So, you know?" A surge of energy shot through his veins.

"A house. On—on…" Chiba began to drift into an unconscious state.

"Chiba!" Elijah shouted as he rushed towards her and shook her by the collar.

"South Road. In—in the Industrial Park," Chiba stammered.

"The number?"

"You can't miss it." She blinked harshly and raised her head with a sense of clarity. "It's the only house."

Elijah reached into his pocket and removed the packet of cocaine and offered it to the dying woman—a last supper of sorts. Chiba raised a hand to suggest, *Thanks, but no thanks.*He considered having a taste himself, but he had never used it and he wasn't about to start experimenting then. Instead, he hovered over Kelvin and then Batal and emptied the contents over them. When the police arrived, it would look like a drug deal gone bad, and with any luck, Chiba would come out of it squeaky clean. Her funeral would be honourable, celebratory. It was ironic really, but Elijah didn't have time to dwell on irony.

As he began to cross the room, his gaze firmly set on the exit, Chiba grabbed at his sleeve. "It's a recovery mission, Eli," she wheezed, "nothing more."

"I know," Elijah responded, "but I still need to go."

Chiba nodded her head knowingly. She knew of love, and such thoughts were preparing her for the end.

"And what are you going to do?"

"I'm gonna sit here and wait."

"Wait for what?"

"I'm tired, I can't keep doing this," Chiba concluded as her hand dropped to her side. It's funny how the inevitably of death can highlight past errors and allow for final acts of redemption. Perhaps the two combatants would meet in the next life. Possibly roles would be reversed. It all just rested on the fall of the dice.

Elijah again patted his pockets and located the remedy supplied by Ricks. He raised the vial and studied the transparent fluid. There was only one course of action left to pursue, and thankfully he still had one syringe at his disposal.

He hastily became a silhouette himself and made his way into the cold night air that had fallen upon the dock. Still, the world seemed abandoned, at peace, as if humans had yet to fuck it all up.

Accompanied by the soundtrack of his pounding heart, the young escapee made his way to the awaiting chariot, a shiny new Bentley courtesy of Kelvin, and, as he opened the driver's side door, another loud explosion erupted from the warehouse, this time fired at point-blank range. The search party would find remnants of her skull first. But they would have a tough time piecing it together.

(RE)UNITED REPROBATES

By the time Elijah had arrived in the industrious part of town, the evening's ominous clouds had ruptured, and the damp streets glistened beneath the glow of tireless lamps and yearning headlights. In the morning, the rain may have offered a fresh start, but in that moment, it was yet another affliction to endure.

Elijah knew he was on the wrong side of the tracks, but those tracks had been ripped up and relayed so many times, it was difficult to know where danger ended and salvation awaited. He wouldn't have been surprised to find alligators in the newly formed puddles. But it mattered not, his objective was clear, and his actions would not be derailed.

Water cascaded from cracks in the ceiling—the overhead plaster bulging from the weight of the downpour—and, as Elijah entered the house, he knew that if it all came crashing down, many hidden skeletons would be exposed. It was some sort of safe house, but the title seemed ill fitting, contradictory, and the Spikies crew knew that very few would come knocking if they wanted to, say, extricate a junkie from the street or even mothball a defiant employee.

From the outside, the property had looked like any other building fit for demolition, and from inside, the point was proven. Rats scurried in the hallway in an attempt to outrun the rising water, and the whole place smelled of rubbish that had never been correctly bagged nor collected.

Elijah hurriedly ventured farther into the property, unsuccessfully trying each of the locked doors in the passageway before arriving at the kitchen where he was shocked to discover appliances of every kind in working order. Domestic bliss in abhorrent surrounds.

The house had, in fact, been a home, and he would have to take care of any cables that hung like tentacles from the walls.

He then saw the stiffened bodies of Good Cop and Bad Cop lying facedown on the floor. The last time they had crossed paths was just prior to Elijah's deployment, and because of that, he would never forget their faces. Suffice to say, he neither held fond memories nor had time to grieve their passing, which was abundantly clear from the odour and the dried blood that had spread across much of the floor. Elijah had initially been wrong about the origins of the aroma, and both officers were well past their shelf life.

But still, there was no sign of Nathalie, which, given the circumstances, provided a glimmer of hope. Elijah couldn't shake the many questions that stirred in his head.

Why her? Why here? Why not him? And why hadn't anyone before him thought of burning this place to the ground?

In spite of the improbable events that had transpired, logic still prevailed.

There were no answers to be found in the proximity of the two dead cops. Elijah would have to head upstairs, something he had hoped was avoidable. Not only was it dark and foreboding, but the saggy ceiling would become unreliable flooring. He turned on his heels and, with an increasing limp and vision blurred by ecchymosis, made his way to the flight of steps located near the entry of the building.

Using the rail as a support, Elijah ascended the staggered rungs, each one threatening to collapse underfoot as thunder threatened to open surrounding fault lines. The second floor was even more pungent than the first, and the darkness made it difficult to navigate the landing which was home to cages that looked like they may have once contained chickens. Elijah knew they were fans of torture and ego fragmentation, but he didn't want to know what the fuck happened here. Perhaps, at one time or another, the place had been self-sustainable, replete with a cow in the yard, if only there had been a patch of grass.

The first knob he tried turned in his grasp and he entered a sizeable bedroom. Bunks lined the walls like a youth hostel, each bedspread tucked tightly, pillows plumped, and brown paper bags tied with twine, like a gift from the tooth fairy, awaited recipients at the head of each mattress. In the murky light, Elijah noticed a vintage armoire wardrobe in the corner. He turned the key and found an array of neatly pressed suits and cocktail dresses, along with lovingly polished shoes. It was a resplendent collection fit for wining and dining and belonged far from its current location. It also posed further questions but offered very few answers.

Although tempted to explore the room further, Elijah knew the doomsday clock was ticking and he made haste back into the foyer.

The sound of a scratched match from the floor below caught his ear momentarily, but a second door beckoned him forth and again offered no resistance as he leaned into it.

It was neat, tidy, habitable, and Nathalie was draped across a finely made, floral bedspread. It looked almost peaceful. A shrine to an angelic presence amid the bedlam.

Elijah ran to be by her side, but before he offered comforting words or an affectionate caress, he removed the syringe and filled the plunger with the last of the revitalising concoction. Ricks had been right: he was no killer, and he had never intended to take the life of another. This one deed could turn back the clock, perhaps make it all better.

The house shifted and the staircase creaked. Elijah shot a glance at the doorway but found nothing. He continued to prepare the needle and a vein by squeezing Nathalie's forearm and then slapping at the pale skin. Finally, he caught a glimpse of a blue streak, and with heightened optimism and trembling hands, he released the contents into Nathalie's stagnant blood. He had to kickstart the current in the stream. She had done it for him, and the least he could do was return the favour. It was an act of true love and an experience they would never share with another.

At that moment, Elijah heard a sound that had become familiar: the hammer of a gun shifting into a readied position.

"What the fuck do you think you're doing?" a man said from behind the raised weapon. He was young, handsome, clean shaven, and well dressed, and his hands were much steadier than the man he was facing.

"I was just…" Elijah fumbled for an answer like a schoolboy caught with contraband.

"No need. Save it," the man insisted. He clearly wasn't there to make friends. "What matters is that I know who you are and I know what you've been up to."

"Who are you?" Elijah asked, gathering his bearings. "Do you live here?" He looked familiar, but Elijah couldn't place him. Was he the driver from that day in the park? His shadow?

"Live here? Do I look like I fucking live here?" The man peeled of his gloves and tossed them aside.

Through swollen eyes, Elijah glanced at the Rolex, the shined leather shoes, the impeccably straight teeth, the glint in his eye. He clearly lived elsewhere.

"Then who are you?" Elijah demanded. All he wanted was to be left alone with Nat,

but as yet, she hadn't flinched, hadn't coughed up that final breath stuck in her lungs.

The man ran a hand through his hair and rolled his eyes. "I'm Patrick Svoboda," he said proudly, his pronunciation shaming Elijah's past attempts. In fact, he wore the name much better than he ever had.

"You're a Spiker?" Elijah was stunned, dumbfounded, but he realised Kelvin had promised as much.

The entrusted assassin kinked a neck muscle, and Elijah noted a tracking-device-sized lump, a red glow filtering through the skin. It was government issued and they were following every second of the exchange. He then placed a mint in his mouth as if he had somewhere else to be and the current situation was leaving a sour taste in his mouth.

The unmistakable scent of burning embers wafted through the air. Somewhere in the house, a fire had been started and the scattered fuel would ensure that it consumed all in its path.

"Spikes, yes, but that's only half of it. I mostly just do what I'm told, and we don't take too kindly to traitors."

"You don't have to do this," Elijah pleaded. "They're all dead. It's over."

A movement from the bed caught the corner of Elijah's eye. Was it his imagination or had Nathalie twitched? Possible reanimation? Or was it the lingering effects of Casey Ricks? Had the passengers returned?

He placed a hand in hers, but she was still unresponsive—the fingers cold and stiff. Smoke from the floor below entered the room. He knew his mother had exited the world long ago, but if he allowed his mind to slip just a little, he could picture her lying on the mattress, inhaling the fumes.

"On the contrary," the other Svoboda professed, "an army is only as strong as its parts, and we are many." He was clearly a disciple.

"We are not at war," Elijah tried to reason.

"Oh, but we are." The man was deranged, fanatical, and he had stepped from the cliff long ago. "And we're only just getting started."

And with that, his lips curled upward, he tenderly squeezed the trigger and lightning lit up the room.

Polite
Sharking

For my family.
For my loved ones.
For letting me drink from my own cup.

A very special thanks to Gayle, Reece and Emma for all their love and devotion. Without your ongoing kindness, honesty and generosity, I would not be the person I am today.

Also, a big thanks to Rhiannon Birch who was a rock and an unrelenting inspiration through the writing process and provided annotations longer than the novel itself. Not all revisions were made so there is a better version that exists out there, somewhere between the stars.

A notable mention must go to those who invested in the early Patreon days and those who rolled up their sleeves and trudged through the bones of many drafts – DirtBag MudCrab, Michelle Hope and Karmen Wells your advice was invaluable.

And finally, a huge shout out to the unbelievably talented design team of Julian Akbar and Matt Revert who breathed new life into the world of Spikies (who would have thought a story about inflicting such harm could turn out so beautiful – it's going to be a trip to see this kaleidoscopic grenade on the shelves).

www.ingramcontent.com/pod-product-compliance
Lightning Source LLC
Chambersburg PA
CBHW020131120726
47903CB00007B/2199